The Story That Cannot Be Told

"By turns surprising, poetic, and stark,
The Story That Cannot Be Told is one
that should most certainly be read."
—Alan Gratz, *New York Times*
bestselling author of *Refugee*

"Stories have immense power to change lives.
J. Kasper Kramer's beautiful novel is proof of that.
A compelling story of a history that
should never be forgotten."
—Jennifer A. Nielsen,
New York Times bestselling author

★"A thrilling, emotional tale."
—*Kirkus Reviews*, starred review

★"An engrossing read that will raise questions about
how to determine the truth of past events."
—*School Library Journal*, starred review

"An affecting account of a historic event
characterized by monsters, hope,
and the power of words."
—*Booklist*

The Story That Cannot Be Told

J. Kasper Kramer

atheneum

Atheneum Books for Young Readers

New York   London   Toronto   Sydney   New Delhi

ATHENEUM BOOKS FOR YOUNG READERS

An imprint of Simon & Schuster Children's Publishing Division

1230 Avenue of the Americas, New York, New York 10020

This book is a work of fiction. Any references to historical events, real people, or real places are used fictitiously. Other names, characters, places, and events are products of the author's imagination, and any resemblance to actual events or places or persons, living or dead, is entirely coincidental.

Text copyright © 2019 by Jessica Kasper Kramer

Cover illustrations copyright © 2019 by Isabella Mazzanti

All rights reserved, including the right of reproduction in whole or in part in any form.

ATHENEUM BOOKS FOR YOUNG READERS is a registered trademark of Simon & Schuster, Inc.

Atheneum logo is a trademark of Simon & Schuster, Inc.

For information about special discounts for bulk purchases, please contact Simon & Schuster Special Sales at 1-866-506-1949 or business@simonandschuster.com.

The Simon & Schuster Speakers Bureau can bring authors to your live event.

For more information or to book an event, contact the Simon & Schuster Speakers Bureau at 1-866-248-3049 or visit our website at www.simonspeakers.com.

Also available in an Atheneum Books for Young Readers hardcover edition

Interior design by Tom Daly

The text for this book was set in Adobe Garamond.

Manufactured in the United States of America

0820 OFF

First Atheneum Books for Young Readers paperback edition October 2020

2 4 6 8 10 9 7 5 3 1

The Library of Congress has cataloged the hardcover edition as follows:

Names: Kramer, J. Kasper, author.

Title: The story that cannot be told / J. Kasper Kramer.

Description: First edition. | New York : Atheneum, [2019] | Summary: In Romania in 1989, when people who say or do the wrong thing disappear, ten-year-old aspiring writer Ileana copes with fear, hunger, and cruelty by writing new endings to stories, including her own.

Identifiers: LCCN 2018043167 (print) | LCCN 2018050428 (ebook)

ISBN 9781534430709 (eBook) | ISBN 9781534430686 (hc) | ISBN 9781534430693 (paperback)

Subjects: LCSH: Romania—History—Revolution, 1989—Juvenile fiction. |

CYAC: Romania—History—Revolution, 1989—Fiction. | Family life—Romania—Fiction. |

Authorship—Fiction. | Dictatorship—Fiction. | Revolutions—Fiction.

Classification: LCC PZ7.1.K696 (ebook) | LCC PZ7.1.K696 Sto 2019 (print) | DDC [Fic]—dc23

LC record available at https://lccn.loc.gov/2018043167

To Mr. Howell, my fifth-grade teacher.
The first one was always for you.

Prologue

Once upon a time, something happened. If it had not happened, it would not be told.

To the west of the Black Sea was a beautiful country, with ancient forests and rivers and a great mountain range that stretched for a thousand miles. This country was called Romania, and it is where my story takes place. There were times when Romania was ruled by princes and kings. There were times when it was ruled by Roman emperors. But not so very long ago, Romania was ruled by the Communist political party, which took control after a dishonest election and chose a selfish man as its leader.

At first, the people of Romania believed things would be fine. The leader had once been just a shoemaker's apprentice from a rural farming village—a common man like many of them. He said he wanted what was best for his country, and maybe, at one time, he meant it. But his power grew and grew and grew, and, as often happens, it consumed him.

The leader held parades in his own honor. He took control of the newspapers and television and radio to make certain they only said things that he liked. He demolished churches and hospitals and forced forty thousand people from their homes in Bucharest, the capital city, so that he could begin building an incredible palace all for himself. It had spiral staircases and marble floors and a bathroom made of gold.

Under the leader's rule, Romania and its people fell into poverty and despair. Orphanages were flooded with children. Gasoline, water, and electricity had to be rationed. Families stood in line for hours and hours every day just to buy food, and sometimes there was no food to be bought. Perhaps even worse than all this was the secret police, the Securitate—which used a network of everyday people to spy on neighbors and friends for the government, and which sometimes kidnapped, tortured, or killed those who seemed like a threat.

Romanians were never sure who was watching them,

so they lived constantly in fear. Everything became dangerous: reading the wrong kind of books, listening to the wrong kind of music, watching the wrong kind of films.

But the most dangerous thing of all was to write.

Because if you wrote the wrong words—if you told the wrong kind of story—sometimes you just disappeared.

Some Poetry About Socialism

When my father arrived home from the university, his face sallow and sagging as if he were sick, he dropped his briefcase on the kitchen floor and braced himself at the sink.

"He's gone. They've killed him," he said.

At the table, my mother set down her copy of *Femeia* magazine. She glanced at me before she stood, took Tata's hat from his head, pulled him toward their bedroom door, and shut it quietly behind them.

It was mid-July in 1989, and the electricity in Bucharest was off more often than on. Our tower-block concrete apartment building baked us like cabbage rolls in a clay pot, so we always let in the breeze through the balcony doors. I had been sprawled out on the living-room floor beside my Great Tome, the warm air tugging at the pages of my stories. Now I laid my coloring pencil aside and stared, my heart thudding faster with each sound that came through the wall.

The apartment was so small you could see it all at once: the balcony where we dried our clothes, the living room and kitchen stuffed together, the tiny bathroom, my parents' bedroom, my bedroom. My mother liked to say—when my father wasn't there to stop her—that if we were again forced to move, they would squeeze our whole family into a closet. She missed the apartment we'd had before, with the dining room and the pantry and the corner office that held her piano. I didn't remember it, since we'd had to leave when I was a baby, but I knew my parents had only been able to keep what could be carried. I knew they'd only been given a day.

As I sat there, tense and listening, I couldn't stop thinking it would happen again—that whatever had frightened my father would force us to pack up without warning and leave. I wondered how much worse things would get if we moved. When the Leader had torn down our first home to make room for the wide, gaping boulevard and the palace, he'd stuck us, like everyone else, into horrible gray concrete buildings, stacked one after another, all the same. Sometimes I would imagine my family's life before then: our pantry stocked full of bread and jam, my father's books lining the walls from ceiling to floor. In my memory of a place that I didn't remember, we always had enough food, and the hot water worked on more than just Saturday nights. We could bathe whenever we wanted, even in winter when the central heating went out.

But I collected stories, both made-up and true.

And I was usually good at spotting the difference.

My family had never had enough food. We'd never had enough hot water, enough space, enough light. At ten years old, I could already see how everyone, even me, talked about *before* in a special kind of voice and with special kinds of words. If we believed that *before*, things were better, we could imagine they'd be better again. This was the way we survived.

There was a loud thump behind my parents' bedroom door, something striking their dresser. I jumped when it happened again. Muffled sounds came in great, rolling waves: my father's words rising, my mother suppressing the swell. I knew she didn't quiet him because of me, not really. She did it for the neighbor whose ear might be pressed to the wall, for the passerby in the corridor who might pause, fingers feeling in pockets for a pen. It was always best to assume someone was listening.

When the door finally opened, I knew I must have looked frightened, so I pretended to be busy writing in my Great Tome. I was working on "The Baker's Boy," a retelling of a parable from school, but my eyes couldn't focus on the words. I kept glancing up at my parents, who had settled into silent preparation for dinner. I tried not to think about who might have been killed, distracting myself by drawing loaves of tan-colored bread around the edge of my title page. But when the sun dipped low, its fading light turned all the Great Tome's colors to ugly shades of gray, so I tucked the book under my arm and carried it to the couch.

With the power still out, the TV screen was just a dark reflection of me holding my stories, but I sat down and stared at it anyway. Thinking about the movies I loved made me feel a bit better, even if I knew there was no chance I'd see them. We used to get two channels that had shows all day long. My mother still talked about when they'd aired the one from America with the man in the cowboy hat, which always ended with somebody shot or in a car that exploded. But now we only had one chan-nel, just two hours a day during the week, and it didn't air shows like that anymore. The programming was usually boring: speeches given from inside the grand palace; televised sessions of the Communist Party, the little men on the screen all cheering together, booing together, raising their fists; broadcasts that reviewed the state guidelines on "rational eating" or politely reminded viewers of local curfews.

On Sundays, though, *Gala Animation* would come on, and we'd get five whole minutes of a cartoon. Everyone I knew who had a television made sure not to miss it. Last summer, over the course of several weeks, I'd caught all of *101 Dalmatians* and bragged to the other children when we went back to school. This summer they were showing *The Aristocats*, and the last episode had left the poor kitties scared and alone out in the country. I wouldn't get to see the next five minutes till the weekend, but if the power came back tonight, our handmade antenna might pick up something good from Bulgaria, and my whole family might sit down to watch. Then, just like always, we could leave behind whatever horrible thing had happened.

Luck seemed to be on my side, at least for the moment, because as we were setting the table, the electricity flickered to life. I asked my father, "Can I turn on the fan?"

Sometimes he said no. The taxes were very high if we

went over our energy allotment. But tonight he didn't even look at me. He just gave a little gesture with his hand, which I took for a yes, then sat down in his place. The lines around his eyes and behind his big glasses looked deeper than usual, and I began to worry he might really be sick. At the table, the wind blowing through my choppy brown hair, I turned my gaze down and picked at my food. Pie with eggplant and potato but no meat. The queue had been too long at the butcher's. When the line manager had told me and my mother that it would take five hours, maybe six, to get our rations, I thought she'd make us take turns waiting, but instead we'd simply gone home.

Nibbling a stale piece of bread and avoiding as much eggplant as possible, I did my best not to complain. My father was still quiet. The sickly look had not left his face, and I kept glancing up, wanting someone to speak. I knew they wouldn't tell me who was killed or why, because they'd never told me before, but the longer everyone went without talking, the more anxious I grew, thinking that this time it had been someone important.

When I could no longer take it, I did what I always did with silence. I tried to fill it with a story.

"Do you want to hear the new one?"

"Maybe another night," my mother replied.

My stomach fluttered. My cheeks flushed. They never said no.

I returned to poking at my dinner, suddenly frightened as I tried to guess who was dead, because it had never been this bad. It had never meant this much.

My father put down his fork. "Is that what you did today? Work on your stories?"

I thought he was mad about me not doing my summer homework, so I said quickly, "It's a school story. Mrs. Dumitru told it to us before vacation."

"Another night," my mother repeated, and this time I took her words for what they were—a warning.

"No, I want to hear it. I want to hear what they're telling my daughter. I want to hear what she's writing."

I looked between them, shrinking into my chair. A chime from the clock let me ask, "Can I be done?"

My mother glanced at my plate with a frown but nodded. "Bring in your dishes. And turn off that fan. You'll catch cold."

"What about your story?" my father asked.

"I forgot it's not ready," I lied.

After filling the sink with soapy water, I switched on the TV and sank down into the worn couch. My parents began to clean up. When the dark screen filled with static,

I peeked out onto the balcony, worried that someone had climbed up and stolen our wires, but everything seemed okay. I looked at Mama. I hesitated. She was elbow deep in dirty dishes, my father helping dry. They were both still silent—a bad sign.

Usually, after supper, I had to turn up the TV extra loud because my mother loved to sing and my father loved to join in and bellow off-key. If it wasn't that cacophony, they would at least be chattering away about work.

Back in the old apartment, my mother had given music lessons from home. But once she'd lost her piano, she'd had to take a job as a secretary. Now she filed stacks of papers and made calls and typed up copies of documents, since copy machines were illegal. Sometimes there was so much work, she had to get special permission to take a typewriter home.

"I have the worst job in the world," she would say.

"At least it's safe," my father would answer.

Tata was a professor at the University of Bucharest, where he lectured in literature and composition. He'd never been a very good writer, but he loved stories almost as much as I did, so he'd spent his whole life learning how to listen to them. He could hear what was inside a story's heart—what made it beat or let it die—and he'd shared that gift with me. Most nights after supper, if he wasn't singing with Mama or talking away, he'd patiently critique all my new ideas. And if we couldn't watch television because the power was out, he'd get a candle and I'd go find his reading glasses and we'd snuggle up on the couch with our books.

Usually, after supper, our family found something to be happy about, even in the hardest of times. But tonight my father was silent and slouched like an old man—like he was carrying a sack of stones on his shoulders—and even though the kitchen was so close I could almost reach out and touch him, I felt as if he were standing a hundred kilometers away.

Whatever was eating him up started eating me, too.

I crawled over to the TV and twisted the knob frantically, searching for a Bulgarian station. We didn't speak Bulgarian, but they got much better shows, and sometimes when *Columbo* came on my father would pretend he knew what everyone was saying, making up silly things till we were all a giggling mess. If that happened tonight, life would go back to normal, I was sure, and whoever had died wouldn't matter, not really, just like they'd never mattered before.

"Mama, the TV's all fleas," I called, getting desperate.

My mother glanced at the clock. "Then watch the news."

"Mama, *please*."

She dried off her hands, sighing loudly, and stepped out onto the balcony to fiddle with the antenna. When she came back inside, there was still only static, so she changed the channel to the nightly state broadcast.

"I want to watch a Bulgarian show!" I said, panicking. Turning on the news was a terrible idea. Most of the time it just made my parents upset.

When I kept complaining, Mama shushed me and gave a few gentle smacks to the back of my head. A newscaster was talking in front of black-and-white pictures of the Leader, an aging man with slick gray hair and puffy little boy's lips. His wife was beside him in a skirt suit and fat, shiny pearls. She was always photographed from the front so her nose would look small. The two stood before a huge crowd of people, giant posters of the Leader's face plastered all over the wall at their backs. The people were applauding. Flags were waving. I slid dramatically to the floor and rolled onto my stomach, groaning till my mother shook me to silence with her foot on my butt.

A clip of the Leader must have started playing, because I heard him then, speaking to the cheering crowd about the importance of loyalty to the country, about the importance of poetry.

"Everyone enjoys a good love poem," he said. "But of course the highest form of all art is socialist poetry."

My mother sat down on the couch. She called to my father: *"Lucian."*

He came over and I stopped fussing, lifting my face up from the thin carpet.

The Leader read some lines from a poem. I knew the poet they were from. We all learned about him in school. This particular poem praised the state and the Communist Party.

But I knew other poems from this poet, as well—ones the teachers did not read in class.

I knew them because the poet had gone to university with my uncle Andrei, my father's brother. The poet had written many things that he shouldn't have written, many things that did not praise our country. And before he died—before his spine was crushed late one night under the wheels of a tram—he had inspired my uncle to write poetry too.

I tensed and looked up at my father.

"What wonderful lyrics," the newscaster said with a smile when the clip ended. "Our writers must always strive for such beauty."

My tata's face drained of what little color was left. When he started to sob, my whole body went numb. I thought I might start crying too, but before I could, my mother got up and ushered me into my room.

"Don't worry. He's just not feeling well," she said.

But I collected stories, so I knew that was a lie.

I knew my uncle, the poet, had not been home in a week. I knew now that my father thought he was dead.

But recognizing a lie and knowing the truth are two different things.

My father wasn't crying just because he was afraid for his brother—his brother who wrote dangerous poems.

He was also afraid for me.

Infestation

For as long as I could remember, I'd fallen asleep to the voice of my father. My mother said he'd started telling me stories even before I was born, when I was still curled up inside her, and that the stories had gotten into my soft bones while I grew, shaping who I'd become.

My favorite story of all had no ending. It was the one I'd been named for, "Cunning Ileana," a folk story as old as they came. In the tale, a clever princess must defeat three evil princes, each more terrible than the last. But in a lifetime of telling, of my father beginning again and again every night by my bed, we'd never managed to make it all the way through. Sometimes it was he who fell asleep first, head nodding to his chest, glasses slipping from his long nose, his words slurring and slowing. Most of the time it was me.

"I'm staying awake for the whole thing tonight," I'd always say. "So you better stay awake too."

Tata would swear on his life that he would, which of course was all part of the dance we did that made the story so special to us both.

On the night my father cried at the broadcast, I lay awake in my bed, covers up to my chin, waiting for him to come tell me my story. I tried to convince myself everything was okay. Tata couldn't possibly know whether or not my uncle was dead. If the Securitate had taken him, they might still let him go. Things could still find their way back to normal. I strained my ears, listening for a sign, listening for my father on his way to my room. I squeezed my eyes shut and swore to myself I wouldn't fall asleep before he was through with my story—really, this time—no matter how tired I was.

But that night my father never came.

He did not come the next night either.

Nor the night after that.

When I woke up Thursday morning, I could feel my bones going hollow, the stories that made me who I was seeping right out. It had been three days since my father had cried. I had eaten three dinners with barely a word, watched my parents do dishes silently three nights in a row. Three times I'd been sent to bed earlier than usual, and three times there'd been no story at all, not even one from a book. Worse than all else, it was clear that the trouble wasn't only my uncle—each time I took out the Great Tome, my father's eyes would fill up with worry and regret.

It began to feel as if our whole apartment had been placed on a cracking glass shelf. I tiptoed all over, sure that even one tiny misstep would be all it took to send the world crashing down—one meal where I forgot and started to complain about eggplant or liver, one night when I whined about not wanting to brush my teeth.

It didn't make things any better that, since school had let out for summer the previous week, I'd been stuck at home all alone. There'd been no other choice. My mother's parents lived up in the mountains all the way across the country, and even if they'd been closer, she wouldn't have called them. Mama had run away from her village as a teenager. She hadn't even spoken on the phone to my grandparents since I was born. The summers before, when he was still frequently sober, Uncle Andrei had watched me when needed. My grandmother on my father's side, my bunica, who'd outlived her husband, had often watched me as well. But now Bunica and Bunicu were both dead, and maybe Uncle Andrei, too—or hiding or dying or worse.

There were no neighbors my parents trusted. No friends whose loyalty was not in question.

"You'd leave her alone in our apartment?" my mother had asked my father of a gentle old woman they'd both known for years. "She'll touch our things. She'll look through my recipes."

"What are you afraid she'll find?" my father laughed.

"Everything. Anything. Nothing at all."

Of course, getting to stay home alone had at first felt like a great victory. I'd fussed about it for months, convinced that ten was old enough by far. My mother, always a champion for the independence of young women— especially when older men tried to question it—declared she trusted me with her life. But my father thought I was irresponsible and impulsive. He believed that if I was left to my own devices, something terrible would happen.

Unfortunately for us all, he was right.

The first of my sins involved the fan, which I'd promised not to use.

It wasn't my fault. Not really. With all those bad feelings whirling around—no one speaking at dinner or singing at the sink, no one saying silly things during the Bulgarian shows or telling me stories before bed—I was halfway to bursting already. By that third day, I understood that my father was frightened and angry, that Uncle Andrei was gone and in danger, but no one had actually sat me down and told me anything. My imagination was filling in the blank spaces. Alone in that apartment, I was on the edge of a breakdown.

So when the electricity came on, I started up the fan.

Sitting with the air blowing down my shirt at the kitchen table, I reveled in my rebellion. If my parents wanted to keep secrets from me, I could keep secrets from them, too. Disobeying one rule quickly led to disobeying another. I'd promised to start on my homework, but there was no way that was happening. I slid aside my book report and science worksheets to make room for the Great Tome.

Its flimsy cardboard cover was decorated with pasted-on plastic gems and a whole cup of glitter. Its pages were torn from spiral notebooks and yellow notepads and colorful packets of construction paper. The tome was my life's work—a massive collection of handwritten tales that rivaled anything I'd ever seen on a shelf. Some of the stories I'd copied from books, changing the parts that I didn't like. Some were retellings of stories people had told me, though at times it was hard to know which ones were true. Of course, the best stories of all were completely made up in my head. I always kept the pages unbound so they could be rearranged or replaced with new versions, and over the years, the Great Tome had grown fatter and fatter, until eventually Tata had had to give me an old belt to hold it closed.

Thinking hard about what I wanted to write, I took my colored pencils out of their dented blue tin and lined them up by height, cracking my knuckles just like Uncle Andrei. Without my father telling me stories at bedtime, it felt more important than ever that I keep writing them down.

But nothing was coming to mind.

For a long while I sat staring at a blank page, my hope for inspiration fading by the second. Just when I was about to give up and do math, someone knocked on the front door.

I went rigid. No one had ever come by while my parents were away. My father had lectured me a half dozen times on this exact scenario, though, so I forced myself to stay calm.

"Just don't answer," he'd said. "Try not to make any noise."

"Play dead, then," I'd suggested with a smile.

He'd rolled his eyes and replied, "Sure. Fine. Play dead. Just don't answer."

So I stayed where I was, listening to the fan whir. There was a second knock, followed by an "Anybody home?"

Still I was quiet. The person would go away. Certainly he would leave. My father hadn't given me a lecture on what to do if the person didn't leave. Clearly it wasn't a possibility.

The stranger started to fumble with the locks at our door.

I rushed across the kitchen with a cry and grabbed the doorknob, grabbed the latch, tried to keep it all from moving.

"Don't come in!" I screamed.

I heard the man in the hall back away. "You scared me half to death! I knocked two times!"

"I'll call the police on you, burglar!"

"I'm not a burglar! I'm an electrician. The landlord gave me the key. I have to do some rewiring."

I hesitated. It sounded logical.

"Listen, kid, I've got a lot of other units to cover. Are you gonna let me in or am I gonna have to call my manager?"

"What kind of rewiring?" I asked. "I'll know if you're trying to trick me. I read a whole book on electrical code."

This was only half true. I'd mostly just looked at the pictures. My father had brought home the manual in a stack he'd saved from the library dumpster. Books were always being thrown away, sometimes for the strangest of reasons. Tata didn't like sneaking them into our apartment, but he had such a hard time finding enough for me to read. I was always reading faster than he could keep up.

There was a long pause on the other side of the door. I often had that effect. Then, slowly, the burglar said, "Your unit's been using a lot of energy. Your father wanted the landlord to get someone to figure out why. You understand all that? Your father asked me to come."

I glanced at the fan and cringed.

If I called my father to make sure the man was telling the truth, there was a chance I'd have to admit I'd broken the rules. If I called my mother—who was generally much more understanding about these sorts of things—there was a chance her boss would catch her on the phone and get nasty.

Either one of those things could be it. The final misstep that sent my world crashing down.

I gritted my teeth and unlocked the door, pulling it open just a crack. The man outside had a gray jumpsuit, a cap, a utility belt, and a bag with lots of tools. He certainly looked like an electrician, not a burglar, though I knew that sometimes burglars came in disguise. I would watch him closely, and if it didn't seem like he knew how to do electrician things, I would grab the Great Tome and dash to the neighbors' to call the police.

My collection of stories would likely slow me down. It was bulky and heavy and awkward. But I couldn't leave it behind. I'd die to defend it.

"Can I come in now?" the burglar asked.

I narrowed my eyes and opened the door just enough to let him pass. I followed him through the kitchen, watching as he went into the living room. He looked behind the furniture. He tapped the walls. I hefted myself up onto the counter, dirty feet and everything. There were big knives next to the stove, by the chopping board and the empty bread box. I kept glancing at them. If he was a really evil kind of burglar, he might try to kill me. Then I would have to use the knives to stab him before I grabbed the Great Tome and escaped. Things were getting pretty exciting. Suddenly I had a great deal to write about.

The burglar set down his tool bag and looked over his shoulder. "Does your mother want you on the counter?"

"Yes. She likes it when I sit here."

"Don't you have something to do?"

"I am doing something. I'm keeping you from stealing our stuff. We have a very nice TV."

"I told you, I'm an electrician. I know your TV is cheap."

He took off a metal panel on the wall and started messing with the parts inside. He got into the place where the phone was plugged and pulled out a bunch of wires, clipped them, twisted them, and utterly lost my attention. My eyes darted to the Great Tome at the table. I was already trying to decide what colors were best for a burglar's tool bag and cap, already thinking about what sort of twist this story could have at the end.

Would the burglar kill the girl and steal all her family's precious things but then realize he'd broken into the wrong apartment?

Would the girl get away at the last moment but then reveal that she's really a bad guy as well?

By the time the electrician went into my room, I didn't even care anymore. I was convinced the man was what he said he was, which was no fun. The story in my head was much better. Before the electrician left, I was back at the table, scribbling away in my tome with wild eyes. He told me not to bother telling my father he'd come—that the landlord would be in touch—and since this meant I might be able to keep my secret about using the fan, I was deeply relieved.

That night at dinner my father asked, "Did anything interesting happen while we were at work?"

I crunched down on an onion, forced myself not to gag, and said with a pained smile, "No. Nothing. Super boring today."

My father nodded. He wasn't even really paying attention, but my mother's eyes grew suspicious, so I shoveled more gross soup into my face.

That evening I worked on my new story. And by the following morning my head was so full of burglars in disguises, I'd forgotten the real electrician entirely.

No one noticed anything strange till the weekend, when my mother, while talking on the phone, became frustrated with the bad connection. This was followed by my father complaining that something was wrong with the volume on the TV. Then I started getting weird calls when my parents were away at work. I'd answer and there would be nothing but creepy popping and hissing, obviously a ghost prank-calling the apartment. My parents didn't believe in ghosts, so I didn't bother to tell them, but I started to feel a bit anxious.

If we'd stuck our ears up to the walls, we might have figured it out.

We might have heard all the little bugs crawling around, tick-tick-ticking through our cables and telephone wires, their tiny, sticky feet stealing secrets. But I guess we still thought we were safe in our home. So by the time we realized what had happened, it was already too late.

The Baker's Boy

It was evening and my parents were in the living room, talking in the quiet, short way I had grown accustomed to since the night my father had cried. My window was open and the gusty breeze pulled and pushed at my cracked bedroom door as my parents whispered on the couch.

On the floor by my bed, the Great Tome was closed beside me. In my lap was one of my father's books. I was supposed to be asleep, but no one had come in to check, just as no one had checked on my homework or on whether or not I was sad or angry or scared.

My back was propped up with pillows, the prettiest of which was small and dark green, embroidered with a round-faced bird—one of the few relics from my mother's childhood. The electricity hadn't come on in two days, not even once, so I was reading by candlelight. Our city was conserving power, diverting energy to the factories. We should have been panicking about the food in our fridge, but there was nothing left to spoil.

"We have to pay our debt," my father used to tell me. "The austerity is for our benefit."

But in late March, the Leader had given a speech, announcing that all of Romania's debts had been paid. More than three months had passed, yet the power kept going out. The queues at the stores kept getting longer. More and more often, we'd make it all the way to the front and there would be no food to buy.

"We just have to be patient," my father told me. "Things will get better if we wait."

My father told me lots of things, but it was hard to know which ones he believed. Like his father before him, who'd survived both the purges and the Second World War, my tata was an expert at speaking softly, especially when it came time to express his opinion.

I leaned closer to the page, eyes straining in the orange light. The words in my father's book were long and unfamiliar, so I had to fill in the blanks with my own definitions. Growing frustrated, I read the sentences again and again to try to make everything fit.

Writing was better if it was simple and easy to read. When my uncle Andrei had worked for the city newspaper, for instance, he used small words and wrote about things that lots of people liked—football, theater, local stories with happy endings. My favorite was the article where the little girl found her kitten after it had run away. REUNITED! the title proclaimed.

I'd talked to Uncle Andrei about his stories all the time back then. I'd grilled him for advice. I'd blindly praised each thing he wrote, even when I could sense that something was off. His poetry was colorful, full of movement and emotion, but his stories for the paper often felt empty and lifeless. Once, over dinner, he admitted to us that most of them weren't even true. Often his interviews were pretend, or he'd change people's words to make them say nicer things.

"I'm just writing what everyone wants to read," he told us, looking ashamed.

I couldn't figure out why this was a problem. Shouldn't writers try to make people happy? Besides, who cared what he wrote? Uncle Andrei's words were in print. They had been given the blessing of publication. He was a real writer.

I pinned the article about the kitten on my wall next to an essay of my own about how much I loved Romania. I'd just written what I knew the teacher wanted to read, and it had won me first place in my school's competition, then made it all the way to the national judges before someone else's essay—about the Leader's fantastic teeth—knocked it out of the finals. Standing in front of my class, a wreath of bright flowers on top of my head, I'd thought, *This is writing. This is what writers do.*

When I pestered Uncle Andrei about his stories in the paper, though, he never shared in my enthusiasm. He didn't like to talk about the pieces he wrote for work and was confused by my reading them.

Often he asked my father, "Why that? Why has she latched on to that?"

"She reads everything." My father would shrug.

"And you let her?"

My uncle didn't like to talk about his writing until he was fired—until his editor friend helped him publish a story that would nearly get the paper shut down. After that, writing was the only thing Uncle Andrei talked about. He would come knocking on our door at the craziest hours, smelling of *palinca* and slurring his words.

The last time I saw my uncle before the night my father cried, it was past midnight, and instead of knocking, Andrei called our names through the front door.

"Liza! Lucian! Ileana!"

I was the one to answer, rubbing my eyes as I let him into our kitchen. My parents were still in their bedroom, fussing about the time and putting on robes. My uncle knelt with a dangerous smile and pushed a crisp manila envelope into my hands.

"You want to read? Read this."

I scurried into my room before my parents could see. I closed the door and listened, still as stone. My father was furious. My mother, who had always been close to her brother-in-law—who had always sided with him even when my father had not—hissed that if Uncle Andrei didn't take a bath and wash his clothes, that if he came stumbling to her door with glassy eyes one more time, she would never allow him to see his niece again.

My hands trembled as I pulled the papers from the envelope. It was a poem, a long one. There was a stamp that showed it had been published in a different country. The name under the title was not my uncle's, which I didn't at first understand because I hadn't yet learned about pen names—because I couldn't imagine a writer not wanting to take credit for the thing that she wrote. I was jittery as I huddled in bed, trying to read by moonlight, trying to block out the raised voices in the kitchen. The poem told a story about students at the University of Bucharest. It took place long before I was born. The whole thing was hard to figure out, with strange, lyrical words, abrupt spacing, and references to philosophers and authors and politicians I didn't know.

But it was clear the students were listening to the radio a lot. It was clear they were not supposed to.

Radio Budapest. Radio Free Europe. They heard jazz for the first time on the Voice of America.

It was clear this was an act of resistance.

Even with all the pieces laid out before me, though, I didn't realize what my uncle had written till the poem described special security troops arriving at the University Square, carrying guns. The students were arrested for a protest they hadn't even had the chance to perform. Terrible things happened to them in the jails—things that shouldn't have happened to anyone anywhere, no matter what they did or didn't think or do or say.

I sat up in bed, my pulse racing, my eyes scanning the pages feverishly. In a panic, I realized just what it was I was reading.

A poem that did not say good things about our country.

A poem that, if discovered, could make my uncle disappear.

It had been a month since the poem's publication, since Uncle Andrei had stumbled into our apartment that night. But for some reason, sitting on my bedroom floor and reading by candlelight from my father's book, the poem came back to my mind. Perhaps this was because on both occasions there was something being said outside my door that the adults did not want me to hear. Perhaps this was because I was again awake when I shouldn't have been, reading in dim light with the pages so close.

In truth, though, I am sure it was that I had finally admitted to myself that Tata was right. My uncle must be dead.

Feeling queasy and weak, I didn't react fast enough when the wind gusted again into my room and flung the Great Tome open. My little flame flickered wildly as mismatched sheets of paper, different sizes and colors, were snatched up by the wind and went flying. I cried out, rising to chase them, and my father rushed into the room to see what was wrong. He dove across my bed, shutting the window, and then moved my candle to safety as the pages fluttered all around.

"You were supposed to be in bed."

"I was just reading."

"You were supposed to be asleep."

My mother peeked in. She looked so tired, as if the exhaustion in my father's long face were a disease that had spread.

"It's fine," he assured her, and she left.

I slumped to the floor and grimaced at all the mixed up pages. "I can't leave it like this."

Tata sighed and then knelt. In the quiet, side by side, we put the stories back together. Sometimes my father would pick up a sheet and pause, lingering. Sometimes, as I sorted and stacked, I would glance over because I realized he was reading. It made me flush. It made my heart shiver.

For as long as I'd had the Great Tome—which was basically all my life—I'd rarely let anyone read from it but me. I collected stories in class, at the store, off the TV. I changed them to suit how I felt, most often rewriting the endings. But when I decided to share what I'd created, I was careful in choosing which tale and how to tell it. There were things I wouldn't read in front of a classmate but might read in front of my parents. There were words I would use during the day but not at night.

In fact I had whole stories, more than a few, that were

meant only for me—that I never intended to let out into the world.

My father didn't know I'd written about his time as a university student or about my mother running away from her village. He didn't know I'd written about the boy in the Pioneer club who'd died during our city parade. We'd been marching in the hot sun for hours, singing and waving flags in front of the palace, and he'd just dropped without warning, skull thunking onto the pavement. I'd never told anyone about the girl in our class whose parents were arrested for whispering things that she whispered to me in the bathroom. I'd never told anyone about the history teacher I loved who'd said our textbook was wrong when we studied the Second World War—who'd repeatedly used the term "Holocaust" and insisted our people were not simply victims of fascism but responsible for the brutal murders of hundreds of thousands of Roma and Jews. Shortly after her lecture, she'd suddenly, inexplicably, vanished.

My father certainly didn't know about Uncle Andrei's poem—that I'd copied down all the best parts and told them in those smaller, simpler words I preferred. How could Tata have guessed I'd remember so much? He'd taken the poem from me the morning after I'd read it, when he'd found me sleeping with it clutched to my chest.

My father stopped helping. His eyes were trained on a pale blue piece of construction paper with shiny black ink.

"Tata," I said, trying to pull him back to me. "I want to hear my story tonight. I want to hear about Cunning Ileana. If you promise to stay awake till the end, then I'll promise too."

But my father's eyes were still on the paper.

"I need you to tell me a story first," he said.

His voice was too calm, the timing of his request strange, but when someone asked me for a story, I almost never said no.

"Which one do you want?"

"Last week you mentioned a story at dinner," he said. "One your teacher told you before summer break."

For a moment I watched him uncertainly, but then I nodded and began. "Once upon a time, something happened. If it hadn't happened, it would not be told. There once was a baker's boy. He was a very good boy. He took his homework seriously and did his chores every day. He liked to play football and basketball and kept himself healthy and clean." I hesitated, glancing down at my tome, still a mess. "I don't—can I find it first? I don't remember what he liked to study."

"Trivial details. Just go on."

"It develops the baker boy's character," I insisted.

"I very much doubt that. He liked physics and math, I'm sure."

I paused. "Wow. I think that was it."

"Please go on."

"One day this boy, who was a very good boy, who liked football and basketball and physics and math, one day he was walking home and passed a dark, dirty alley, and down at the end he saw his father talking with a bad man."

My own father's eyes narrowed. His face danced with shadows as my voice changed.

"The baker's boy and his family were very, very poor, Tata. Poorer than us. So poor they lived in just one little room behind the bakery, and even the mice wouldn't sleep there in the winter because it was so cold. Every morning, before his parents woke up, the boy would knead all the dough and fire up all the ovens. He liked to work very much. And he loved his country very much. And the thing he wanted most in all the world was for the Leader to come to his bakery and taste his family's bread. But if he couldn't have that, he would be happy enough if his mother just gave him a baby brother or sister. She'd only had one child, and that made the Leader very sad. She was a disappointment."

My father's voice was low when he asked, "Would you tell this story to your mother?"

"I'm telling this story to you."

"It's rambling. And you've developed the characters quite enough for my taste."

I licked my lips and tried to remember where I was. "The boy . . . the baker's boy saw his father in an alley talking to a man who was bad. Very bad. He was selfish and lazy. He didn't love his country. He didn't want to work. And the baker's boy almost started to cry, because while he was watching, his father gave papers to this bad man and got money in return."

"And what were these papers?"

"Papers that said mean things about the Leader. Papers that would hurt the country. But the baker's boy knew what was right to do." I began speaking faster. "So that night, when his parents were sleeping, he ran to the police and told them the truth. They came at once. They took his father, the baker, to jail, and everything seemed perfect and happy."

I scrunched up my face. "But secretly, the boy's mother was furious. His relatives were furious too. Because they loved the baker, and who cared what stupid things he said about the stupid Leader anyhow?"

My father's eyes widened, but before he could speak, my voice dropped to a whisper, coming faster still, and when I leaned forward, my shadow grew like a monster. "The next night, the boy's family came into his room and they took his limbs, one for each person, and they ripped him right to pieces! They ground him up and baked him with the dough, and when the Leader came to visit the shop of the brave young man who'd told on his father, they gave him a loaf of Baker's Boy. He ate every last bite, saying it was the best bread he'd ever had. So, in the end, the boy got his wish after all."

There was silence for a long time before I started to cry.

"It's Uncle Andrei who's been killed, isn't it? You think the Securitate will come after us next!"

My father's face flushed. *"You cannot tell such stories."*

"They told it to us at school!"

"You've changed it. That's not your teacher's ending."

"The teacher's ending was boring. And the baker's boy was a snitch."

Tata grabbed a fistful of papers from the Great Tome, and I pulled back in surprise as he shook my stories and hissed, "Can you not understand what is happening?

Don't you realize that I'm praying, for all our sakes, that my brother *is* dead—that he hasn't given our names out of desperation? Haven't you figured it out? *Your mother helped him publish his poems.* She typed the copies herself! If he's even alive, do you know what they'll do? Do you know what happens to people who make stories like yours? They'll beat him bloody and chain him to the wall. He won't eat for days or bathe for months. Do you know how many die in those jails? How many wish they were dead?"

I shrank away till I bumped the little table beside my bed. The candle rattled, nearly tipped, and my father's eyes fell to the paper in his hands, to the rest of the Great Tome spread out on the carpet before him. It took me a moment to realize what was happening, to realize what he meant to do as he started snatching everything up, stuffing and crumpling the stories in the kind of reckless way that let me know he never meant to put them back together.

"I'm sorry. I'm so sorry, Ileana," he said, and his voice broke.

Then I was screaming, my hands grasping for any part of him I could reach. "Tata! *Tata, no!* Please, Tata! No!"

My fingers caught the edge of my tome as he rose, glitter raining down, paper ripping in my hands. He shook himself free of me. Then he was striding through the door. Then he was out of the apartment. I stumbled into the living room, my mother already ahead of me, shouting and running after him down the hall. I meant to follow too, but my legs went weak and I fell to my knees.

When my mother returned, I was sobbing, curled up on the floor and clutching bits of torn paper. Surely, all the neighbors had woken by then. Surely, they'd all made little notes in their books. But my mother just lay down beside me. She held my body with hers, stroking the knots from my hair.

"I'll hate him forever," I cried.

"He's just afraid," she said. "He doesn't realize what he's done."

For the rest of my family, the world had not yet come crashing down.

That would happen the next day, after my father returned home from work. The cuffs of his sleeves would still be stained with ash when I showed him what I found in my bedroom.

For the rest of my family, the world had not yet come crashing down, but for me, all that really mattered was gone. Because my stories made up who I was, and that night my father—whom I loved best of all—had destroyed them.

Somewhere Safe

I was alone when I found the first bug, nestled tight with tape in my very own room. No one else would have noticed it, no one but a distraught girl searching more desperately than ever for an escape—for hidden passageways inside closets or doll-size families that might become friends, might just live anywhere in her apartment that normal people wouldn't look, like deep, deep inside a child's beside table.

When my fingers fumbled across its cold metal casing, I snapped my hand back as if I'd been bitten. I hesitated, then pulled out the small drawer.

In the corner, tiny wires squirmed from a gray, segmented shell.

I stepped away slowly, my breath coming shallow and quick. In the kitchen I climbed onto the counter and hugged my knees to my chest, thinking of everything my father and I had said the previous night. About my uncle. About my mother. I pictured the cell they would put me in because of the story I'd told. I wanted to cry, but all I could do was stare into my room at the open drawer.

When my parents finally arrived home from work, I jumped down and ran over, grabbing my mother by the wrist.

"What? What? Ileana, wait! Let me put down my bag."

But I must have looked so frightened. I must have struck something ingrained so deep—she'd lived this way her whole life, just like me—that when she saw my finger over my mouth, my wide eyes, she went silent. She followed me. My father followed her. And I showed them. I showed them, still hoping I was wrong.

My mother's hand trembled up to her mouth. My father went white.

In silence, my parents and I gutted our apartment. Every piece of furniture we owned was flipped upside down. The cushions and pillows of every sitting or sleeping place were torn open and scattered. Every electronic was unplugged, every light switch and outlet unscrewed.

We didn't speak as we searched. We didn't need words to share what we knew.

Our apartment was infested.

When the place was fully wrecked and my father had finally sat down on the overturned couch, his brow damp, my mother took a pad of paper from her work bag and began writing. She passed it to my father. He read and wrote and passed it back. When they were through, they passed the notepad to me. The ink was black, the paper muted yellow with faint blue lines. For the first time in a life of secrets and half sentences, I was allowed to know every last word. I read quickly.

Last night. This was underlined by my mother.

Below was my father's handwriting. *We can't stay here.*

Leaving is as good as a confession.

They already have one. And then, underlined not once, but three times, *Ileana.*

My mother had looked at me before she'd written, *There's nowhere safe.*

Yes, there is.

They don't even know what she looks like.

We don't have a choice.

We could go with her. Together. My mother's cursive tore holes with its loops.

She'll be safer going alone.

Below this, Mama had scribbled something out, then written a few lines about where I was going and what I needed to pack. When I finished reading, my stomach flooded with fear.

No, I wrote back, and looked up, the pen trembling in my hand. *I want to stay here with you.*

My mother pursed her lips and pulled me close, pressing my forehead to hers. My father turned his face away.

That night I chose clothes from the floor by my closet. We put them in my schoolbag with my toothbrush and comb. My mother picked up the kitchen table and set it straight. She picked up a chair. She sat down to write—first the directions, next the letter. We could not call ahead. Not from our house. Not from a public phone. Everywhere, the Securitate were listening.

For a few hours Mama held me while I dozed, but before the sun rose the next morning, we were all at the front door, dressed and ready to leave. I strapped on my schoolbag, trying to be brave. But when my mother handed me the white envelope with her letter, she started to cry, so I started to cry too.

"Don't give it to anyone but her," she whispered, her lips close to my ears, her cheeks wet.

No one had spoken in hours. She was risking everything just to feel the words in her throat. My father glanced out into the hallway, checking for eavesdropping neighbors. He looked at his watch, then into the hallway again. I stood up straight as a soldier, trying to catch my breath. I wiped my eyes and walked out the door.

In the street on the way to the North Railway Station, Tata, Mama, and I passed the queue at the grocer. Already, people were lining up for their rations—two hundred fifty grams of bread per person per day, one kilogram of sugar per month, seventy-eight liters of milk per year. The tickets for each trimester were printed on off-white paper. The official stamp was red. The little boxes with numbers, the ones the man with the uniform would X off so you couldn't get in line twice, those were light blue. There were tickets for flour, tickets for eggs, tickets for meat. They had our name and our address and said that we were three people.

But when I got onto the train all alone, my family would be only two.

I wondered if my parents would still buy my rations when I was gone. I wondered how, without a ticket, I would eat.

The sun, just beginning to rise, peeked above the tops of the gray public-housing complex, but on its heels were dark, angry clouds. The streetlights flickered. Only one in five worked. My mother held my hand, humidity sticking our fingers together. The palace was behind us, the boulevard, too—my school and my bakery and my butcher. The turn to the university came and went on our right. It was a long walk to the North Railway Station, but my parents didn't risk hailing a cab. We passed Romarta, where my mother bought all our clothes—where everyone's mother bought everyone's clothes. Through the storefront's glass panes, I could see the same plain T-shirt and shorts I was wearing. In my once-white tennis shoes, with my school-sanctioned bag bumping along on my back, I blended into my city so well, it would have taken almost nothing to make me disappear.

We had nearly reached the train station when clouds filled in the sky overhead, hiding the sun so that the dawn couldn't arrive. What little color remained of the world became dark and muddled. I pressed close to my mother and tugged on her hand.

"I'll be out past curfew," I whispered when she bent down her head.

"You won't be in the city by then."

A block later I tugged again. "Someone might ask

me where I'm going, and if I can't think of a lie, I'll get found out."

"Tell them the truth, then—just not all of it."

Another block, another tug. "I'll hate the village. I know I will. I'll want to run away."

This time my mother only glanced down, frowning.

The North Railway Station was just ahead, its clock tower in sight. The Romanian flag was flying from a pole at its top, and when we neared, it snapped to attention in the wind, lightning flashing behind it. Inside the building, we joined the queue. A few people grumbled and pushed, but my father, as always, stood stoic, pretending he didn't see. Along the wall were identical posters: red, yellow, and blue with a painted picture of the Leader and his wife— the People's Genius and his Scientist Spouse. One of the posters was torn, ripping the Leader's smiling face right down between his eyes.

At the ticket counter, the woman pulled out a map and charts, pointing. My father made notes while she talked. I didn't start feeling truly frightened till we walked to the platform and he knelt down beside me, handing over a paper with the times and stations and names of lines. He showed me the tickets one by one.

"You'll have to change trains twice," he said, his voice

almost lost in the ringing bells and crackling announce-
ments from the loudspeakers above. "Ask for help if you're
lost, but try not to draw any attention."

There was a long, loud whistle, and I turned to see
the train approaching in the distance. My mother knelt
down too.

"When you can, sit next to a woman," she said, "especially if she's traveling with children."

She tightened the straps on my backpack as the train
reached us, slowing. Warm wind and the smell of wet
pavement gushed up into my face. Mama gave me a quick
hug, kissed both my cheeks, and then stood, facing away.
I could tell she was holding her breath.

When the train stopped and the doors opened, people
began boarding. My heart started to race. I held tight my
directions, my tickets, my letter. Next to me, my father
put his palm on my cheek, and I suddenly understood
how much my life was about to change.

"Don't make me go," I said, panicking. I clutched his
arm, trying my best not to cry, but I was so scared I felt sick.

"I'm so sorry, Ileana." Tata's eyes went glassy behind his
wire frames. "When you come home, I'll take you to the
movies. I'll read to you. I'll finish your story, I promise.
On my life, I won't fall asleep till the end."

He tried to smile, and for a moment he looked very much like the father I loved—the father who'd taught me about character and setting and theme, who'd taken me on secret adventures, who'd walked with me to the boulevard to work together on writing by the light of the construction cranes. For a moment my father looked so much like the person I loved that I almost gave in—almost wrapped my arms around his neck and kissed his stubble and begged him to forgive me for letting in the electrician and telling stories that put our family in danger.

And then I remembered the Great Tome.

Every story I'd ever written—a lifetime of collecting, of reordering scenes, of making outlines, sketching plots, fine-tuning dialogue—everything was gone, gone, gone.

There was nowhere to write down the end of our story.

There would be nowhere to write the next story I found.

"I don't forgive you," I said, ducking out of my father's reach. "I hope I never come home!"

And then I ran through the doors, not looking back as they closed.

Cunning Ileana and the Three Princes

Once upon a time, something happened. If it had not happened, it would not be told.

There once was an emperor with three daughters who lived in the land to the east. The princesses were, of course, perfectly beautiful, because stories would have us believe that the daughters of powerful men are never plain or hawk-nosed or born with moles and frizzy hair. So even though the emperor's oldest daughter was certainly more beautiful than you or than I, it is said that the middle daughter was more beautiful yet, and that the youngest daughter, Ileana, was more beautiful than both her sisters. In fact, Ileana was so beautiful that the sun itself sometimes stopped and sighed while admiring her perfection, and everyone knows that's absurd.

One day this emperor received news that the Great Monarch, who lived in a massive golden palace to the west, had been disgraced by an unforgivable slight—someone had made fun of his teeth. This was such a tremendous insult that the monarch had called forth all the rulers from neighboring kingdoms to ride with him around the world on a campaign of terror, slaughtering anyone who might have started the rumor.

Now, the truth is, the rumor had been started by the emperor himself. In fact the princesses' father had whispered a lot more than just the thing about the teeth. The emperor hated the monarch. The neighboring kingdoms hated the monarch too. For decades he'd wielded terrible power and been, overall, just a really mean guy. Even worse were his three vile princes. As you can probably guess, though the monarch's oldest son was incredibly cruel, certainly crueler than you or than I, it is said that the middle son was crueler yet, and that the youngest son was crueler than both his brothers.

But no matter how much the emperor hated the monarch and his sons, he was too afraid to defy them. So when the call came forth to go fight, the emperor rallied his soldiers and sent for his princesses.

I hate to break it to you, girls, but I've got some bad news, he told them.

Has the ship full of my new dresses been lost? cried the oldest princess.

Have you decided to marry me to someone terribly ugly? cried the middle one.

You're leaving to fight for that awful monarch, aren't you? Cunning Ileana accused him. And then her eyes widened, her heart already aching, because even with his many flaws, she loved her father best in all the world. *You're going to send us away.*

The emperor put his palm to the youngest princess's cheek. *If you were any more clever, Ileana, you'd ruin us all,* he said fondly. *Yes, my daughters, it's true. You must go live in the mountain castle while I'm at war. It's the only way you'll be safe.*

The mountain castle? cried the oldest princess. *But it's so plain! The chandeliers aren't even made of real diamonds!*

The mountain castle? cried the middle princess. *But it's so remote! There won't be any cute stable boys for me to tease!*

I want to stay with you, Father, said Ileana. *I want to protect you. Please, please don't make me go.*

No complaints! said the emperor. *Now, remember, girls. Even while I'm away, you must always keep faith with your family. If I return and you've broken my trust, I will know.*

Cunning Ileana kept her eyes on her father. *If you choose the monarch over me, I'll never forgive you. I'll hate you for the rest of my life.*

But either the emperor didn't hear or he didn't care, because with a few surely touching, forgettable fatherly words, he turned and was gone, off to watch his soldiers valiantly die for no good reason.

Now, as chance had it, right after the monarch went to war, the three vile princes discovered that it was the emperor who'd started the rumor. Eager to please their evil father, the boys decided that instead of revealing the truth right away, they'd first make the emperor's daughters fall in love with them. Then, once the sisters had been wooed, the princes would steal the rest of the emperor's secrets. When he discovered his princesses' betrayal, he'd be so heartbroken, he'd die.

The oldest prince leaped onto his horse and rode straight to the mountain castle. For three days and three nights he stood in the gardens under the princesses' wall, but none of them appeared at their windows. On the fourth day, in the damp gray before dawn, shivering, starving, and irritated, he marched up to the window of the oldest princess and banged on the glass till she arrived.

It is I, little sister, the prince began, but she cut him off.

I know who you are, and I know you've been out there doing heaven knows what for three days and three nights. I don't care what you want. Go away. May thorns spring up before you and thorns remain behind.

But for love— the prince started, and she slammed the window shut in his face.

Taken by the oldest daughter's beauty, and never having been rejected even once in his life, the oldest son of the monarch forced himself to wait three more days, three more nights, and then again at gray dawn he approached the window, tapping softly this time.

After a moment the oldest princess appeared, and she opened the window quite gently.

It is I, little sister, the prince began. *For love of you I wait still.*

Go away, she said, but her voice wavered a bit. *May thorns spring up before you and flowers remain behind.*

The princess closed the window again, but not before taking a rather long look at the prince's perfectly chiseled chest and dashing blue eyes. The oldest son smiled, quite sure of himself, and was content to wait three more days, three more nights, till the gray dawn of the tenth day arrived. He smoothed down his hair, flexed his biceps twice for good measure, and approached the window once more. He didn't even have to tap before the princess opened it.

It is I, little sister, said the prince. *For three times three days and three times three nights, I have stood under your window and longed to gaze into your eyes. I have imagined myself by your bed as you sleep, by your vanity as you dress in the morning.*

That's not creepy at all, said the princess, and she meant it, because she had foolishly fallen in love.

Relieve me of my torment and invite me into your room.

Goodness no! My dear younger sister would never forgive me for falling in love with our father's enemy's son, said the princess, taken aback. But after a moment she added, *Unless, of course, she fell in love too.*

The prince smiled. *I'll send my younger brother right away. But first, a kiss to make more pleasant my travels.*

And before she could protest, he reached up and stole one.

Go away! the princess shouted, wiping her mouth with her silken sleeve. But as the prince mounted his steed and rode off into the rising sun, she called after, *May flowers spring up before you and flowers remain behind!*

When the oldest prince returned home, he sent the middle prince off to the mountain castle at once. Staggered by the beauty of the middle princess, he did not find it difficult to wait after her first, and even second, rejection. And, just like his brother, by the gray dawn of the tenth morning the middle prince had won the princess's foolish heart. She came running to her window before he even approached.

It is I, little sister, he said. *For three times three days and three times three nights, I have stood under your window and longed to gaze into your eyes. I have imagined myself by your bed as you sleep, by your vanity as you dress in the morning.*

How romantic, the middle princess sighed, for she, too, was an idiot.

Relieve me of my torment and invite me into your room.

I wish that I could, the princess swooned. *But my dear younger sister, she'd never understand how passionately we feel for each other. Those rock-hard abs . . . that slicked-back hair . . . oh, but for my sister!*

The prince's face reddened handsomely and he tugged at his tunic collar. *Perhaps, my love, I could send my younger brother to meet your younger sister. First, though, a kiss to hasten my journey?*

To the prince's great surprise, the middle princess nearly toppled outside, pulling him into her arms. When she'd freed him, and he rode off, she called after, *May flowers spring up before you and flowers remain behind!*

After hearing of his elder brothers' trials, the youngest son of the monarch was not looking forward to his ten days of solitude in the damp, chilly gardens. In fact he wondered why—if the girls were so easily found in their bedrooms alone—he and his brothers didn't just break the emperor's heart by murdering his three daughters while they slept. But when the youngest prince reached the mountain castle, he found himself pleasantly surprised.

Cunning Ileana was already at her window. She smiled as he approached.

You're a prince, aren't you? she asked. *I can tell by that perfect royal face. To where are you hurrying that you urge your steed so hotly?*

The youngest son of the monarch was unable to look away from Ileana's beauty. He spoke boldly, puffing out his chest. *I hurry to you, little sister.*

Oh, not me, surely!

The prince was full to bursting with passion. *It is true! I have imagined myself by your bed blah, blah, blah . . .*

By now, certainly, you know the rest.

Cunning Ileana's mouth turned up into a smirk. *If your soul is like your face, I will gladly invite you into my room. Here I'll pour you drinks and offer you kisses.*

The prince's eyes widened, quite shocked. He'd never kissed a girl, after all.

Little sister, do you know who I am? the young prince asked.

I do, Ileana replied.

But what of your two elder sisters? Do you not fear their disapproval?

Ileana only smiled wider. *My sisters have fallen in love with your brothers, so what need have I to consult them?*

The youngest prince couldn't believe his good fortune. *I swear to you, my soul is like my face. Invite me into your room and you shall never regret it from dawn till nightfall.*

I'm certain I won't, she called sweetly, then whispered to herself, *But you will.*

Ileana gestured, allowing the prince to climb up through her window. Once inside, he went straight to a table laden with fruit, meat, and wine. When he reached it, the floor dropped right out from beneath him, and he fell into a deep vault where the emperor's important scrolls and books were kept.

Help! Help! Ileana shouted to the guards outside her door. *A burglar is trying to steal my father's secrets!*

The guards discovered the prince entangled in paper and dripping with wine and sliced beef. They shackled him and brought him before the throne to be sentenced at once. Cunning Ileana was already waiting, arms crossed.

My father betrayed me, but don't think I'll betray him so quickly, she said. *Twelve women are to carry you down the mountains. And when they leave you at the border of our lands, each one is to give you a kiss.* She leaned forward daintily. *May flowers spring up before you and flowers remain behind!*

The order was obeyed, and when the youngest prince arrived home, furious and disgraced, the three sons of the monarch concocted a terrible plan. The oldest and middle sons sent messages to the oldest and middle daughters, insisting that they could love them no longer unless Ileana's insult was paid for. The two elder princesses must steal all the emperor's secrets and help the brothers take their revenge.

Being foolishly in love, and rather lousy daughters and sisters, the two princesses agreed.

The Village from My Mother's Stories

The train lurched forward before I was settled, and I almost fell over—almost dropped my letter. The compartment listed on my ticket had eight seats in two rows facing each other. Since I was the last to arrive, I had to squeeze into an empty one in the middle, and when I finally sat down, the weight of everything that had happened flooded in, unexpected.

My father had betrayed me. My mother's life was in danger. My uncle was probably dead.

I was traveling alone to the other side of the country—to a place that I knew only from pictures. With nothing more than a letter, I'd have to convince people who'd never met me to take me in and use their rations to feed me. I'd have to convince them to keep me a secret.

My heart sank. It felt as if a chunk had been gouged out of its middle. I thought it was fitting: a hollow heart to match hollow bones.

Outside, the tower blocks stretched on forever. Somber morning light reflected off thousands of dark glass balcony doors. The first drops of rain speckled our window, and it looked like the buildings were melting. The factories came next, smokestacks puffing behind chain-linked fences with rusted NO TRESPASSING signs. The grays and browns and blacks of the city blurred. Then the buildings grew older and shorter. Red brick peeked from between concrete structures. Blue shutters, green ones, yellow ones, too, patterned the fronts of homes built long before we were all told to look the same. Somewhere beneath the weary plaster and wood, there was still color. This was the part of town where my father's parents had lived—the last familiar place I would see.

The train sped up outside the city limits, droplets of water streaking the glass. Buildings distorted, then vanished, replaced by rolling hills and empty fields. I checked the directions my mother had given me. I clutched the letter in my hands.

When I changed trains at the first station, the storm really started to pick up. There were only two platforms, each covered by an aluminum roof, so it was easy to find where to go, but the wind was blustering like mad and spraying rain every which way. Standing in front of a bench with water pooled in the plastic seats, I turned my back to the tracks, getting soaked, and again checked my mother's directions. I counted my tickets to make sure none had been lost. Then I looked over my father's note with the times and train lines. My stomach knotted at the sight of his handwriting, so I stuffed all the little papers down into my pockets.

On the second train, my compartment had only an old lady inside. She was sitting by the window, so I sat by the door. She smiled politely and gave me a handkerchief so I could dry off. She asked me where I was going, and I told her, but not everything. She asked me where my parents were, and I told her, but not why. She stopped asking things after that, and I watched through the glass as the platform whizzed by and the train pulled out of the station. Thunder growled over distant treetops. The forest and mountains edged closer.

Around lunchtime I opened my bag and took out the food my mother had packed. Two pieces of bread, one with apple jam, one with butter. And, wrapped in a tissue, a small chunk of dark chocolate. I gaped. I had no idea where my mother had found it or how long she'd had the sweet stashed away. I closed my bag and looked at the old lady suspiciously, in case maybe she'd seen. I ate only the bread with apple jam, just to be safe.

Early afternoon came and went. At the next station I had to wait almost an hour, but the rain finally slowed. I clutched the letter to my chest and avoided the eyes of anyone who passed by. It was strange for a child to travel unattended. Someone was bound to get curious soon. Someone was bound to ask questions I wouldn't be clever enough to deflect.

The third train was almost empty, so I rode in my compartment alone. Sometimes I peeked in my bag at the chocolate, making sure it was still real. It was nearly seven o'clock when we arrived at my stop—the very end of the line.

I gathered my things and got off, surprised to find little more than a raised slab of concrete outside. No roof, no benches, nowhere to buy tickets or ask for help. The platform looked like it was clinging to the edge of the world, floating in a sea of waving green wheat flooded with bright, golden light. I'd never seen such a wide-open space. Nor had I ever really seen mountains, not like the ones to my left, so giant they blocked out the entire horizon. I felt anxious all over again, just as I had felt when I was about to board the first train, but I pulled out my mother's directions and puffed myself up.

A few other passengers had gotten off with me. They looked like factory workers or businesspeople on holiday. One man had a camera around his neck, taking pictures of the countryside. Everyone was walking toward a small patch of pavement to meet cars. My mother had drawn a little map to show where she thought the bus stop would be, but she didn't actually know, and she'd never been a very good artist. The last time she'd seen this place, there hadn't been any buses at all. Before I could get too worried, I spotted a woman with three children standing next to a sign past the pavement.

"Hello, there," the lady said when I walked over. "Are you by yourself?"

Her children, all younger than me, looked up with frog eyes and runny noses.

"Yes. I always travel alone," I said. "I'm going to my grandparents' house."

"Well, so are we." The lady smiled. "Are you having a good summer vacation?"

"Oh, it's been super great," I replied. "I even finished my homework."

"Good for you," she said with a wink, then gave her three children a *did you hear that?* kind of look. When they boarded the bus, I sat with them, and the driver didn't even blink once.

We rode through tall, swaying grass for some time, stopping every once in a while to let somebody off at a lonely old farm. The lady asked which village my grand-parents were from, and I told her, but then I mentioned how tired I was, and that kept her from asking anything more. The sun hung low in the sky, warming my cheeks through the windows. We turned toward the mountains and the bus drove into the forest. Trees stood guard on both sides, their boughs scratching the roof. I pressed my face to the glass, tilting my head to see up to their tops. I squinted, peering into the undergrowth, thick with ferns. I had never seen so much green. The sound of the pave-ment beneath us was traded for the loud crunch of gravel. Up we went. Up, up, up, twisting and winding, bumping along like a ride at the fair.

The setting sun flashed red between the trunks of the trees, growing weaker. The lady and her three children got off, and I saw her whisper something to the driver, who looked back in my direction. I ate my piece of bread with butter, then bunched up my backpack under my head, assuring myself I would not fall asleep. Unfortunately, the seats were soft in the way only used things can be, and it wasn't long till my eyelids grew heavy. The last of the sunlight dipped below the forest floor. Shadows blanketed the narrow mountain road. Dark, unfamiliar shapes darted past my window.

I woke to the honk of a horn.

"Come on now, kid. I want to go home."

I sat up, blinking, and climbed out of the seat. Before waddling up to the front, though, I wiped my crumbs off the torn upholstery. The bus was stopped in the middle of the road, its taillights washing the gravel behind us in red. There was no one else left on board.

"Lucky that lady told me where you were going. Would have driven right past it," the driver said. "You should pay better attention."

Flushing, I muttered an apology and stumbled down the steps with sleepy feet. The cool air was a shock. I'd never been so high up, so far north. When I reached the ground, I stepped into the orange glow of a blinking streetlight. Inside the glass were dead moths. Outside were live ones, fluttering and frantic. I rubbed my bare arms, thinking the bus driver would hesitate, would make sure someone was coming to get me, but he just gave me an uncomfortable look, closed the door, and drove off.

All alone in the near dark, I tightened the straps on my backpack. Night birds cried above. Branches cracked, echoing like gunshots. My eyes were wide as I listened, but I couldn't see where the sounds came from. The world had shrunk to only what the humming orange light touched.

For the last time, I checked my mother's directions. She had warned this would be the hardest part, and I'd promised I would not be afraid.

I stepped out of the lamplight and peered up a narrow dirt road through the forest. I took a deep breath and began walking. It was a minute before my eyes adjusted to the dimness, and even then the holes and roots in the earth were well hidden. I picked my way carefully along the steep path, mostly looking down, but when a strange prickle went up my spine, I lifted my head.

There, through the trees, was a glimmer of light reflecting off yellow eyes.

I froze, my fingers grasping at the straps of my bag. The creature was watching me—whatever it was. Something monstrous. Something hairy and fanged and half-starved. Any moment now it would leap out and gobble me up. I forced myself to look back down and keep walking, faster now. I considered taking out my chocolate and stuffing it into my mouth, so it wouldn't go to waste if I died.

And then, all at once, the trees receded, and I emerged into a huge moonlit valley nestled beneath a cluster of great mountain peaks. Stars speckled the darkening sky. Candles flickered in shuttered windows.

It was the village from my mother's stories—the village where she was born, which she hadn't seen since she was seventeen.

The dirt road led past an abandoned, crumbling church, through a series of outlying houses, and then straight into the center of town. It dead-ended at a stone well, and that was where I finally paused, turning in a circle. I had drawn pictures of this place for much of my life, copying from the handful of photographs my mother had taken with her when she left. Not much seemed to have changed, so I quickly spotted a trail between houses, pointing into the fields. I took it, the grass waist-high on either side, and it brought me to a steep, wooded hill with uneven stone steps going up a shadowed path through the trees. My pulse pounded, but I went up the steps two at a time and kept my eyes straight ahead.

I was close. I knew I was close.

When the ground flattened again, I ran till I was free from the shadows and standing in a grassy yard. There, in the moonlight, was the tiny old cottage. It was built on a tall stone foundation with a pair of lattice doors that opened into cool, dark storage beneath. A stone walkway led to a little set of stone stairs, which led to a porch. This I followed.

And then I was standing in front of the big wooden door.

And then I was knocking.

When she opened it, I was already holding out the letter for her to take. I was already shaking.

"Who is it?" a man's voice, thick with a rural accent, called from somewhere inside.

She didn't answer. Instead she stared at me, and I stared at her. I didn't think I would know her, but I did. I knew her wispy white hair, struggling to free itself from the bright scarf tied under her chin. I knew her blue, diamond-patterned apron, wrapped around her wide waist, and her yellow cotton skirt. I knew her hands when they took the letter. I knew her hazel eyes when she read it, when she looked straight into mine.

But she did not know me.

The man hobbled to the door behind her, trying to see around.

"A girl from the village?" he asked.

She passed him the letter, still silent.

But I knew what to do—something not noted in any directions, something neither my mother nor father had thought of. I opened my bag and dug deep inside. From the bottom I pulled out a small embroidered pillow. It was dark green with a black border and a big, round-faced bird. I hugged it to my chest, then held it out for her to see.

"I keep it on my bed beside the little red one you helped my mother make, the one with the tiny bird flying off." I tried to keep my voice steady. If she turned me away, I wouldn't know what to do. No one had written directions for how to go back.

Her hand rose to her mouth and she dropped to her knees, pulling me to her and kissing my cheeks over and over.

"Ileana," she said, starting to cry. "It's Ileana!"

And with that, Mamaie led me into her home.

The Words You Hide

After I was swept into the cottage with kisses and embraces and long looks at my face, my mamaie sat me on the bench by the long wooden table and immediately started cooking.

"I knew someone was coming," she said. "I set three plates out at lunch by accident and then a bee got trapped in the house!"

Tataie was reading the letter, his bushy eyebrows raised high. He kept looking up at me, as if surprised all over again that I was there. Mamaie took out leftovers from supper and blew on coals in a clay stove. I tried to explain that I wasn't hungry, that I'd eaten a whole piece of bread on the bus, but my grandmother still put down dish after dish, only stopping when I started to fall asleep at the table.

In the morning, I squinted awake to shutters flung open and strange, foreign smells—cut grass, fresh air, and sausages. For a moment I didn't know where I was, and when I remembered the journey to the mountains, it was like recalling a dream.

"These are real eggs," said Mamaie. "And this is real milk. Have you ever tried pork? Does your mother serve cheese with her *mămăligă*?"

Again I sat at the table. Again my grandmother offered plate after plate. Slices of ham. Raw tomatoes and cucumbers and peppers. I'd never seen so much food. I took one bite of egg and nearly gagged, it was so rich. I took one sip of milk and went pale. I didn't even touch Mamaie's mămăligă—the cornmeal porridge piled high with sheep's-milk cheese.

"I'm not hungry," I said, and my grandmother looked at me like I was dying.

"Let her be," said Tataie.

I washed my face with water from a painted ceramic bowl and changed into a new set of clothes from my backpack. Then Tataie took me by the hand and the three of us went down the porch stairs and down the walkway and down the stone steps to the valley below.

The village was a farming community, as it had been since the first settlers arrived—hundreds or thousands of years in the past, depending on who told the tale. Most of the people lived along the one stretch of dirt road that cut through the center of town. There was no other way to get in or get out, though that didn't matter much, since only the old butcher had a truck. He used it to help carry livestock down the mountain.

The fields where everyone grew crops and raised animals took up most of the valley, and the houses that sandwiched the road almost all served more than one purpose—the one-room shop to buy goods in was also the house of the shopkeeper, who was also the barber; the tavern was also the inn, though there were only two rooms for rent and they hardly ever got used.

Dense forests of pine, ash, and fir climbed up the mountains, some so high their jagged tops touched the clouds. I tilted my head back as we made our way through the waist-high grass at the bottom of the hill, blinking in the light and the vastness. In the center of town, at the well, I surveyed the strange houses, avoiding loose animals wandering in the road. None of the buildings were more than one story, though I'd learn later that some had basements for keeping fresh food and attics for smoking meat. The roofs were made of red tile or thatched with hay topped in bright moss. The walls were unusual colors: pink and blue and pale green, white with dark yellow bands. Some houses were tall and thin and stuffed up against one another. Others were fat and low with lots of small windows. A few were cracking in disrepair, the foundations crumbling and sections of wooden skeletons showing beneath plaster, but most were quaint and well managed, with little fences penning in little yards, or pretty bunches of flowers painted on the walls by the doors. Almost every last one was decorated with some kind of wolf carving.

As Mamaie and Tataie led me through the town, people stepped out of their houses. They poked their heads from windows. They looked up from work in the distant fields. We stopped at a slanted, peach-colored home with brown shutters and a wild, buzzing garden. There was a large tree out front, and on the low branches, near the open kitchen window, cups were hung up by their handles, clinking together as they dripped dry in the sun.

At the door, Mamaie stuck her head inside, calling out before she let herself in. Neighbors peeked around hanging laundry and peered over from porch steps. My tataie stayed down at the street, where he'd been stopped by a man on a horse-drawn cart. I heard him say that I was his granddaughter, that I had come to stay for my summer holiday from school—the truth but not all of it.

Mamaie and I walked down the hall inside the peach house. My grandparents' cottage didn't have electricity. They didn't even have indoor plumbing. But this place was twice the size of the cottage and had both. I looked into the living room and spotted a TV and a sofa.

"Is someone here?" a voice called, and a wisp of a woman appeared from the back door, hands dirty up to her elbows. Her hair was pulled back in a long braid, and she had a purple scarf around her head. When she saw my mamaie, she pattered down the hall, wiping her hands on her apron. "Oh! Doina! How are you, love? Are the goats feeling well?" Then she noticed me. "Who's this?"

"My granddaughter, Ileana. She's just arrived from the city. I was hoping I might phone her mother."

"Granddaughter! Since when did you get one of those?" The woman took my hands and I could feel the bones in her joints. She was such a small thing she had only to bend a bit to kiss me on each cheek, but her fingers were strong and calloused. "Welcome to the village, dear girl! Look at those clothes! And that hair! Please call me Sanda, and come by when you're settled. I have a daughter who's about your age." She turned and yelled through the cracked back door, "Gabriella! Gabi! Someone here for you to meet!"

Out of the corner of my eye I saw a shaggy dark head peek over the sill of the living-room window, then vanish. I bristled but didn't speak up.

"Where could she have gotten to?" the small woman mused.

"Sanda is the veterinarian," my mamaie said, and at this I looked over, eyes widening.

"The veterinarian?" I asked, a story surfacing in my memory. "What about Pig-Nosed Petre?"

Mamaie's mouth dropped open, but Sanda just burst out laughing.

"Pig-Nosed Petre! I haven't heard that in years. She's certainly Liza's daughter, isn't she?" The veterinarian patted my hand once more before letting go and wiping her eyes. "Petre was my husband. He passed on some years ago, I'm afraid. The practice is mine. Has been since he died."

Sanda led us into the kitchen, where there was a refrigerator and a green phone on the wall. I felt bad about having called her dead husband pig-nosed, so I tried to smile back when she smiled at me.

"You come by anytime, Ileana," she said. "Gabi could use a new friend."

Mamaie picked up the phone and dialed, and Sanda left us to return to her backyard. When the veterinarian was out of sight, my grandmother's expression turned serious. At first I thought she was mad about what I'd said, but then she checked down the hall to see that Tataie was still guarding the front door.

The phone must have connected, because her eyes lit up.

"Liza? Liza, hello."

My heart skipped a beat, but I couldn't really hear my mother's voice, just a tiny squeak through the speaker.

"Yes, I'm doing well, dear. Yourself? Oh yes, the weather's quite nice. Your father will be heading out to the fields soon, but it's been a rather busy morning."

I didn't understand. I stared, blinking.

"The thing is, dear, I've called to tell you about Old Constanta. She's not doing well. A doctor came by town and they've put her on bedrest. It's unlikely she'll ever get up again. Do you remember that walk you took with her through the forest?" A pause. "What do you mean, *no*! How could you forget? You nearly scared the life from your tata and me! We woke up and you were missing— followed her through the woods in your nightdress! You must at least remember the trouble you got into when you returned. You shoveled manure two weeks in a row!" A pause, then a laugh. "Yes, that's right. See, you do recall."

Mamaie looked down at me and grinned. I opened my mouth to speak, but she put a finger to her lips.

"Listen, dear, it's been so good to chat. I've missed you so much. *So* much, Liza, really. But I've things to tend to this morning, so I'd best be off. I just wanted to let you know about Constanta. You give a call here at Sanda's anytime. *Anytime.* She won't mind at all. The number might have changed since she got the new line. Do you have some paper? Good."

Before I realized what was happening, the phone was back on the wall. Mamaie hadn't let me speak to my mother. No one had even said my name. My eyes started to well up, but then Mamaie took my hand, and we were suddenly back in the sunlight with my grandfather. People were waiting to meet the little girl from the city, and there was no time for questions or tears.

Later that day, after lunch at the cottage, I found the letter on the table and slipped it from its envelope. I read what my mother had written:

> *Mama,*
>
>   *We're in danger and it's not safe here for Ileana. I don't know when it will be safe again.*

*I'm sorry that this is how you meet her. I'm sorry I've
kept her from you. I'm sorry for all the things that I said
on the day that I left, and I'm sorry for all the things
I didn't say but I should have. Perhaps when this is
through, when her father and I come to bring her back
home, we can sit together and have a long talk.*
*But for now, Mama, keep my baby safe. Please don't let
them find her.*

*After you read this letter, call me, but don't mention
Ileana over the phone. Our lines are tapped—our whole
apartment. They listen to every word. So instead, tell me
something only you and Tata would know. Then I'll rest
assured that she's safe.*

Liza

I read the letter again, then once more to be sure. I
repeated in my head the pleasantries exchanged, the bits
of story about Old Constanta. And I realized that my
mother and grandmother were doing the same thing my
uncle had been doing all these years with his poetry.

Sometimes, the words that you say aren't what's important. Sometimes what's important are the words that you
hide.

The True Story

My mother's first phone call home after running away was to tell my grandparents I'd been born. In my memory of a memory that is not mine, the story changes with my mood. If I'm angry, my mother sounds angry, and her parents sound angry too.

"I have a girl of my own now, and you'll never get to meet her!" she yells into the phone.

"Well, we don't want to anyway!" my grandparents yell back, slamming down the receiver.

If I'm sad, my mother sounds sad, and her parents sound sad too.

"Tata? Mama?" she says, her voice shaking. "You have a granddaughter now."

"Liza? Liza, my sweet? Is that you?" Mamaie gasps. Tataie cannot talk because he is crying.

Most of my quirks as a storyteller I picked up from my father or uncle, but my habit of never telling the same story the same way more than once, that came from my mother alone.

"How can anyone learn to tell your stories like you if you're always changing them?" Uncle Andrei complained.

"They shouldn't tell my stories like me," I replied. "They should tell my stories like *them*."

"You can't keep writing a story forever," said my father. "Someday you'll have to accept the thing's done and let go."

At this I just rolled my eyes.

My favorite story to change was the one I was named for. This was easy, of course, since I'd never heard the real ending. If I was having a particularly bad week, for instance, Princess Ileana would realize right away that her sisters were tricking her, and instead of completing their ridiculous tasks, she'd chop off their heads.

My mother's favorite story to change was the one where she ran away from the village.

In the version she told me most often, it was spring and she was seventeen, and more than anything else in the world she loved music. All her free time was spent down at the butcher's, listening to the radio. Maria Lătăreţu and Irina Loghin and folk singers like them were her favorites, but if there wasn't anyone else around, and she kept the volume down low, Mr. Ursu sometimes let her try to catch Radio Free Europe's signal. For hours and hours she'd press her ear to the speaker, humming along through the static to songs from America. Her face was always so close to the radio, it was no surprise that the music seeped through her skin and soaked into her bones. It was no surprise that she got the idea in her head to move to the city for school, where she might become a musician herself.

She'd been chittering to her parents about this for months, about what sort of classes she wanted to take, about what sort of life she would have far away—no more chickens, no more goats, no more farming at all. They must have known she was serious, that soon she really would leave, because one warm afternoon, when she twirled into the cottage, my grandparents were waiting for her at the long table by the wood-burning stove.

"We've been talking to the veterinarian," my mamaie said. "His son's taking over the practice."

"Oh?" my mother answered, pretending to care.

Her long dark hair was kept braided under a head scarf.

She had a cute, modest nose and striking hazel eyes, a figure forming in curves beneath her dresses and skirts. She was beautiful and everyone knew. The village boys—the veterinarian's son included—often vied for her attention, but my mother's head was always too full of songs to make room for them.

When she looked up and found her parents staring, she snickered. "Some veterinarian Pig-Nosed Petre will make. Do you remember how he used to squeal when I chased him with frogs?"

Tataie wasn't smiling. "Please, Liza. Listen. We have something to tell you."

"Oh?" my mother responded again, but this time her eyes were unsure.

"Petre's started to look for a wife," said Mamaie.

My mother cocked her head. She folded her hands and put them in her lap. And then she said quietly, "I can't imagine what this has to do with me."

"The match is well made. And it's already settled," Tataie said.

My mother looked between her parents, brow rising. "You're serious."

"He's a nice boy," said Mamaie. "He's been fond of you since you were children."

But my mother began shaking her head. She stood up from the table. "You couldn't have thought I'd agree to this! I'm going to the city! I'm going to be a musician!"

"Please, Liza, end all this nonsense!" said Mamaie. "If your songs bring you joy, sing to yourself every day, but you can't expect that to feed you!"

"When I was your age, I saw cities," Tataie said, looking grim. "I promise you'll be happier just staying here."

"I'm not marrying Petre," said my mother, "and on my life, I won't stay one more night!"

And with that she started packing her things.

Or she waited till her parents were sleeping.

Or the conversation happened again, several days later.

Or it never happened at all.

In most versions of the story, there is a confrontation with yelling and tears. In most versions, there's the threat of an unwanted marriage. In most versions, my mother leaves bitter.

In every version of the story, though, no matter how else it gets told, a girl of just seventeen realizes her parents love her too much to let her live the life that she wants, so she leaves without saying good-bye. She packs her clothes and her songbook and her two favorite pillows from bed. She lights a lantern and steals a small wad of money from her parents' dresser. She leaves a letter on the long table by the wood-burning stove.

In some versions of the story, told to me when I was young, my mother walks down the mountain in the dark. She holds her lantern out before her and straps her bag to her back and takes the narrow, twisting road through the trees. The forest creeps in, but she keeps her head high and her eyes straight ahead. In some versions, the butcher stops to pick her up and she rides in the bed of his truck with the sheep. Eventually she reaches the train station at the edge of the world.

On nights when I raged over eggplant or television, when I threw fits where I threatened to leave—to run away as she had—my mother would tell me about the sounds of scurrying creatures in the woods, about the sight of yellow eyes staring back from the brush.

On nights when I knew my mother secretly missed home, she would describe the smell of grilled sausages, the taste of fresh milk and eggs, the sound of Mamaie weaving at the loom.

I often tried to discover which version of the story was true. Did my tataie sob by the door? Did my mother ride in a truck full of sheep?

Was she always still happy she left?

My father taught me most of what I knew about stories. My uncle made being a writer seem possible. But it was my mother who showed me that after a story has been told for so long, truth is not something that can be picked out like a single thread from the rest.

Something Eating Me from Inside

For three days and three nights, I did not leave my grandparents' cottage. I couldn't stop thinking of my mother's voice on the other end of the phone, close enough to almost hear but not quite. I couldn't stop thinking of how she'd run away from the very same place where I was staying. So for three days and three nights, I paced the wooden floors and wandered between the kitchen and the one little bedroom. I stared at the piece of chocolate tucked away in my bag, considered eating it all in one bite, then wrapped it up and hid it instead. When Mamaie and Tataie were out in the fields sowing crops, I climbed the ladder to the attic, lifted the boards, and peeked my head up inside. A thick, heavy smell clogged the air, and large, chunky shapes hung from the rafters. In the darkness it took me a moment to realize these were animal carcasses—meat being smoked and preserved—and I almost fell down the ladder in my fright.

I didn't want to be cramped up in the creepy old house, but I didn't want to go into town even more. Becoming acquainted with the rest of the village meant accepting that I was staying. And how long would that be? For a week? For a month? Forever?

The only way I kept calm was by telling myself that my parents would arrive at any moment. They'd discover that the wrong apartment had been bugged. My uncle was just away on a holiday. The Great Tome was safe under my bed.

There was no need to go into town, because the next time I walked out the door, I'd be going home.

So when my grandparents asked if I'd like to see the farmland, I just shook my head.

"No, thank you."

When they offered to introduce me to the local children, I politely declined.

"That's okay. I like being alone."

When my tataie brought a newly hatched chick right into the cottage, trying to tempt me to come out and see the animals they kept, I petted its head with a finger and followed him in a trance all the way to the front door. But then I started thinking how great it would be to draw tiny fuzzy chicks around the border of a page—to write a story where one falls in love with a girl just like me and becomes her best friend.

I shriveled up before making it to the porch.

"Actually, I don't like animals so much. Even really cute ones. And I don't like trees, either. Or farms. Or little villages in the woods. So it's really better if I just stay here."

I moped about, plucking at Tataie's fiddle and counting embroidered pillows. Thirty-six. Some were as tiny as my palm, with a single rosebud stitched in the center. Some were wide enough and stuffed so full that I could barely get my arms all the way round. After I ran out of pillows, I counted woven blankets. But I couldn't decide where to begin and kept starting over. Did I include the ones used as rugs? The ones nailed up like wallpaper? The ones draped over my grandparents' two narrow beds and across the backs of each chair?

I lost interest and stopped counting. In fact I lost interest in doing anything at all.

By the third day, I'd gone from sulking to irritable. I was missing my tome and my TV. The Aristocats had surely been rescued already after being abandoned out in the country, but now I'd never get to see how. I was missing my bookshelves, my bed, and my bathroom. At the cottage, there were no books at all. At the cottage, I slept on a pallet made of pillows and blankets on the kitchen floor. At the cottage, I had to pee in a stinky wooden outhouse and bathe in a metal tub in the yard.

My mamaie, who believed all ailments could be cured with good food, prepared a country spread fit for the Leader himself. I knew I shouldn't, knew I *couldn't*, test their patience any longer, but the bad feelings slipped out of my mouth in the most familiar of ways.

"I really appreciate all your hard work," I said to my grandmother, "but there are a lot of foods I don't eat. Not eggplant. Not liver. Not onions. Not peppers. I can make a list. My mom knows it. She knows everything. So it's not that your cooking isn't nice or something, but I just really only like bread and jam. Chicken's fine too. My favorite part is the legs, but heads and feet are okay."

I made a face at my mincemeat cabbage rolls and cheese mămăligă, eggplant salad and potato goulash. I pushed my plate out away from me.

Mamaie's eyes narrowed. "I see," she said.

After dinner, as the summer sun set, she took away the food dish by dish. Tataie had to go check on the goats. He put on his blue felt hat with the wide brim. He buttoned up his vest. If I hadn't seen the goats from the little window in the bedroom, I would have thought he was going all the way into town.

When the door closed behind him, Mamaie and I were alone.

"Well, let's have it out. I've kept my peace, but now the thing's filling up the place and we just don't have room," she said.

I blinked. "Don't have room for what?"

I was half ready to drop to my knees. If my mother discovered I'd been evicted from her parents' home for complaining about dinner, I would never sit properly in a chair for the rest of my life.

"Something's eating you up from inside. I want it out," said Mamaie. She poked my stomach and then picked up another stack of dishes. "It's not just sadness. I know sadness. I know loneliness, too."

I placed my palm on my stomach. When she returned to the table again, my grandmother pushed into my hands a large box of matches.

"Light the lamps," she said.

It was the first time in three days anyone had told me to do anything at all. I sat staring at the box. In my apartment I wasn't allowed to touch matches. My parents always lit the candles when the electricity went out. I stood up from the bench, looking over my shoulder to make sure Mamaie hadn't made a mistake. She was busy at the table, so I opened the box and pinched a matchstick in my fingers. Excitement swept through me. Relief, too. And, quite suddenly, I realized how tired I was of feeling bad.

It took a few strikes to light my first match, and when it caught fire I stood too long gaping. The tiny flame burned my fingertips. My second try was better. By my third, I got the first lamp lit.

"We're so happy you've come to stay with us, your tataie and I. We want you to be comfortable here. We want you to feel welcome," said Mamaie. "I don't know what your life in the city is like. I've only ever lived here in the village. But it takes a lot of work to make things grow and get ready for winter. There's the farmland to tend, the gardens to care for, and the animals, too. Your tataie and I aren't young anymore. We have trouble sometimes just keeping ourselves. If we're going to keep you, too, Ileana, we'll need help."

I looked up as I lit the last lamp, the room glowing orange. My grandmother held out a wet towel, wiggling it in my direction, and I hurried over to take it. She motioned to the dishes and I began scrubbing—another job that was not mine at home. My mamaie hummed as she dried.

"I could be a farmer, maybe," I finally said. "Or I could be the one to take care of all the baby chicks."

"That would be a good start." Then she added, "We could also use someone to do a bit of cleaning. Someone to go into town to run errands. And since you have such particular tastes, you'll be helping me with the meals. People with lists like yours need to learn how to cook for themselves. Your tataie doesn't cook, but he doesn't complain. I won't be hearing it again at my table."

She didn't sound angry, but I flinched anyway.

The wood-burning stove was made of brick smoothed over with white plaster. There were shelves like steps that went up toward the ceiling. Even with the lamps lit, the stove still put off the brightest light in the room, so when the dishes were done, Mamaie pulled up a chair and took out her embroidery. I sat down on the woven rug next to her, scooting back a bit from the heat.

"In the city, I didn't have those kinds of jobs," I said. "I mean, I cleaned my room when Mama got mad. But mostly I had a different job."

"You can do your city job here."

I shook my head. "I can't."

"What was it, then?"

I pulled at the frayed ends of the rug, and she reached down and smacked my hand with her crewel needle. I looked up and considered whether or not to react before saying, "I was the storyteller."

Mamaie raised her eyebrows. "That's an important job. And for someone so young."

"Well . . ." I started to pick at the rug again but stopped and put my hands in my lap. "I'm going to . . . I wanted to be a writer when I grew up. My uncle Andrei is a writer— or at least he was before the Securitate took him away. And my tata, he teaches at the university. He taught me all about stories and how the parts go together, like character and setting and the climax." I realized what I was saying and clamped my mouth shut. It seemed that perhaps Mamaie was right, because something inside started gnawing like mad. "But I'm not going to be a writer anymore. Stories are stupid and so are people who like them."

Mamaie watched me for a long time, narrowing her eyes beneath her red-and-black scarf. She watched me so long I got nervous and shrugged. "What? Why are you looking at me?"

"I'm trying to see what's eating you up." She leaned

forward, squinting. "It's there, all right. Nasty little thing. I wonder how we'll ever get it out."

I touched my stomach again, uncomfortable, and said stubbornly, "There's nothing eating me. I'd know it."

"Maybe I'm wrong." She sat back, sighing. "It's too bad, really, about the storytelling. Everyone would have been so excited."

I frowned. "What do you mean?"

"Well, stories are very important in this village. We have a long tradition of telling tales. It's how we remember our history, how we pass the time when the winters are harsh or a day in the fields has been long. And good tellers are hard to come by, you know. I suspect the other villagers would have been quite thrilled to hear someone new."

"Oh," I said. And then, feeling defensive: "What kind of stories do people tell here? Like kissing stories and ones for little kids about animals? Like that kind of thing?"

"My goodness, no," said Mamaie, taken aback. "Have you heard about the *balauri*? The twelve-headed, finned dragons whose spit turns into precious stones?"

I shook my head.

"How about Muma Pădurii, the Mother of the Forest, who steals the sleep of little girls and boys or kidnaps them to cook in her sour soup?"

I shook my head again.

"The *pricolici*, maybe? The dead who return as giant wolf-beasts and attack travelers in the woods? Or the *iele*, who dance in the moonlight on the tops of the trees with bells tied to their ankles?"

This time I scrunched up my nose. "Your storytellers tell stories like those?"

"Of course. Really wonderful tellers can cast a spell over the whole audience, too, entrancing people so they forget even to breathe! I expect you'd be a teller like that." But then she raised her hands, laughing. "What am I saying? You don't like stories. They're for stupid people. And I can see you aren't stupid."

I chewed my cheek. "I mean, I still like *some* stories. I'd probably like those if I heard them. It's just . . . all my stories are gone. Tata took them."

Mamaie scoffed. "You can't take someone's stories."

"But he did," I insisted. "He burned the Great Tome. It's gone, really. He thought my stories were dangerous."

"Stories *are* dangerous. He was right to be wary. But once a story is told, it stays with you forever." She tapped my forehead with her crewel needle. "If you want them, you'll find them."

When I thought about it, it seemed this was true. Most

of the time I didn't need the Great Tome to tell stories. I looked up, suspicious. "Are you a storyteller, Mamaie?"

She chuckled. "Your tataie would say so, but not in the way that you mean."

"Can you tell any stories like the ones you talked about, though? About the Mother of the Forest and the balauri? That sort of stuff?"

"Well, I couldn't tell you about characters and climaxes and all those things from the university. But I have a few stories I know. Your tataie and I often sit by the stove while I work on my pillows and blankets. Sometimes he'll play his fiddle and we'll tell stories to keep away ghosts."

My eyes widened. "You have ghosts here too?"

"There are ghosts everywhere, child. The world is full of them."

I twisted my fingers together, looking back down at the rug. "I think I'd like to listen to your stories."

"I think I'd like to tell them to you," she said. "And perhaps if you find your own stories again, you can do your job from before. Your tataie and I are good listeners."

My grandfather came in through the door then, the smell of the night on his clothes, and Mamaie smiled.

"But tomorrow I have to get up extra early to help in the fields," she said. "So it's off to bed now. You can come with us in the morning if you like. The other children will be there. In this village, we all work together."

After a moment I nodded. "I could maybe go for a while. I still don't know if I want to be a storyteller again, so if I'm going to be a farmer, I'll have to start practicing."

"A farmer?" my tataie repeated, hanging up his hat and taking off his vest. "Well, I'll be."

The next morning, when I sat down for breakfast, I found a small yellow notebook and a ballpoint pen at my place.

"Oh, don't mind that," my mamaie said, pushing bread with plum jam in front of me. "It's just a little thing. In case you start to remember."

I watched the notebook as I ate, fingers twitching. I set it by a painted bowl of water as I brushed my teeth. Before we left, I opened it just long enough to flip through the pages, and then again to draw a little puffy chick. The notebook could fit in my pocket, so I took it with me to the fields. And at lunch, after weeding around potatoes and feeding the cows, I sat down and made a few notes about the people I'd met and the things I'd seen.

Slowly, bit by bit, the something eating me from inside trickled out.

The Wasp Nest

After my first couple of weeks in the village, my grandparents became concerned because I hadn't made any friends. This was fine with me, though. There was no reason to make friends when I'd be leaving so soon, and I was busy anyhow, learning to cook and take care of the animals. I spent lots of time in the fields where everyone worked, and it was much more fun to see how many buckets of water I could carry before I collapsed, or to fork hay into giant piles, than to talk to the children from town.

Sometimes, when there was a lot to do at the cottage, I stayed back and fed the chickens or pulled weeds from Mamaie's garden. I started making lunch for everyone all by myself and collected eggs and goat milk to trade for bread or cheese or a salve for Tataie's leg cramps. I'd walk to the store for cornmeal or thread, or to the old butcher's to get bones for broth. I liked Mr. Ursu and his big chopping block. He had a great gray mustache and was always telling jokes and playing tricks, sticking his hand under his bloody apron and shouting that he'd cut it off. Even better, he kept his portable radio on pretty much all the time and talked often about how he missed my mother's singing. When I asked him if he'd let Mama ride down the mountain in his truck with the sheep, he laughed till he started to cough.

"Of course not. Where did you hear such a thing?" he asked, a hand patting his chest.

I shrugged, pretty sure he was lying.

The truth was, I was content being useful and spending time with my notebook. And even in the city, I didn't have many friends. There were no other children on my floor of the apartment building, and most of my classmates had brothers and sisters to play with at home. That just left the other kids in the Pioneer club, and I hated them. In fact I hated everything about the Pioneers—our matching red triangle scarves, our dumb songs, our "patriotic work," where we had to clean up trash or sort potatoes. My father had made me join the club in second grade with all the other students in my class, and there'd been a long, boring oath ceremony at the Communist Party Museum. One time we got to go camping, and that was fun, but mostly we just went to meetings and practiced marching or reciting bad poetry about the Leader.

"It's good for you to do things you don't like," said my father. "It makes you appreciate the things you like more."

I knew that really he was just scared of how it would look if I got kicked out. Already, long before the electrician, our names were on lists.

Mamaie pressed me to make friends, though, insisting that I'd like the village children.

"You'll meet someone who changes your mind. I'm just certain," she said. "Have you walked into any spiderwebs recently? That's a strong sign. You know, Mr. Bălan, the innkeeper, has a son who's just turned eleven. And there's Sanda's girl, Gabi. Have you thought about playing with her?"

I had, but whenever I saw her, she ran away.

"I'm really okay just hanging out with the goats," I replied.

"The goats!"

"Leave her be," Tataie said. "If she wants to make friends, she'll make friends."

Mamaie gave him a look, then innocently examined the

stitching on her apron. "If you humor me and play with the other children tomorrow, I'll tell you a story about your mother."

My eyes widened. "Like from when she was a kid? Like what you told on the phone?"

"If that's what you want."

The next morning, while Mamaie and Tataie were out, I searched around the cottage for a spiderweb, then walked into it on purpose, shivering and frantically rubbing my hair. After that I went down the hill with the intention of finding friends—any would do. It didn't take long till I spotted some children hanging out near the well. The girls were holding hands in a circle. Two of them looked much alike, but the third was smaller, with shaggy dark hair and a metal leg brace with an extra-tall shoe—the veterinarian's daughter. In the middle of the road, the boys were sitting in the dirt looking at a shared collection of brightly colored candy wrappers. I crept closer to hear what they were saying.

Most of the collection belonged to Ioan, the innkeeper's son, who had an older cousin who went abroad for work, but one of the other boys was showing off his own addition—a full-size candy-bar wrapper he'd found next to a trash can at the bus stop. It was white with some blue decorations and an English word in red letters. He tried to read the name, but all he could figure out was the number three, which anyone could have done, since it was the same in Romanian.

"I bet you stole it," said Ioan, making a face. He had dirty-blond hair that grew past his elephant ears. Back in Bucharest the police would have stopped him, since hair that long on boys was illegal.

"Some foreigner threw it on the ground," said the other kid defensively.

"I bet you're the one taking palinca from my father's tavern, too," accused Ioan.

One of the older boys ruffled Ioan's long hair, snickering. "Still sore from that whooping?"

The innkeeper's son shoved him off. "I didn't deserve it. Someone's coming in and stealing things. There were footprints."

I cleared my throat and the boys finally noticed me hovering. They put their hands protectively over their treasure.

"Hey, look," Ioan said to the others. "It's Ileana. Do you have candy in your city? Did you bring any with you?"

"No," I said.

"Well, go away, then. Go play with the girls."

"Yeah, go play with the girls," said the older boy.

"They're teaching Gabi the Spitter how to dance."

It mostly just looked like they were laughing at Gabi. She kept trying to copy their steps, but with her brace she couldn't move quite the same way.

"She'll get mad and start spitting any second now. Just watch," said Ioan.

I started to get the feeling these kids weren't very nice, but I was determined to hear Mamaie's story, so I took a seat on the edge of the stone well. When Gabi spotted me, though, she turned and darted out of the circle, vanishing down a little alley between houses. The other two girls looked to see what had scared her off, and I stood up, offering my prettiest smile. It seemed to have no effect.

"Why do you always dress like a boy?" asked one of the girls.

She was wearing a skirt and a blouse and a scarf tied under her chin. The girl standing beside her was dressed almost the same. I bit down on my tongue to keep from saying something nasty and pretended I hadn't heard. Being in the Pioneers had at least taught me how to do that much.

"Do you want to come play at the cottage? I can't play for long 'cause I'm really, really busy today, and my parents could show up to take me back to the city any second, but I could use some help making flower necklaces for the goats. And a lot of my tataie's chickens still haven't been named," I said. Then, thinking of a story, I added, "Also, there's a place under the house where we can crawl around in the dirt and look for buried curse boxes."

The girls blinked in unison till one said, "You're really weird."

They went right back to doing their dance.

I thought about just leaving. I had to pee anyway, and these children seemed pretty much the same as the ones at home. If they told any stories at all, very likely none of them would be worth writing down. But when I remembered Mamaie's promise, I hung my head and scrunched up my nose and muttered, "I have a piece of chocolate I'll cut up and share with anyone who plays with me."

Ioan leaped to his feet. The girls' eyes got huge. By the time I was halfway through the fields and up the hill, I had a whole troop of children trailing after me. When everyone started playing in the yard—and I started counting—I realized that if I divided the chocolate into so many pieces, we'd each only get just the tiniest nibble. The other kids might say I'd tricked them, but I didn't really care, since Mamaie would certainly admit that I'd held up my end of her deal.

The girls were playing a clapping game that determined

how many children they'd have. The boys had just begun sniping one another, belly down in the grass, clutching long, knobby sticks. I was trying to decide which group to join, when I remembered again that I had to go pee. Back home this wouldn't have been a big deal, but at the cottage, of course, there was no toilet inside. Instead, in the yard was a little wooden house with a door.

And under the cusp of the tiny roof was a wasp nest.

Country wasps were much bigger than the ones in the city. Their abdomens had black and yellow stripes. Tataie had warned me about them. He'd said last fall he'd been stung, and his finger swelled up till he thought it would burst. For days it looked like an overstuffed sausage. When he'd noticed the new nest on the outhouse, he'd warned me about that, too, promising to get rid of it. But he'd been busy—my grandparents always were busy—so I'd taken to sneaking around and peeing in the backyard or the bushes. If I did that now, the other children would tease me for sure.

I crossed my legs. I bit my lip. I toed a step closer. The wasps dove around the door and skimmed the grass. My skin prickled at the sound of their hum.

"Where's the chocolate?" Ioan called from the porch.

"Hold on," I called back, then stood there grinding

my teeth and squeezing my thighs tight together.

"What are you doing?" He came over. "Is this one of your games?"

I shook my head, then reluctantly pointed. "I have to use the toilet, but there are wasps."

He followed my finger, brow raised, and the other children started to take interest too.

"So what?" He shrugged. "Just go really fast."

"They might sting me."

"So what?"

"Tataie said when he got stung it hurt for forever."

"So what?"

I started to hate him.

"They won't bother you if you don't bother them," said one of the girls.

"That's bees, not wasps," corrected the other. "Wasps can smell if you're afraid. And if you are, then they chase you."

"Yeah, but if you move really, really slow and hold your breath, they can't figure out where you are," added the boy with the full-size candy wrapper.

None of this appeared to be sound advice.

"I've been stung lots of times," said Ioan. "It doesn't even hurt. I guess your tataie's just a baby like city kids."

I didn't really care what he was saying, since all I could think about was how I was seconds away from peeing my pants. Groaning, I made a run for the outhouse. I knew a wasp might be hiding under the handle—that was how Tataie had been stung—so I checked before I opened the door. Relief swept over me once I was safely inside. I crumpled up some newspaper for wiping. Real toilet paper was almost impossible to buy in the country. Everything seemed all right until I was pulling back up my shorts— until I heard the children out in the yard go quiet as pigs in a cornfield.

When someone shushed someone else, I knew something was wrong.

"What are you guys doing?" I called, but the only response was a spatter of laughter.

There was a sound, something small and hard clipping the side of the outhouse and smacking the roof. That was when the buzzing started—loud and mad, first around the outside of the door, then everywhere all at once.

"What's going on?" I yelled.

The village children began laughing. Through the cracks between the wooden boards, I could see them all running and jumping. My heart raced.

"This isn't funny!" I shouted.

"Come out, Ileana! You've got to come out!" one of the girls screeched.

"I can't! They'll get me!"

"You've got to come out," she repeated, breathless from giggling. *"They're going inside!"*

I looked up. The wasps had squeezed through the space between the roof and the wall. They were dashing around over my head. I cried out and grabbed the handle, but the door wouldn't budge. Pain shot through my shoulder and straight up my neck, so terrible that for a moment the whole world turned white. I tried the door again, desperate now, sobbing. The laughter only grew louder. I threw myself against the outhouse so hard that it tilted. I started to scream.

Then the other children started screaming too.

"Gross!" shouted Ioan.

"Get away! Get away!" cried a girl.

"Make a run for it! Hurry! She's spitting!"

There was chaos. A stampede of feet. Then, finally, silence outside. I was still banging on the door, yelling and kicking, when all of sudden it swung open. I fell out onto the grass.

First I saw feet. An extra-tall shoe. A brace attached to a short leg. I looked up into the face of the veterinarian's daughter. In her hand was a stick, which I realized the other children had used to prop closed the door. Gabi looked like she wanted to run away again, but before she could, I said, "I got stung on my shoulder," and started crying once more. That must have made her feel bad for me, because she put down the stick and helped me to the porch.

"Could you go get my grandparents?" I asked, sniffling, and she nodded and hurried off toward the fields.

Mamaie and Tataie showed up soon after, while I was still sitting there nursing my wound. My grandmother fussed and fumed and finally just stomped right down the hill, knocking on parents' doors and wagging her finger. Tataie stayed behind, quietly chewing tobacco and packing it wet on top of the welt. My whole shoulder was still throbbing when my grandmother got back. Since the village didn't have a doctor, Sanda came up to check on me and gave me a paste made from ground oatmeal to put on the sting. Then she washed my shoulder and covered it with a tied cloth.

"Sorry, but we're all out of bandages," she said. "I could have sworn I had some left. Maybe Gabi knows where they are."

I told the veterinarian how her daughter had saved me. "Please tell her thank you," I said. "I'd do it myself, but I'm afraid she'll just run away."

Sanda sighed. "She's very shy, isn't she? The other children aren't always nice to her. I guess they aren't always nice to anyone who seems different. Give Gabi some time, though. I'm sure she'll warm up."

Later Mr. Bălan dragged Ioan to the cottage and held him by the ear on our front porch.

"It was just a joke," the boy muttered. "Besides, if you weren't so scared, then they wouldn't have stung you."

His father smacked him on the back of the head till he apologized properly.

The other children came too, one at a time, to say sorry. I could tell, though, that really they were just thinking about the chocolate I owed them. And it was funny, since the only person I wanted to share with hadn't asked for any at all.

After supper Tataie took out his fiddle and played while Mamaie sat at the loom. Looking pitiful, I said in the quietest voice, "I think I'd feel a lot better if I had a story."

My grandmother glanced up from her work. "Are you still wanting the one about Old Constanta?"

"Yes, please."

I didn't expect any resistance. The story was technically mine. I'd done just as she'd asked and gotten stung, too. And I'd been so good recently. I was even eating all my sour cabbage these days—though, truthfully, that was mostly due to the fact that Mamaie swore that leaving leftovers on your plate meant you'd grow up to marry someone terribly ugly.

It was a surprise to watch my grandmother hesitate, to see her share an uncertain look with my grandfather.

For a moment Tataie stopped playing, and the cottage went quiet except for the crackle of wood. But then, after a twist of a peg, he nodded, and my Mamaie's eyes went back to her work. She passed the shuttle through yarn as she spoke, the rhythmic slide of the reed and creak of her feet at the treadles weaving the story into the world.

"Once upon a time, something happened," she said.

I took out my notebook and readied my pen.

The One About
Old Constanta

There once was a devout woman named Constanta who lived in a village in the mountains. She prayed every day, and though she could not read, she always kept close her psalm book. Her house was modest and yellow and right across from the lovely old church, which had colorful paintings of icons all over the walls. She appreciated that she never had to walk far for services.

Constanta's life largely consisted of tending her garden and taking care of her family, but eventually her children, all girls, married and left. Soon after, her husband, who'd survived the First World War, was killed in the Second. Some women might have crumbled, but Constanta stood strong. With the church so nearby, and with such a nice priest, she wasn't lonely at all. Most of her time she spent praying and generally minding her own business.

She was still a mild, sensible woman back then.

She was a mild, sensible woman until the night the priest vanished right out of his home—right out of his bed—never again to be seen.

The man had been kind but so simple. He'd spoken his mind far too loudly. The Red Army's occupation since the Second World War was nothing to bring up in a sermon. Soldiers appeared in the village soon after the priest disappeared. Everyone gathered to listen as an official in a brown suit and tie explained how the land and the animals and the tools now belonged to all the people.

The property of the church became the property of the country—as did the property of the farmers. And the villagers came together to churn the dirt and grow the crops. And the state came to take the crops far away.

The church across the road from Constanta's house sat quiet and empty. Vines grew through its glass windows and painted walls. The colorful icons chipped and faded.

Constanta became Old Constanta, though she'd been old a long time already.

Her neighbors took pity, believing she was a tame, fragile thing, liable to break at a whisper now that so much had been lost. They checked on her regularly. They brought her food and helped with her chores. When she called them nasty names or spat at their feet, their only reaction was to shake their heads.

"Poor old dear, hardly knows where she is."

The village children were not quite as forgiving. They were frightened of Old Constanta's sagging skin and sharp tongue. When she approached, they scattered like mice, but behind her back they were vicious. They left pig dung and dead birds at her door. They told stories claiming that she'd eaten her daughters, cooked them up in sour soup— that she'd cursed her husband so he'd die in the war.

The stories only got worse when Old Constanta started taking walks up the mountain.

Every Sunday, in the dark before dawn, she'd disappear into the woods.

When my mother was still a little girl, it was all the rage around harvest time to loiter in the road that ran through the village. The trucks would come up and stop to load crops. And since the trucks were driven by young, eligible bachelors from down the mountain, the girls would scurry out of their homes and stand in little groups near the well. The brave ones would lean into the driver's-side windows and bat their lashes and smile with teeth. Old Constanta always watched from her porch, palm flat on the top of her prayer book. She would stare with cold eyes till the trucks drove away.

My young mother, unloading vegetables and fruit from horse-drawn carts, would not talk to the men in the trucks, though they always tried to get her attention. She would not giggle with the girls by the side of the road. Instead she would hum to herself as she watched Old Constanta.

To the rest of the villagers, the woman was a shame and a burden. She celebrated holidays thirteen days after everyone else, refusing to change to the Gregorian calendar. She prayed in the ruins of the old church.

To my mother, Old Constanta was the most interesting person in town.

Some Sundays before dawn, my mother would sneak out the front door in the dark, take the stairs down the porch of the cottage, and hurry beyond the stone walkway to the edge of the trees. If she timed it just right, she could catch Old Constanta in passing. Eventually, these Sundays became ritual—my mother rose in the dark as if to a call, watching the wrinkled old woman creep up the mountain step by haggard step, a great hump under the shawl on her back.

Then one early, early morning, while the world was still

black as night, my mother tiptoed out of the cottage and crouched down in her usual place just as a lantern appeared through the trees. Cloth shuffled. Bones creaked. A cane tapped on the stones.

"I'll have a word with the one who's been watching me," a croaking voice called.

My mother froze, terrified. She imagined Old Constanta pinching her by the ear and dragging her back into the cottage. But even though she was frightened, she peeked her head out from the bushes.

"I'm sorry, Old Constanta. I didn't mean anything rude. I just wanted to find out where you go every week. Will you tell my mama?"

Old Constanta scoffed and again began hobbling up the mountain.

"If you want to know where I'm going, then come." With a glance at my mother's nightdress and shawl, she added, "But make sure you cover your head. We'll soon be in the house of the Lord."

My mother didn't hesitate. In a breath she was trailing the old woman's heels. "Is it far? What sort of house could possibly be out in the forest?"

"There's an ancient monastery at the top of the world," Old Constanta replied, "one of the few in these mountains left standing. The monks there have kept themselves hidden, copying books. Their brains are still all their own—not washed and dried up like the others."

"How exciting!" my mother said, but then looked over her shoulder. Already her cottage was out of sight through the trees. "Will I be home before dawn, Old Constanta?"

"If we hurry," the woman said. After a moment, though, she looked back. "But you'll cover your head or I'll guide you no farther. And don't ask me to stop and let you rest, because I won't."

My mother covered her head with her shawl, eyes wide. Up the mountains they went. Up higher and higher. For an hour they walked in the dark, the lantern swinging from Old Constanta's wrist. Then, quite unexpectedly, following no sign in the path that my mother could see, the woman turned away from the worn stone stairs and stepped into the trees. Farther and farther they traveled this way, till a wolf howled in the distance and my mother stopped in her tracks. Ahead, Old Constanta did not slow.

It was in that moment that my mother realized no one knew where she was. No one even knew she had left. She was in the middle of the woods, in the night, off the path. Already she was tired from hiking.

And something was wrong with the trees.

The deeper into the forest they traveled, the higher and higher up the mountain they climbed, the stranger the trees looked. Some bent at their trunks in the middle. Some spiraled round and round and up like a screw. Some had branches jutting out of their thick, exposed roots.

Worst of all, my mother wasn't even sure it was still Old Constanta she followed.

Watching the feeble, hunched woman ahead, she feared she'd been tricked by the Mother of the Forest and was being led away to the witch's dreadful little house.

But my mother had no choice. Surely, she couldn't find her way back on her own. She hurried forward and kept near the old woman, night sounds edging closer. The twisted, ugly trees grew stranger and larger in size. Again the wolves howled. Ferns shifted at my mother's ankles as dark shapes were disturbed from their hovels. When she reached up to move a low-hanging branch, something long, slick, and heavy dropped with a thud to the grass and slithered away.

Finally, moonlight from a distant clearing could be seen through the trees. Old Constanta crossed herself again and again. "Not much farther now," she said.

But my mother was exhausted. She had to rest. Her feet were aching. She was hungry, and her nightdress was stained brown and black at the hem. Mud stuck to the soles of her boots.

"I don't think I can go on. Could we stop for a minute, Constanta?"

The old woman didn't even glance back. "It's not safe here in the forest."

They walked a bit farther, and again my mother complained.

"Just for a few minutes. Please, Constanta, please."

"Didn't you hear me, child? It's not safe. Just over this hill, then we're there."

They walked a bit farther, and this time my mother could take it no more.

"Constanta, I must catch my breath. There's a stick in my shoe and my shawl won't stay put. Can't we just sit down on that rock while I fix it?"

Old Constanta looked over her shoulders, and sure enough my mother's shawl had fallen, dragging now through the leaves. The old woman peered around. All was quiet, moonlight spilling down through the boughs. A few paces away was a white-faced rock, jutting out from the earth.

"Just for a moment. Just to tidy your shawl. We shouldn't linger," she said.

So together they sat on the rock. My mother unlaced her boot to fish out the stick, and Old Constanta picked the leaves off the shawl with her knobby, pale hands.

And then the wolves howled again.

One call came from below. A dark figure dashed through the trees. The other call came from just at their backs. They didn't have time to look, time to turn, time to duck before it leaped right over their shoulders.

A massive white beast.

My mother's scream caught in her throat as he slid to a stop on the trail just below, then looked up—straight into her eyes. The wolf's silken coat shimmered, and in the space of a drawn breath, he darted into the woods and was gone.

My mother couldn't find her feet fast enough.

She ran past Old Constanta, not stopping till she'd reached the top of the world. There, outside the monastery, she collapsed to her knees, gasping for air. When the old widow finally caught up, she pursed her lips disapprovingly.

"Perhaps next time you'll listen," she said. "Always remember, in this forest you're never alone."

Together they went inside the monastery to pray, and on the way back down the mountain, my mother did not ask once to rest.

Tracks

It had been nearly a month since I'd left home, and still there was no sign of my parents—not a letter, not a phone call, not anything. School was set to start in a little over three weeks, and it was becoming a serious possibility that I'd have to attend class in the village, so Mamaie and Tataie took me down the hill to meet Mrs. Sala, the teacher.

On our walk through the valley we passed the two-room schoolhouse, which in the summer was used to store produce and seeds. I peeked through a window and saw the desks all pushed up to the walls, piled with tools and burlap sacks. The floor was covered in dirt, and from the tracks on the wood, it looked like a goat or two had gotten inside. I thought it was funny, picturing a goat in the school, so I made a note in my book.

Mrs. Sala's house was little and blue, with a fenced-in place out back for the pigs. Right down the street was the abandoned old church, where vines grew through broken glass and over the faded paintings of icons. I squinted, looking closer, and spotted a lonely wicker basket sitting outside the busted double doors, which seemed a bit strange. The townspeople thought the old place was haunted. They wouldn't even use it for storing goats.

Since Mrs. Sala lived near the schoolhouse and the abandoned church, that meant she lived near Old Constanta's house too. Everything was nearby in the village. I could see the old woman's cottage from Mrs. Sala's front porch. The curtains were drawn and the grass was overgrown.

"Does she still go for walks up the mountain at night?" I whispered.

"Of course not!" Mamaie said. "She's far too old now. And the monastery has been empty for many, many years."

But Tataie made a noise in his throat. "Well, someone's been traveling up that path. Seen their footprints in the forest."

Mamaie prodded him with her elbow as Mrs. Sala

opened the door. She was plump and she wore her head scarf much tighter than my grandmother. Her nose was straight and thin, and her eyebrows rose right to the top of her forehead when she saw me.

"My gracious, look at those clothes. Do they let girls dress like this in the city?"

"I suppose they do," Mamaie answered politely.

I tugged on my white shorts and looked down at my brown tank top. Here in the village they had many more colors. Some people dyed the cotton themselves or embroidered vests with designs. At first, I'd thought that was the trouble—that I looked horribly plain. Now I realized that the problem was that I didn't wear dresses, but I still couldn't understand why it mattered.

Mamaie explained that my parents were "having some trouble financially" and that I would be staying "till things even out." I knew this was at least partly a lie.

"Don't worry," I added. "They're coming to get me real soon. I probably don't have to go to school with you at all."

"But just to be safe," said Mamaie, placing a hand on my shoulder.

I nodded. "Yeah, you know, just to be safe."

Mrs. Sala's eyebrows were still clinging to the top of her

forehead, but she smiled and nodded and stepped to the side.

"Why don't you all come in, then, and we'll have a nice chat," she said.

Mrs. Sala's husband was out back helping birth some piglets, so he didn't join us. We could hear squealing in the yard as the schoolteacher stepped into the kitchen. It was very difficult to find coffee—my parents complained all the time—so no one was surprised when Mrs. Sala explained she didn't have any. However, since she was a proper host, she returned with glasses of water and tiny plates of chunky black cherry jam for each of us. I picked at the treat with my spoon while the adults talked.

"We were hoping you could give Ileana your homework assignments. That way she won't be behind when class starts," Mamaie said.

My mouth fell open.

"We're so close to the end of the holiday, though," said Mrs. Sala. "Didn't you have homework for your city school?"

I nodded, sitting forward. "So much. Tons of homework. Boatloads of it."

"And how much have you finished?"

"All of it, like forever ago," I said, and Mrs. Sala's eyes

narrowed. I'd always found it both enchanting and frustrating how easily teachers could sniff out a lie.

"You have it with you here in the village, of course?"

I glanced at my grandparents, then looked down at my feet.

"She was so excited to come stay with us," Mamaie said. "Poor dear forgot to pack it."

"I see," said the schoolteacher. She picked up a pad of paper and a pencil and passed them to me. "Could you write down the assignments you remember?"

I smiled, big and cheesy, panicking. It would have been much easier to remember something I'd done—or at least something I'd *considered* doing. After a couple of minutes I passed back the paper with only a few items, half of which I'd made up. Mrs. Sala barely glanced at the list before setting it down. She explained the importance of following the state curriculum, how unfortunate it would be if I got behind. Mrs. Sala was a good Communist.

"If there's even a chance you'll be joining our class here in the village, you'll need to have studied the same material as the other children," she said.

My heart sank to my toes as she brought out books and supplies, calling special attention to the bug project. It was the hardest of all the assignments. It had a list five pages long with little boxes to check and black-and-white pictures to use as a guide. Everyone was supposed to catch as many bugs as they could and pin them to a board. While Mrs. Sala was going over the instructions, I started to feel really awful. I'd been sure I'd left my homework so far behind that there was no way it would ever catch up to me. Now I had three weeks to complete a whole summer's work.

"Since you've already finished so many similar projects at home, this should take you no time at all." The school-teacher smiled—a special, knowing smile just for me. I gave it right back but with teeth.

The next day, in the grass behind the cottage, I spread out my books, lining them up by size and weight, and then made dandelion wreaths for the goats to wear on their heads.

In the back of my mind was the bug project, but I had serious qualms about the whole thing. I'd never liked catching bugs for science. I only liked catching them for fun, then letting them go. I hated the way their tiny bod-ies popped when I poked them through with the pin. I hated how they tried to flutter or climb out of the cotton-ball jar. Earlier that morning I'd tried to catch a few beetles and worms, but they were worth very few points, and I'd wound up freeing almost all of them.

Just as I was wondering how much trouble I'd get in for turning in nothing at all, a thin, white-and-green, veiny butterfly landed on top of my notebook. My eyes darted to the homework sheets on my left. I picked up the checklist, trying to move as slowly as I could, and turned pages till I found the right section. Sure enough, she was there—a type of Pieridae. While playing alone, I'd spotted dozens of butterflies with shimmery blue wings, and more than a couple of the fat, fuzzy kind, but I'd never seen any like this. Because she looked just like a leaf and was so hard to find, she was worth twenty points—a gold mine, more than triple most anything else.

The butterfly twitched up off my notebook and alighted on the gate of the goat pen, balancing on the tip of a wire. I reached for my net without looking. I stood up and inched forward. But a breeze swept through the backyard and the Pieridae took flight.

I was off in a breath, dashing across the grass and into the trees. The sound of bleating goats dulled behind me. I followed the butterfly down the slope of the hill, watching my feet so I wouldn't go tumbling. I ducked under branches, leaped over rocks, slid through a pile of bramble and leaves. Then I came stumbling out of the woods and found myself down in the valley. I stood stunned for a moment, surprised I had traveled so far. When I spotted the butterfly in the nearby grass, riding the edge of a long, swaying blade, I dove forward, swinging, and missed her. Again I went bounding, heedlessly running through the waist-high fields behind houses. In the distance I heard voices, the rumble of a cranky muffler. The farmers were close by, my mamaie and tataie, probably, too. If they saw me, I might get in trouble, since I was confined to the cottage till my homework was done. But catching just this one bug would spare so many others, and it would mean I might actually have a shot at completing the assignment.

The Pieridae landed again, and when I swung this time, I didn't miss. My net smacked into the side of an old out-building, the butterfly fluttering wildly as she was trapped between mesh and rotted, dark planks. I was so pleased with myself—pinching the top of the net in my fist so she couldn't escape, backing away and admiring my catch—that I hadn't even realized where I was.

Finally, I turned my face up. My eyes widened.

The old church.

Not only was this much farther than I was supposed to go by myself—even when there wasn't homework to do—but everyone in the village knew this place was bursting with ghosts. When I helped in the fields, the other kids tried to scare me, telling how they heard crying and moans in the night. I'd try to scare them right back, talking about the ghost who liked to prank-call my apartment, but they always insisted their ghosts were worse, and that, if I had any sense, I'd better never go down to the old church alone.

I took a step closer. I lifted up on my tiptoes at the window, but the stained glass was too grime-covered to see in. I lowered myself back down.

And that was when I saw the tracks in the dirt.

Big tracks. Big boots.

I crept around to the front of the building, following, and they led me straight to the large double doors. One was ajar, hanging on by a single nail. It had an emblem above the handle shaped like a wolf's head. There was a gap just perfect for a girl to slip through, so I looked around to make sure no one could see. Ioan and the other kids would tell me all sorts of nonsense if they found out I'd gone inside, and my grandparents would likely get mad. But the only house with windows pointed my way was bedridden Old Constanta's, so I got down on my knees and crawled through the gap, the pole attached to my net scraping the floor.

The moment I stood up, I knew I wasn't alone.

There was a smell that repulsed me. Muddy boot tracks

went in but not out. I followed them with my eyes down the center of the building. A row of damp, broken chairs lined the left wall. Midday sunlight poked through the places where the roof had collapsed, vines gushing in through the crumbling tiles. Paintings covered the building from ceiling to floor, and the way the light hit them, they looked like they were on fire. At the back wall, where the tracks ended on the other side of the room, dozens of chipped, faded, two-dimensional people were dressed in colorful robes with glimmering circles drawn around their heads.

Beneath them, a man was lying on the floor.

He raised his eyes when he heard me come in.

Despite all the bruises, despite the full beard and the long, oily hair, despite the dirt on his face, I knew who he was—but he did not know me.

The net dropped from my hand with a clatter. The butterfly took off into the air.

"Uncle Andrei," I said.

Soon the Securitate would be coming.

Soon the tracks would lead them here, straight to me.

The House
with Three Eyes

I crept closer.

"Uncle Andrei," I repeated. "Uncle Andrei, why are you here?"

I crept till I was right in front of him, till I could reach down to see if he was real. Before I could touch him, his dirty hand shot up and grabbed my shirt.

"Get out! Leave now and don't come back!"

I tried to protest, but he shook me so hard that I squeaked, "Okay!" and pulled out of his grasp, stumbling. In his free hand were papers, rolled up and gripped tight in his fist. They were muddy. The edges were torn. The black ink was smeared.

When he saw what I saw, he hissed, "Out. I said get out! Go! Don't tell anyone I'm here!"

He didn't know who I was, and it didn't take much for me to understand why. His face was swollen and bruised, his eyes nothing more than slits when they opened at all.

"I—I want to help," I stuttered.

"I don't need the help of a child. Did you hear me, little girl? *I said go!*"

I fell beside a broken chair. I grabbed my net and crawled till I reached the door. He was growling at me, saying nasty things, using words that made me flushed and frightened—words he'd never said in my presence before, not even while drunk.

The sunlight outside in the valley, the bright, hot summer day and the smell of the flowers, made it all seem like a dream. There was no way he was real. No one living could look as he did. He wouldn't have been able to climb up into the mountains. I couldn't even picture him standing. His knees were swollen. He had only one shoe. The fingers on his left hand were dark and fat and twisted in all the wrong ways. His clothing was torn. There was blood. He was gaunt and pale and he stank. The whole church stank with him in it.

There was only one explanation.

My uncle was dead.

The Securitate had tortured and killed him, just as my father had feared, and because he'd died alone, in an unnatural way, he'd come back as a *strigoi mort*—a terrible creature that would haunt my family and feed off our blood.

My stories had taught me about monsters like this, but I hadn't really believed in them. Not till now. Not till I'd seen Uncle Andrei myself.

Tears streaking my dirty cheeks, I ran back through the valley. In the yard by the goat pen, I sat down cross-legged in the grass and rocked till I could breathe, till I could stop crying. When I realized my fist was still balled around the net, I looked down, and opened my hand.

Half of one of the butterfly's wings was stuck in the mesh, ripped and crushed. She'd gotten away, but she wouldn't get far, because the truth is, once you're caught, that's it. My uncle had known the risk when he'd published that poem. He'd known that nothing in our country could stay secret for long.

Once, when I was young, he took an assignment for the paper in a faraway city, and when he returned, he slipped sharp-edged photographs into my palms.

"Look," he said, tapping with his finger.

In pictures of the streets, of the stores, of the homes, he drew my gaze to the sloping tiled roofs. There, little hooded windows peeked out from the attics, sometimes two, sometimes three, sometimes five. It looked very much like the houses had eyes. Tiles surrounded the small, dark openings like eyelids.

"They were watching. Someone is always watching."

We all said one in three, because that was how it felt, but really it was just one in thirty.

Just one person out of every thirty people you knew who was informing for the Securitate. Just one person out of every thirty people you knew who would watch while you ate, while you slept, write down when you came home from work, whom you called, what you said, what you read on the train in the morning.

Uncle Andrei was always telling jokes I didn't get.

"I asked a Russian, an American, and a Romanian how they liked to have fun at a party," he would start.

The Russian, quite confident, says, "Well, the best thing to do is to take out your gun and shoot at your head, but put only one bullet in the chamber."

The American interrupts. "That's so crass! The real way to have fun is to pass out expensive champagne to all your guests, but stir poison into only one of the glasses."

The Romanian smiles, shaking his head at the others. "You've both got it wrong," he explains. "To have fun at a party, all you need to do is get everyone telling anti-Communist jokes, but make sure you've invited only one spy."

My mother would snicker and snort. My father would shush his brother and wife, asking if they'd both lost their wits, because if you were caught—even joking—that was it. You'd wind up in jail, just like my uncle.

Just like my uncle, you'd wind up dead.

My uncle had known what he did was a risk. My mother must have known too. But they'd published that poem anyway, and now my uncle was a strigoi mort, come back to remind me there was nowhere to hide.

When my mamaie and tataie came home, I was so quiet they thought I was sick. They put me to bed early, which was fine, because I wanted to sleep. I wanted to forget what I'd seen. But the vision of Uncle Andrei on the floor of that church would not let me rest.

As I lay on my pallet in the dark, moonlight poured through the cracks in the shutters, striking the skeleton of the vacant loom. Crickets filled the air with the waves of their song, growing louder and louder. An owl called from above. She was perched on the roof, *clack-clack-clack*ing back and forth as she searched for a way in.

I imagined my uncle crawling up the stone steps of the hill.

I imagined him in his cement cell, mangled hand chained to a wall. He was crying because he was thirsty. When he died, he was praying for someone to save him.

And then I imagined the most frightening thing of all.

What if there wasn't a strigoi mort?

What if Uncle Andrei was still alive?

I'd never planned to return to the church, never again in my life, but as I pushed off my blankets and slipped on my sneakers, I knew exactly where I was going. I tried to keep quiet as I opened cabinet doors, searching for food that could vanish unnoticed. Most of the villagers' animal products and crops disappeared on the trucks, carried down the mountains to be sold outside our country. However, unlike in the city, the Securitate simply couldn't regulate everything that the villagers did. Livestock were born and raised and slaughtered without ever being recorded. Gardens were overflowing with fruit and vegetables in the summer. They went into jams and pickling jars before some man in a suit could claim they belonged to the state.

My grandparents had food, if you knew where to look.

Standing on a chair, I undid the rusty latch at the top of the front door and snuck outside. I hurried to the back of the house and climbed into the chickens' rickety coop. The birds clucked, irritated, as I searched under their warm bodies for eggs. I found three.

Using the bottom of my shirt as a basket, I crept past the porch and tiptoed through the path in the yard. At the edge of the hill, though, I paused, frozen with the feeling that someone was watching. Mamaie always said not to look back at a house once you'd left—that if you did, something bad would happen while you were away.

Branches rustled just out of sight. The undergrowth shivered.

I turned toward the path that traveled through the forest, all the way up the ancient mountain. Whenever I walked it with Mamaie to forage for herbs or fat mushrooms, we had to clap our hands and make lots of noise so that we'd scare off any bears.

There were even more reasons not to be out past dark, though.

Shortly after I'd arrived, my tataie had gone to the front porch at dusk and asked me to follow. He'd cupped his hands, howling. I'd thought he was just teasing me, since I was from the city and looked easily tricked. But then the wolves had begun to howl back. Their calls came down through the trees. They came from the path through the forest—the path I was now standing beside.

When I heard the Ural owl hoot behind me, I couldn't help spinning around.

There, perched on the mossy thatched roof, she sat staring. Pale gray and mottled, streaked with dark brown, talons clutching the peak of the cottage just above its one eye. In the attic, my grandparents hung meat from the rafters. Smoke drifted up from the stove to flavor and preserve it.

"The window helps the house breathe," my mamaie had explained.

But I knew what eyes were really for.

I hurried past the path up the mountain and took the steps down the hill two at a time. If I'd missed even one, I'd have gone tumbling and broken my neck, but I made it to the bottom alive. Somehow the eggs didn't crack. I looked back up the hill, afraid of what would be there looking down. The forest was empty and quiet—the cottage out of sight.

When I was sure I was alone, I made my way through town, keeping off the dirt road with the well that led between the rows of closely packed houses. I walked through the tall grass in the moonlight instead. And then I was at the edge of the village—at the abandoned old church, slanted and crumbling.

As I crept up to the front of the building, pulse beating in my ears, my body thrummed, tingling from top to toes. Of all the villages in all the world, he'd come here because of me. I was certain. He loved me and he knew I would help him. As I gripped the three eggs nesting in my shirt, though, I felt anxious. It was such a meager offering— such a worthless reason to return when he'd shouted at me to leave only hours before.

Then I saw it, sitting outside the broken double doors. A wicker basket covered with a yellow cloth. The same one I'd spotted from Mrs. Sala's front porch.

I hesitated before looking around. The grass was unbent but for where I'd stepped. The brush was unmoving. I knelt and lifted the cloth: bandages and a bottle of clear, corked liquid. The gift was for my uncle—that was obvious. Someone was leaving him supplies. Turning in a circle, I scanned the nearby houses, but the lights were off in all the ones close enough for me to see. Still, I couldn't shake the feeling that I was being watched. Equally elated and disturbed, I picked up the basket and added my eggs, then ducked and wiggled through the broken doors.

The darkness in the church was so thick that my body felt weightless.

I stood up straight, trembling, and whispered into the black, "Uncle Andrei?"

No reply. I paced a step forward into nothing at all.

"I haven't told anyone you're here. But I've brought you food and bandages. Something to drink, too."

Only silence. I took another step forward.

"Uncle Andrei, it's me, Ileana."

This time there was a deep, throaty noise that made me go stiff. "Lies. Tricks and lies. Go. Out. Leave me be!"

Clouds shifted overhead, and moonlight coming through the fallen roof flooded the back half of the church. I saw his shape then, lying near the altar, just as I'd left him. I straightened up and forced myself to be brave.

"I remember the poem you gave me. The one that made the Securitate so mad they took you away. Tata stole your poem from me, but once a story is told, it stays with you forever." And then I began, whispering:

> You arrived in the dark while we slept.
> Our paper weapons
> no match
> for yours.

Pen in hand,

name on tongue,

you killed us with words.

I close my eyes and still hear them screaming.

"Stop," he said, and I did. But I also stepped into the light, ice blue and floating with dust.

"I let an electrician into our house, but he wasn't an electrician. He wasn't a burglar, either. He put bugs in the walls and the phones. They were listening when I told stories." After a moment I added, "I wanted to save your poem. I knew someone might try to take it away. So I wrote it in the Great Tome, but Tata took the Great Tome and he burned it."

"Ileana?" Uncle Andrei asked, voice cracking.

I moved till I was standing in front of him. He didn't reach out to grab me this time. In fact he barely even breathed.

"Are you dead, Uncle Andrei?"

"No," he said.

"Are you going to die?"

"Maybe."

I set down the basket beside him. I helped him sit up as he wheezed. I handed him the eggs one by one, and he sucked them down raw. When I uncorked the clear glass bottle, I was surprised by the smell, but Uncle Andrei smirked beneath his grimace. With my hands bearing the weight, he turned the bottle up and drank till he started to cough. The rest he poured over his face and his wounds, breathing hard through his teeth when the liquid touched his torn skin. I wrapped one of the bandages clumsily around his broken hand. I tried to ask him questions, but everything took us in circles, like the fairy stories in children's books.

"How did you get here, Uncle Andrei?"

"I walked."

"But how did you walk here?"

"On two feet."

I was fairly convinced that he didn't really know where *here* was anyway. And the truth is, neither of us was entirely sure that the other was real. I wanted to bring him to the cottage. I swore again and again that Mamaie and Tataie wouldn't tell. But anytime I mentioned getting help, he'd grip the papers in his hand tighter and start cursing, making me promise all over.

I agreed because he was an adult—and not just any adult, but the one I most wanted to please. Never before had I had the chance to prove myself to him. Never once had he needed me. I swore I'd return the next night. I left the empty basket just outside the door. Remembering the owl and the cottage's attic eye, I hid my face, ducking my head when I reached my grandparents' yard.

The next day was the hardest. My mamaie was worried about me, convinced all the signs were pointing to illness, so she forced me to stay put at the table and focus on homework. My whole body was rigged like a bomb in an American cop movie. I was certain that at any moment—with just the wrong question, just the wrong look from my grandmother—I'd explode, telling everything I wasn't supposed to.

"Ileana, take a break and go see if the chickens have anything for us."

"They don't," I spat, then scrunched up my toes. "I mean, I checked already this morning. They should work harder, right? Worthless chickens."

That night I again snuck to the church, this time with two eggs. Outside the door, the wicker basket was full. A hard chunk of aged cheese. A new bottle of alcohol. Uncle Andrei could not sit up anymore. He ate an egg when I offered, but when I tried to help him drink, he got sick.

"Will you wrap me in bear hide?" he chuckled. I could

feel the heat coming off his skin without even touching him. "I've no peace to make, false priest."

I poured alcohol over his wounds, but he barely reacted. I tried to ask him questions and he almost wouldn't speak at all. The only thing that could rouse him was explaining again that I wanted to bring someone to help.

He gripped my wrist till it hurt—strength somewhere still in him—and said through his teeth, "You *promised*."

When I returned to the cottage that night, I looked for the owl and stared straight at the eye in the roof, half hoping someone had seen.

The next day was Sunday, so both Mamaie and Tataie were home. I kept quiet by reading schoolbooks and writing reports.

"Such a fast worker," Mamaie cooed. "Where did this motivation come from?"

I stuffed my face full of garlic chicken liver at dinner so I wouldn't have to talk, careful to not bite my tongue. My grandmother said that was the surest way to know if somebody was telling lies.

And then, for the third night in a row, after I was certain the rest of the village was sleeping, I snuck out again. This time there was only one egg, but the basket, once more refilled by the stranger, was still waiting at the broken doors. I entered the church and called out to no answer. I stepped forward slowly, eyes adjusting to the light.

Below the altar, Uncle Andrei was facedown on the floor.

My heart leaped into my throat as I dashed to him, dropping my things, breaking the egg. When I touched him, his skin was so hot that I jerked back my hand. I started to sob, shaking my uncle as hard as I could, but he wouldn't wake. The run back home was a blur. I burst into my mamaie and tataie's room, completely hysterical, and they both sat up with a fright.

Down the hill, Tataie knocked—anxious and hushed—on Sanda's door, and the two of them helped carry Uncle Andrei through the town and into my grandparents' yard. Under the gaze of the cottage, his eyes drifted to the roof and then lolled into his head. When they laid him down on the kitchen floor and he finally spoke, no one else understood. No one else paid any attention to what he said during that fever, papers always still gripped in his hand.

But I listened. I knew.

"They're watching," he breathed, barely alive.

Cunning Ileana
and the Balaur

Summer in the mountain palace turned to fall, and still there was no word from the emperor, off fighting for the monarch in his wicked campaign. Princess Ileana hadn't gotten over her father's abandonment, but she had found some happiness in her new home. The mountain castle was peaceful and lovely. At night, yellow stars twinkled from a deep blue sky. Woven blankets of rust red and sage hung on the stone walls, and the sweet scent of flowers wafted in through the windows. Unfortunately, while Ileana had been exploring the mountains, her two older sisters had started stealing secrets and helping the evil princes plot their revenge.

Though exceptionally clever, when it came to the people

she loved, Cunning Ileana was far too trusting. She didn't at all suspect that her sisters were out to deceive her, so when the afternoon came that she heard the eldest princess crying, Ileana ran at once to her room and threw open the doors. Her sister was tucked in bed, face pallid and gaunt.

Sweet, sweet Ileana, the eldest princess croaked, *I've fallen deathly ill and look utterly average!*

I can see that, said Ileana slowly. Obviously, her sister's face was only caked with makeup. *Do the doctors know what's to blame?*

Heartache, the eldest princess replied. *I begged my beloved to slay the balaur at the peak of the mountain. Legends say his saliva can harden into the most radiant gems, and I selfishly wanted to have some. But my prince has been gone for three days, and I fear something awful has happened! If you could go up the mountain and check on him, I'm sure I'd get better at once.*

Now, everyone knows that balauri are fierce, finned dragons with far too many heads and that trying to fight one alone results in nothing but death and dismemberment. Ileana was sure the princes were playing a trick, but she would have done anything for her sister's sake, so she packed a basket for her journey and went up the mountain anyway. At the top, she found the aftermath of a great battle. It had taken not one prince, but a whole troop of knights, to injure the serpentlike balaur and tie down his twelve thrashing heads. As Cunning Ileana approached, she noticed the thin line of a trip wire, meant to release the ravenous creature when she got near. She also spotted the eldest prince hiding in the bushes, waiting to watch her demise. Ileana took a careful step forward, avoiding the wire, and the balaur snapped and slashed out of reach, a broken wing writhing beneath its restraints.

Go away! roared the first of his gigantic brown heads.

Be gone, little girl! growled the second, bearing fangs long as swords.

Ileana took another step forward. *I'm not here to hurt you.*

Did you hear me? I said go! hissed the third. *I'm dying of thirst, so if you come any closer, I'll drink up your blood!*

The other nine heads snarled such foul, nasty things that even drunk poets wouldn't repeat them. Ileana ignored all of it, raising her basket and offering the balaur her own rations of water. His twenty-four eyes blinked in surprise. After she'd given each of the beast's twelve heads a drink, she crept forward again and picked spears out of his scales, then bandaged his broken wing.

Thank you, said the balaur when he felt better. *I'm sorry for being so grumpy.*

That's all right. Ileana shrugged. *Everyone says things they don't mean sometimes.*

Before she left, the balaur let her fill a jug with his saliva.

A tiny drop will make a pile of gems, he told her. *You'll be rich for the rest of your life.*

Cool, said Ileana. *By the way, did you know that the monarch's eldest son is hiding over there in the bushes? He's the one who ordered those knights to attack you.*

And with that, Ileana "accidentally" tripped over the hidden wire, releasing the balaur, who immediately descended on the eldest prince and ate both his arms.

At home, the cunning princess gave her oldest sister a vial of balaur saliva.

Oh, Ileana! You shouldn't have! said her sister, mesmerized by the sparkling spit. When she finally pulled her eyes away, she added, *Er, what about my beloved?*

I'm sure you'll hear something soon, replied Ileana, smiling.

Sure enough, when the first prince arrived back at his palace missing half his limbs, the two other sons of the monarch became even more enraged than before. They sent word again to the elder princesses, describing their next horrible plan. Being foolishly in love, and really, really just terrible people, the sisters once more agreed to help trick Ileana.

The White Wolf

I was sure my uncle would not last the night. He looked so much worse with adults all around, with lamps to brighten the cottage. I wouldn't leave his side, no matter what anyone said.

"Don't go," I whispered, tears squeezing out of my eyes.

Somehow he was still alive in the morning. And the one that followed. And the one that came after that. My days ran together, sitting by Tataie's bed, where Uncle Andrei rested, bringing him water and soup when he woke, holding his good hand when Sanda came to see how he was. No one dared send for a doctor.

Since I didn't know when my parents would come—or if they'd ever come at all—nothing mattered more than my uncle. So I kept near him, whispering stories I believed I'd forgotten, hoping they'd keep death at bay like they sometimes did in fairy tales.

Things went on like this till one day my vigil was interrupted by a timid rap on the front door. When I opened it, I found Gabi standing on the porch, holding a parcel of medicine from her mother. Her eyes widened. Mine did too. We still had not spoken since the day she'd saved me from the wasps. She handed over the parcel before hurrying down the steps and into the yard. Even in her brace, she was faster than most kids I knew.

A couple of days later, when Gabi came by again, I looked out the window and saw her set down a new parcel on the porch before knocking, clearly intending to take off. Mamaie opened the door and caught her by the sleeve.

"Gabi, dear! Come in and have a treat."

My grandmother drew out one of the benches and forced Gabi to sit at the table. Then she motioned for me to come join, and the two of us sat there staring at each other in silence. Mamaie gave us bread with quince jam and glasses of fresh, warm milk with cream at the top. Gabi's dark hair was even thicker up close, so bushy it couldn't stay put under her polka-dot scarf. She was short and bony, with a fragile little frame. I gulped down my milk, and she did too, each of us watching the other. After that she stood, a frothy white mustache under her nose.

"Thank you," she said to my mamaie, hobbling to the door. Before she opened it, she turned back, looking at me. I waved, and in return I got the tiniest smile.

The next time Gabi came, I wrote her a message telling her some things that I liked. I folded the paper until it was shaped like a treasure box and put a little flower bud inside. I handed the message to Gabi on the porch steps, and she came back later that afternoon and left her reply on my window. She'd refolded the note and colored it so it looked like a golden apple. Inside, she'd drawn an excellent picture of a cow wearing boots. That was when I was sure we'd be friends.

Uncle Andrei began sitting up by himself. He didn't need me to feed him anymore either. When he started talking in sentences, asking Tataie where his papers had gone—when he seemed to finally know where he was—my grandparents sent for Sanda. She checked his wounds, looking closely at the stitches. She replaced one of his bandages and took his temperature, too. The crease in her brow smoothed. She patted my cheek on the way out the door.

"I think you've done it, dear girl."

"Done what?" I asked, fearful.

"I think you've convinced him to stay."

Mamaie was fussing over my uncle, so I followed Sanda out onto the porch. Gabi was sitting on the bottom step.

"Go ahead," her mother urged, motioning in my direction.

Gabi stood up with her hand on the rail. She licked her lips and then looked at the ground.

"Would you like to play?" I offered.

Sanda smiled, but her daughter stayed silent.

"We could read books if you want," I suggested. When Gabi made an ugly face, I said, "Or would you like to see the baby chicks?" Her eyes widened. "There are seven now. The littlest ones can fit in your hand, but the older ones are starting to look like real chickens. It's my responsibility to feed them and name them."

She turned to her mother, who gave her a nudge. I reached out my hand on the way down the stairs and Gabi took it, her fingers so light it felt like she wasn't even touching me. Together we walked around the side of the cottage to the backyard. I showed her the goats and opened the cage with the chicks. I meant to get out only one, but they all got excited, peeping and hopping, and several escaped. I screeched and Gabi giggled as we chased them, yellow down fluttering everywhere when we stuffed them back in their house.

"Do you have chicks in the city?" she asked when we finally managed to close the cage.

I shook my head.

"How about bugs? Do you have to catch them for homework?"

"Not for homework, but I have to catch the roaches for Mama when we find them in our apartment. She always tells me to smoosh them, but I usually just drop them off the balcony 'cause I think, you know, they're people too."

"Gosh," said Gabi. "You're very thoughtful."

After that, she and I were inseparable. Uncle Andrei continued sleeping for much of each day, so while my grandparents were away in the fields, I'd play with Gabi in the yard. When she asked about my parents and uncle, I told her the truth but not all of it. In return she told me how her father, Petre, had died when she was little. She also told me about how much she hated the other children in the village, and I agreed that mostly they were horrible.

"Why'd you save me from the wasps, anyway?" I asked one afternoon.

She just shrugged. "Everyone's always playing tricks on me, too. And wasps are very dangerous. Their stingers have venom that gets in your blood, and when they're upset, they can send out pheromones that alert the rest of the hive."

"Pheromones are so crazy," I said.

Really, I didn't know what pheromones were, but I was impressed that she did.

It wasn't long till I started telling Gabi my stories. She quickly became my biggest fan. My new friend was better than me at lots of things, though, like science and drawing and catching insects. She taught me how to tell if a pig was coming down with a cold and what plants were good to eat if your stomach felt sick. Sometimes we'd walk to the valley and watch the other kids play, whispering secrets as we peeked around corners. Gabi was good at spying, just like me, and on the rare occasions when the other children caught us watching and started to tease, she'd respond by hocking gigantic loogies. This was one of my favorite things about her, but I was worried, because it was why everyone called her Gabi the Spitter.

"Oh, I don't mind," she said. "They used to make fun of my brace, but now they don't even notice it."

Eventually, my uncle started showing real signs of improvement. He began walking around on his own and sitting at the table for dinner. He was especially talkative when Sanda and Gabi would come up to join us. Uncle Andrei apologized for the things he'd said to me in the church—at least for the things he remembered. No matter how hard I pried, though, he wouldn't answer most of my questions, and sometimes he got grumpy just at me asking.

"But how did you escape from the prison?" I whispered over cheese mămăligă.

"I'll tell you when you're older. Now finish your food."

"But how did you know I was hiding in the village?"

"I didn't. I only knew your grandparents lived here. Stop pestering. Don't you have homework to do?"

For a while it felt like the world was okay. Uncle Andrei assured me that soon my parents would come take me home. He said that after some time passed, the Securitate wouldn't be so mad anymore. He said they'd probably forget all about his poem and my stories. He promised my mother was safe. He promised no one would find us in the village. He promised the salt with the sea.

Because I loved him, I believed all his lies.

About a week before school was to start, my mamaie caught me by the ear, my mouth still full of dinner as I rushed out the door. Gabi was coming up the path in the woods. I could hear her calling my name.

"Wait, child!" Mamaie said. "Chew your food."

I did as I was told, and she put her hand on my cheek to get my attention. My tataie stood up from the table. My uncle's lips were pursed tight beneath black-and-blue eyes.

"Stay near the house tonight, Ileana. Can you do that for us?" asked Mamaie.

I hesitated. Gabi and I had plans to go down the hill. She'd seen me earlier that morning in the fields, when I was picking fat green caterpillars off tomatoes, and she'd told me Ioan had caught a snake and was going to keep it for a pet. This was a tragedy, of course, because Ioan had once done the same with a lizard and it had died in less than a day. We were planning to spy on the innkeeper's son to find out if he still had the snake, and then rescue the poor thing, if needed. The mission was too important to cancel, but all the adults in the cottage had a particular look on their face, so I lied and said I'd stay close.

In the yard Gabi and I concocted a plan. After making a show of singing and running and being generally obnoxious, the two of us crawled under the house and listened to find out if the adults were preoccupied. Through the floorboards came splinters of light, muffled talking, Mamaie at the loom, and Tataie tuning his fiddle. Satisfied, we took off down the hill.

At the bottom we searched for Ioan and the other boys

from town, but they weren't near the school, and they weren't near the little creek by the road. We wound up outside Ioan's house, where he lived with his family in a room in the back. The other rooms were the village's tavern and inn. Even when I was allowed down in the valley, we weren't supposed to play by the tavern. People were always smoking there, and some of the townsfolk called Mr. Bălan, Ioan's father, a slug and a sot because he always showed up late to help in the fields. Gabi and I agreed the innkeeper wasn't so bad, though. He was potbellied, with a big, toothy smile, and when kids were around, he'd reach into his pockets and pass out sugar cubes. Usually, though, we tried to stay away from the tavern to keep out of trouble.

At the back of the building, Gabi peeked through a window; then we both ducked to the ground. The sun had started to set, and in the tall grass we were hidden by shadows.

"Ioan's already in his pajamas," Gabi said. "Probably being sent to bed early for doing something mean."

"What about the snake? Did you see her?"

"No. But he might have her in a box under his bed. That's where I'd hide a snake. We could climb in through a window and check."

"I dunno," I said. "Maybe his parents made him let it

go. I don't want to risk my life for a snake that doesn't need saving."

Gabi sighed and slumped back against the house.

"Yeah. Me neither," she said. Then she turned to me, quite serious. "But if I find out he hurt her, he'll pay. I'll figure out a way to get Old Constanta to curse him. She's a witch, you know. Roma used to come to the village, and she learned magic from them."

I scrunched up my nose. "My tata says Roma can't really use magic."

"They can," Gabi warned. "I've seen it."

Two men came out the front door and stumbled around to the side of the tavern, pulling down their pants to piss on the wall. When I made a grossed-out noise, Gabi put a hand over my mouth, and we both went still.

"Did you hear?" one of the men asked.

"Hear what?" asked his friend.

For a heartbeat I thought they meant us, but then the first man said, quieter, "The White Wolf's been seen."

The second man, clearly the more drunk of the two, started to chuckle. "The what?"

"*The White Wolf,*" the first man repeated. He pulled up his pants and lowered his voice. "The one who used to look like a man? The priest who could talk to the animals?

They say he's been spotted down below the mountains. They say he's headed our way."

"How long till he's here?" the second man asked, suddenly sober.

"Days, maybe. Less. Just giving you warning in case you've got business to see to before he arrives."

"Many thanks, friend. I'll be sure to pass on the story."

The two men went back inside, leaving Gabi and me with wide eyes.

"What's the White Wolf?" I finally asked, feeling nervous.

"I don't know," Gabi said, and she looked nervous too.

We both decided it was time to go home.

Back at the top of the hill, Mamaie was calling my name. When she saw me emerge from the forest, she rushed over and grabbed me by the wrist.

"What did I say!" Then she shouted over my head, "She's here! I found her!"

Tataie appeared, coming down from the path up the mountain. He took off his cap and put it to his chest, crossing himself. I was hurried into the house. There I found Uncle Andrei pacing. He stopped when I came through the door.

"What's wrong with you? Why can't you follow directions?" he asked angrily.

"I just went to town," I said, confused.

"We told you to stay in the yard!"

My cheeks flushed. My knees went weak. He could make me feel awful like nobody else.

"I'm sorry," I mumbled. "I didn't think it was a big deal."

I knew things were serious when Tataie locked the door and Mamaie started closing the shutters. The cottage grew dark, and my voice dropped an octave by instinct.

"We just went by the creek. We were looking for Ioan," I said.

"Did anyone strange talk to you?" asked Mamaie.

"We were hiding. No one talked to us at all." I smiled, trying to reassure her. "We're really good at spying now. These two farmers walked right by us and didn't even notice. They almost *peed* on me."

My grandmother made an unpleasant face, but everyone looked generally relieved.

At least until I added, "They were telling a weird story, though. It was about a wolf. A white wolf."

Mamaie's face paled. Tataie went still by the stove.

"A story about a white wolf?" my grandmother repeated, and I knew I'd landed in a pitfall.

"They said . . . they said people had seen a white wolf.

They said he used to be a priest who could talk to the animals—"

"No more, child! *Shh!*" She turned to my tataie. "How could they be so dense? To let a child overhear! And of all the children in the world!"

Tataie knelt down in front of me till I could see the bald patch on top of his head. He picked up my hands. His were dry, the skin loose and rough. There was a ragged scar on his forearm that I'd never noticed before. He looked at me head-on, unblinking.

"Ileana, are you listening?"

I nodded, suddenly frightened.

"What you heard is a very special story," my tataie said. "Only adults can tell it, and even then, they can't tell it all the time. Do you understand?"

I nodded again, though I didn't.

"What you heard is a story that can't be told to anyone. Not to Gabi. Not to the other children. Not even to us. Not ever. Do I have your word?"

I'd never seen my grandfather look so shaken. I nodded again, and I meant it. I wouldn't tell the story. Not for my life.

The Manifesto

Uncle Andrei left in the night while we slept. No more word than a note by my pillow.

It's not safe here for me anymore. If I stay, it won't be safe for you, either.

He'd folded the little paper into a bumblebee, like I'd taught him.

That morning I woke up crying. It was an hour yet till dawn, and I sat up straight in the dark, knowing he was no longer there. I'd dreamed that he'd lifted me from my pallet and held me, that he'd given me a gift—not the note, something much more important—and he'd whispered, "Remember, Ileana, even while I'm away, you must always keep faith with your family."

When I sat up, I was covered in sweat, my face wet with tears. Rain pattered against the cottage windows. Wind shook the shutters and pulled at the boughs of the trees. A fire had ignited inside me, wild and terrified and furious. I got up and ran outside without even finding my shoes. I stumbled down the porch stairs, the door swinging open behind me, banging against the chair by the wall. I screamed for him from the yard in the pouring rain. I screamed for him till I heard rustling in the trees. Then I ran straight toward the sound, gasping, my bare feet breaking branches and slipping on mud, my toes stubbing rocks. In a matter of seconds I was soaked, clothes clinging to my skin as I hurried along the path up the mountain. I called for him, begging him to come back.

The rustling came again. Brush shifted to my left and I turned.

I stared into the eyes of a wolf.

He was gray, dark points at his paws and his ears and his tail. Neither of us moved. Neither of us had expected the other. Sweat and rain dripped from my nose to the earth.

There was shouting behind me, commotion, and the wolf took off into the woods. He was long gone by the time my tataie reached me and knelt down.

"Are you all right? Are you all right, Ileana?"

I stared into the trees, unable to answer.

Sanda came later that morning, when I was tucked into bed. She felt my forehead, her small hand frigid, and smiled.

"Just a summer fever. A couple days' good rest and she'll be fine."

My mamaie put oversize wool socks on my feet. She kept the windows shut and the woodstove hot to keep out the chill from the storm. She cut an onion in half and left it by my bed to suck out the sickness. My tataie brewed a special tea made of herbs. I slept and woke to eat garlic soup, hardly noticing how bad things were beginning to smell. Two days later, though, I was still burning up. My skin was sore to the touch. I was too weak even to walk on my own to the toilet outside, so my mamaie kept a little pot for me to use in the kitchen. When I breathed, there was a rattle deep down in my chest. When I coughed, there was brown phlegm in my handkerchief. A real doctor, from another, much larger, village, was sent for. He gave me an injection and left me with a bottle of syrup that burned my throat going down.

I missed my mother so much then, more than I ever had in my life. I craved the back of her hand on my forehead. I yearned for her kiss on my cheek. Her humming.

Her scent like a salve. The feel of her presence lingering at the door while I dozed. She could soothe my aches with only her touch.

I missed my father, too, as much as I didn't want to admit it. I couldn't stop thinking about him. Was he walking to the boulevard alone, with no one to hold his hand? Who found his reading glasses for him if he misplaced them? If Tata had come into the cottage and picked me up in his arms, I'd have started to cry. I'd have forgiven him without hesitation for all the things that he'd done, and begged him to tell me the end of our story.

I pleaded with Mamaie, wanting her to call my parents, sure they would come if they knew I was so sick. Finally she did as I asked, but there was no answer at home.

Adults whispered over my bed, their voices drifting in and out like waves, like a radio signal from over the border or the dub on a copied tape that had been watched too many times.

. . . they surely won't bother you . . . told them it's very contagious . . . no one's suspicious; don't fret . . . should be gone in a day or two more . . . a sighting up in the mountains . . .

For days it continued to rain. My grandparents took turns keeping watch. Mamaie embroidered in her chair or wove at the loom in the corner. Tataie played softly on his fiddle. They told stories, and the stories would churn around in my head as I dozed and woke and dozed again. Roma and dragons and magic. The evil box buried under the house. Tataie's three coins and the night he was sure he would die.

Cooped up in that smelly, hot cottage, I felt like my head would burst, it was so full. My dreams were so ripe, gushing, and swollen, so overflowing with color and sound, that one night I floated right out of my bed. Past the stove. Out the door. Off the porch.

In the yard was a girl just my age, humming as she skipped out the gate. She had a basket with a yellow cloth. Her nightdress was dirty and torn at the hem. A shawl slipped over her ears and fell to her shoulders. She paused at the place where the stone steps up the hill to the cottage met the path that would lead through the forest. A wolf appeared from the darkness to meet her—not gray, but white.

I couldn't help following. All the way up the mountain we went—all the way to the twisted trees and the ancient monastery at the top of the world. At times, I tried to catch up, hurrying as fast as my dream legs could fly, but the girl and her companion always stayed just ahead, out of reach.

Inside the high walls of the monastery, its stones covered in moss and cracked at the seams, the girl with the basket tiptoed through the halls, pausing to peek into doorways. When she came to a great vaulted room, she put a hand over her mouth to stifle a giggle, gesturing for me to come look. When I peeked inside too, I saw monks, all lined up at massive oak tables. Tiny flames burned on pale mounds of melted wax, the memory of a hundred candles in each spot. The men were dressed in black robes with big sleeves and metal crosses dangling from their necks. They wore tall, rounded black hats with black cloth hanging like capes halfway down to the floor. They didn't see me. They were chanting and writing, so diligent in their work, making copies and copies and copies of the very same story. I desperately wanted to know what it was, but I knew that I couldn't disturb them.

I snuck through the remains of the dusty old stone halls, the overgrown gardens, and the great crumbling chapel. Back outside, the girl and her wolf came to a stop at the tip of the mountain. There I peered over the edge of the world into the valley below.

My heart caught in my throat.

Armies had come to the village while I was away. They were burning the homes to the ground.

I reached out to the girl, frightened, craving her touch and the hum of her song, so close this time, but when my hand found hers, it glided through like water. She shimmered and rippled, wisping away, the smoke of her sailing over the tops of the pines and ashes and firs.

Then, to my right, there was movement. The white wolf's body changed, growing larger and longer. He shed his fur, his skin turning scaly and slick. He wasn't really a wolf. He never had been. Instead he was a white dragon with a white wolf's elongated head. Six silver tongues darted out from his mouth. When he howled, there was fire, and a thousand wolves howled back in response. I watched them cascade down the mountain. I watched them crash into the armies.

The white dragon-wolf leaped from the peak of the mountain. He soared down to the valley below, and I again heard my uncle's voice at my ear. "Have you kept faith, Ileana? Is the gift that I left you still safe?"

When I woke, I was calm, and I lay for a long time listening to the rain. The lamps had died down, only one left on the windowsill, flickering. Tataie was asleep in the chair by the cold stove. Mamaie was snoring in their bedroom. My fever had broken, but the dream still burned hot in my head. I sat up, and the floorboards beneath me creaked. I looked at the woven blankets that made up my pallet, then lifted them to reveal the smooth wood. One of the planks was uneven—a corner sticking up above the rest, nails loose and wiggly. I pulled the blankets up more, and light from the one tiny flame shone into the space underneath the loose board.

Something was there in the dark.

I glanced at Tataie. Quiet as I could be, I removed the plank and reached down inside. I had to put my arm in up to my elbow. I had to feel around in the air, fearing what creatures I might touch by mistake. My fingertips scraped old stone. Something squirmed past my wrist and made my spine stiffen. But then the thing I sought was in my hand and I was pulling it out.

The papers Uncle Andrei had left us were torn at the edges.

They were muddy, and the black ink was smeared.

I remembered his left hand wrapped tight in a bandage, the fingers unable to move.

"I guess they weren't fans of my writing." A wink and a smile.

My eyes scanned the first page. Not his *T*s. Not his *F*s. Not his *M*s. But I'd know his voice anywhere. If he'd published a grocery list, I could tell.

It was only a story in the broadest of terms: a history of the pains of our people, a series of demands to relieve them. Attached to the end was a list of names in different handwriting. Beside the names were professions: teachers, scientists, artists, musicians. My uncle was one of the first. The list went on and on, page after page after page. At the very bottom, Sanda and my grandparents had signed.

I thought for a long time. I stared.

Of all the writing in all the world, this was what Uncle Andrei had carried with him over the mountains. This was what he'd clung to with his broken hands, what he'd hidden away.

There was no mark of publication. And it certainly wasn't the kind of writing people wanted to read. It would make them uncomfortable, anxious, afraid. It would make them question our whole way of life.

This. This is what writers can do.

I crawled across the floor to my little yellow notebook. I took the pen back to my bed. And before returning the manifesto to its hiding place, on the very last page, I printed my name.

Beside it I wrote, *Storyteller.*

What Belongs to Us

After I'd been bedridden for almost a week, Sanda finally proclaimed that I was well—just in time, of course, for the start of school. On our last day of vacation, Gabi showed up at the cottage barely after sunrise. I was awake and already dressing, fiddling with the straps on my overalls and lacing my boots. It had begun to get chilly in the mornings—the leaves already tinting red and orange—and since I'd only brought summer wear, Mamaie helped me go through my mother's old clothes. Unfortunately, most of it was too big for me to wear, and to be honest, the dresses and skirts and head scarves didn't look like they belonged to my mother at all.

At my request, Mamaie traded one of her blankets with

a neighbor for some used children's clothes. Though she muttered about how she'd prefer to see me in things meant for girls, my grandmother got me some brown overalls and big boots, which hardly smelled like boy feet at all. Mamaie's comments were delicate enough to ignore, and besides, when I wore my overalls, I looked like a real farmer. Tataie said so more than once, and it made me beam bright as a radish.

After securing the last button, I met Gabi in the kitchen. She had a net and a stubborn look on her face.

"There's some *Bombus lucorum* down near the school-house," she said, her jaw set. When I didn't react, she rolled her eyes. "White-tailed bumblebees."

My brow raised. "Those are worth extra credit."

Perhaps there was hope I'd finish my homework after all.

Since, of course, I'd completed all the summer reading, I'd helped Gabi fill out her worksheets with questions about characters. I'd even written book reports for her to copy, just different enough from my own that we shouldn't get caught. In return the veterinarian's daughter had brought me slugs, beetles, grasshoppers, and moths. She'd dropped the cotton balls into the jars and pinned the bugs to my board.

"It's all right," she said as she pushed the needles through their backs and caught my expression. "They're dead now. It doesn't hurt."

"It's just so sad, though," I said. "Why do they make us kill them?"

"Adults are pretty messed up." She shrugged. "But I guess it's better than keeping them alive trapped in a jar, feeding them grass and stuff that they don't want to eat."

"Maybe," I said. Though at least in a jar there was hope. Your captor might let you go. Or the jar might get knocked off the table and break.

Even with Gabi's help, though, my bug collection was unfinished. If I wanted the project to pass, I'd have to catch something really fantastic.

"I saw the bees yesterday in some witch's bells. Probably the last of the year," Gabi said. "I wanted to get one for you, but I was bringing formula to the Salas' piglets and my arms were full. They might be back today, though, and you need the points. You won't get any credit for those mushed caterpillars."

I looked at Mamaie, who was near the door collecting her things.

"You're sure you're feeling all right?" she asked, touching a hand to my head. I nodded, and she said, "Go ahead, then, but no running. And no drinking cold water out of the well. And keep away from the man at the inn."

She still hadn't said out loud who he was, but I knew.

While I'd been sick, a stranger had arrived in the valley. He claimed that he was on vacation, traveling the country-side, and had promised to meet a companion in our town. Every day he walked around the village, describing his friend to the townspeople, asking if anyone had seen him. The description sounded just like my uncle.

My grandparents' first instinct was that I should stay hidden. But the man never mentioned anything about a little girl, and once school started tomorrow, it would be more suspicious than anything else to keep me locked up at home.

"Don't worry," I said to Mamaie. "Ninja Robo-Gabi and I will use stealth mode."

With that I dropped to the ground and snuck across the front yard like Chuck Norris in one of the action movies I'd seen with my father. My mamaie gave me a worried look before going inside.

Gabi and I were about to dash off into the woods, but at the back of the cottage we heard someone curse, so we went to investigate. Tataie was bent down in the goat pen, his arms up to the elbows in hay.

"What's wrong?" I called.

"Ah, nothing." He pulled an arm out to wave me off, but I exchanged a look with Gabi and we moved closer. The bale of hay was dark in large patches, white and fuzzy in others.

"Mold," Gabi said.

My tataie shook his head. "No choice but to see if they'll take it. Too much rain. This is the second bale gone bad."

"You could try salting them," Gabi suggested, but then shrank away at his look. "I mean, you know, next time."

After a moment he just sighed. "Haven't had enough salt to spare, anyhow."

On our way down the hill, nets bouncing on our shoulders, I asked Gabi, "What happens if the goats eat moldy hay?"

"They probably just won't eat it," she said, her brace clacking as she walked.

"But what if they do?"

"I guess they could get sick."

When we reached the schoolhouse, we walked up to the windows and peered in. Someone had recently wiped them down. Inside the little building, the desks had been returned to the center of the room and were lined up in rows. The chalkboard was dark and shining, cleaned spotless with *borș*—a pale yellow liquid for cooking that made everything sour. Mamaie's soup was made out of the same stuff. It had to ferment for days. Every time she'd pass by the pot, she'd pull on my hair.

"Is it sour yet?" she would ask.

"Yes!" I'd screech, ducking. The one time I'd said no, and it really hadn't been sour, she'd told everyone it was my fault.

I pointed at the wooden floor of the schoolhouse.

"No more goat prints," I said to Gabi, disappointed.

Bookshelves along the walls had been revealed from beneath the protective cover of old bedsheets and tarps. I peered at the spines and pressed my nose against the glass as I tried to make out the titles.

Outside, we searched for bees in the witch's bells. The little violet flowers sprang up in patches, their thimble heads drooping down from their necks. I tipped them up and peeked inside to no avail. After a while, my attention was drawn down the row of pastel-colored houses to Old Constanta's cottage across from the church. I squinted because I thought I saw movement at her curtains. A pale shape in the center of one window caught my eye.

It took a moment to realize someone was standing there, staring back.

I gasped and went still.

Gabi glanced up from where she was bent in the grass, mistaking the direction of my gaze. "That's where your uncle was, right? Where you brought him the eggs?"

I pulled my eyes away from Constanta's window and turned toward the abandoned church. The gnawing in my stomach—long forgotten—started up again without warning. I couldn't help looking back at Mr. Bălan's tavern, where a tall man was leaning near the door, cigarette trapped between his fat lips. The red tip glowed as he nodded to villagers passing by, everyone polite but not friendly.

"Don't worry," whispered Gabi. "Once that guy realizes this place is just a bunch of pigs and vegetables, he'll get bored and leave."

"Tataie said more people will come looking. Mamaie got mad and told him he was calling evil into the town."

"Your uncle's way far away. No one will find him."

When the man with the cigarette glanced in our direction, though, we both decided it was time to hunt white-tailed bumblebees elsewhere. We steered clear of the fields where the adults were all working, wary that someone would give us a job. Harvest had already begun, and the chores seemed never-ending. Everyone—the butcher, the schoolteacher, even Sanda—was digging in the dirt and hauling crops. It was best to stay out of sight.

As we walked along an unpaved road, balancing on the dried hump built up between tire tracks, Gabi slowed beside me, her gait becoming more burdened. Since I knew she wouldn't be the first one to suggest it, I told her I thought we should take a rest and eat lunch.

The field we picked to stop at had recently been cut. Much of the hay was stacked up in great, loose heaps held together by sticks. The piles formed rounded golden towers almost as tall as the cottage. We wandered till we found a shaded spot and plopped down to eat bread and fruit. When we were full, we danced between the haystacks, pretending the golden towers were under siege. Before, when I hadn't had any friends, I'd run through the wheat fields alone, beating down sections of stalks to square off into houses and shops and factories that I'd have to people all by myself. Spending time with Gabi was much better. I made up a story and we took turns playing parts—the evil prince, the witless monarch, the wolf-dragon that helped the cunning princess escape.

"Let free the Lady Ileana or prepare to meet your doom!" Gabi roared, breathing fire into the crumbling ramparts as she spread her scaled wings.

Since I was very clever and brave, I wanted to leap from the tallest tower onto her back and have her fly us both away. I lugged around small rectangular bales to make stairs and climbed the nearest stack, then slid down, drenching us both in a shower of hay. When I got to my feet and tried to wrap my arms around Gabi's neck, though, I realized she wouldn't really be able to carry me, so I changed the story. The wolf-dragon, drained from the battle with the evil prince, used the last of her magic to give the princess enormous butterfly wings. Gabi latched on to my back and I ran between the haystacks till I was exhausted.

Finally, we collapsed to the ground, fits of giggles coming in waves as we both caught our breath.

"I love your stories," Gabi said. "I hope you'll always be here to tell them."

I made a face. As much as I didn't want to leave my new friend, the thought of staying in the village forever could only mean bad things.

"My parents are probably gonna come get me soon," I said. "But maybe, when I go home, you can come visit me in Bucharest."

"Maybe," said Gabi. "I don't really like cities, though. The last time I went to a city, it was for surgery."

I sat up slowly, biting my lip. "For your leg?" After she nodded, I asked, "Does it hurt when you walk?"

We'd never talked about Gabi's leg or her brace before,

and a pang of shame stirred in my chest. I was worried she'd be upset, but she just shrugged.

"Sometimes, yeah. Mama says it's good for me to get exercise, though." When she caught me looking at her brace, she asked, "Do you wanna see?"

I nodded, and Gabi pushed up her red skirt to the thigh, then undid the metal brace. Her left leg didn't look very much different from mine, except for a big birthmark shaped like the moon. Her right leg, however, was thin and short with tight skin and scars. Her foot, which curled strangely, fit into the special tall shoe.

"It's always been like this," Gabi said. "It's just how I was born. When I was little, it was worse and I used crutches. But then I turned six and got my first surgery, so I'd only have to wear a brace."

"Surgery sounds really scary," I said.

"Yeah. And that was the year Tata died, so it was just me and Mama when I got home. She had to take care of all the animals by herself. Plus, the other kids made fun of the metal pins in my leg, and I had trouble walking."

My calves prickled, and my hands found them unconsciously. "Will your leg get longer when you grow up?"

"I don't know," Gabi said. "The doctors told Mama I should do surgery again. Maybe next year. But I don't want the pins and stuff like before. Besides, I'm the fastest kid in the whole village already."

"I know," I said. "You're really great."

"You're really great too," Gabi said. Then her eyes lit up and she reached into her pocket and pulled out a folded piece of paper. "I forgot I drew this for you. It's no big deal or anything."

The picture was of the two of us holding hands in front of the cottage.

"You wanna hear something weird?" she asked with a smirk.

I nodded. "Uh, duh."

"A long time ago, like a *really* long time ago, your mama was supposed to marry my tata."

I smiled. "But then my mama ran away."

"You always know the stories," Gabi said, rolling her eyes. After a moment she added in a sad kind of way, "It's sort of funny, 'cause even though it's been a long time, I still miss my tata like every day."

"I don't miss my father," I said, and the gnawing started up again.

The sun had fallen far in the sky, and the clouds were painted orange and yellow, so Gabi put her brace back on, and we headed toward the road.

"You know what?" I said before we got too far. "A lot of hay here is dry. Could we bring one of the bales to the goats? That way they won't have to eat mold."

At first my friend seemed delighted, but then her face fell. "I don't think we're supposed to take things from the fields."

"But everyone works on them, right? My tataie, too. The hay is for everyone."

The logic was sound, so Gabi helped me pick out the best bale, and together we pushed and pulled, hefted and dragged, till we were back through the valley. On the way up the hill, Gabi asked me about the white-wolf story we'd heard outside the tavern. She'd told her mom about it, and just like me she'd gotten in trouble. I admitted that, for all my snooping, I hadn't learned anything new about this story that couldn't be told.

Once we'd made it to the yard, Gabi left for home, and when Tataie heard me calling good-bye, he appeared at the front door. The light from inside spilled down the porch stairs. Hay was everywhere. In my hair. Under my overalls. Deep inside my boots. Mamaie would cluck and cluck—and I was itching all over—but I couldn't help grinning. I patted the bale with a hand.

"For the goats," I said, proud.

At first it seemed Tataie didn't know what he was looking at. He squinted. But then the blood drained from his face.

"What have you done?" he whispered. "This doesn't belong to us."

My smile vanished as panic set in. "I thought . . ."

Tataie took the stairs two at a time and pushed me out of the way, then dragged the bale to the edge of the trees where the undergrowth was thick. The yard was fully dark now, and the whites of his eyes stood out as he turned back to me.

"Don't you realize? It's all theirs, not ours," he said, terrified. At the walkway he peered down the hill. "Did anyone see you take it?"

"Just Gabi."

My grandfather squeezed his eyes shut, then urged me toward the door, his voice shaking. "Not a word to your mamaie. I've just gone to scare off a fox."

And before another thing could be said, he was back at the edge of the forest, dragging the hay down the hill in the dark.

Tataie's Three Coins

When the bomb went off, my tataie had been stationed outside Romania, at the port city of Odessa on the Black Sea, for only two weeks. Sixty-seven men whom he'd not yet had time to meet were scattered in pieces along the sidewalks. He stared, gaping, as he was handed a broom.

"I—I don't think I can . . ."

The German soldier beside him narrowed his eyes. He readied a trash bin. Tataie closed his mouth and started to work.

My grandfather was eighteen. The son of a farmer who was the son of a farmer, he'd never before left his mountain village. He'd never been to the seaside. He'd never watched anyone die. In fact he'd spent his whole life trying to keep things alive—sheep and roosters, wheat and fruit trees, his little old mother. But like the rest of the men in his family, Tataie didn't have a choice about going to war. Refusing to serve was deemed treason—its punishment death.

So that morning by the water, my grandfather rolled up his sleeves and swept. He tried not to look so afraid. He did just as he was told. It was late October. Back home the harvest festival had already passed. The ground would be hard, first frost come and gone. But here the air was still almost warm, thick with the briny smell of the coast—seaweed and fish and damp wood. As Tataie struggled to coax a chunk of flesh into the rusted metal bin, he focused on the salty breeze.

Months before my grandfather arrived in Odessa, our country's army had set siege to the port. Textbooks and tavern storytellers alike would dub the coastal town a Hero City. It should have been an easy take, they all said. We'd shown up with sixty thousand soldiers—Odessa had barely half that. It should have been quick and clean. But instead, it lasted and lasted. Instead, it was a bloody mess.

"Poor organization. Shoddy command. Unexpected reinforcements," they said.

"Pride," Tataie whispered.

Before he arrived in Odessa—before the bomb detonated inside our army's headquarters—the "easy take" had cost us more than ninety thousand men, wounded or dead. It would be Romania's second worst loss in all of the war.

Tataie had come by train to the port on the Black Sea carrying just one bag, his state-issued gun, and three silver coins in his pocket. They weren't magic coins. They weren't even particularly large, but they twinkled like starlight and sang like chimes when he rolled them over his knuckles.

"Use them wisely," his old mother had warned. He was the youngest of seven boys. The last to leave home. "They'll be worth a man's life at the right place and time."

After the bomb's detonation, Odessa was ordered to pay for our losses: one hundred Jews for every soldier, two hundred for every officer. Five thousand civilians were marched from their seaside homes, lined up in long, straight rows, and shot. Hundreds were hanged in the streets. Tataie hefted the dead who'd been shot into trucks. He was told to leave the hanged where they were. At night he cried himself to sleep.

The remaining Jews in the city were woken by banging at their doors—a violent, dreadful sound that made mothers sit up with a start. Fathers fumbled into slippers and robes, searching for their glasses as they called down the stairs.

Children peeked into the hallways and were told to keep quiet. Some were rushed into secret compartments under the floor or into the false backs of wardrobes. Almost all were found.

They were not told where they were going. They had no time to pack. The ones who thought to grab provisions or possessions on their way out the door had their belongings confiscated, though a handful of items slipped through.

A portrait of a great-great grandmother, held under the arm.

A porcelain doll with crystal-blue eyes, gripped by the hair.

The people were herded through the streets. Thousands, mostly women and children, were forced into ditches and warehouses outside the city, where indescribable horrors took place. Others were led to a public square by the harbor. Five. Ten. Fifteen thousand. More still. Tataie blinked in the sunlight, his heart racing. One very old man, separated from his family, squeezed a small, yipping dog to his breast. He was shoved left, then right, then back again, people packing in tighter and tighter.

"I can't do this," Tataie whispered.

But he did.

My grandfather's job was to hold a hose and aim a nozzle

with a bronze tip. The German soldier behind him, the same one as before, had a large red canister and was pumping away. The smell of gasoline filled the air as it soaked clothing and skin. The scent would linger on Tataie's hands for days after, for weeks, for the rest of his life.

His task that morning should have been simple.

It should have been easy to do.

But my grandfather couldn't stop shaking. He couldn't hold the nozzle straight. And when full panic broke out in the square, people sprinting in every direction, bullets singing past Tataie's head, he dropped the hose and stumbled away, vomiting.

Only a thousand, maybe two thousand, died before the flamethrowers ignited.

My grandfather got to his feet, the fires of hell at his back. He might have run then. He might have made for the docks and dived into the sea, though he'd never learned how to swim. But at the last moment his comrade, the German, caught him by the shoulders and forced him to stand still. The man didn't make a scene of it. He kept his eyes pointed forward.

Facing away, Tataie went numb—first from inside, then out. He didn't know that the other soldier spoke his language. In two days together, there hadn't been a word. So he was surprised when the man scowled and said through a thick accent, "You think we'd be better at killing by now."

A small group of Soviet resisters, no more than three hundred strong, was holding out in the port. They had infested the catacombs beneath the cobblestone streets. They were spreading like roaches, scurrying past at the edge of one's sight, creeping from cracks in the wall after dark. They could not be flushed out. The catacombs were too complicated, too large—bigger than those even in Paris or Rome. The resisters were in communication with a similar movement in Moscow, using radios to organize their attacks, but surely, they had help from someone nearby. Surely, a homestead or village was supplying food, water, and ammunition.

Tataie and a few other men were sent to scour the surrounding forests. A week of searching brought nothing. Everything was already in ruins. Villages smoldered. The soldiers passed through an abandoned vineyard, sour and reeking. White muscat grapes hung in sagging, dripping bunches as far as the men could see. The ground was littered with decay—great rotting heaps, a whole crop never harvested.

As Tataie walked through aisles of dead vines, the fumes in the air became so overwhelming, he didn't even notice a bloated corpse till it was right under his feet. He cried out, and all around, men readied their guns. They cursed at him when they realized what was wrong. Tataie swallowed hard. He muttered a prayer for the farmer before stepping over his body.

Almost a month passed with still no sign of the resisters. The world changed to chilly, then frigid. The first snow came without warning. It didn't stick to the ground but hung in the air, freezing breath and bone alike. It would be the coldest November in sixty-nine years. Luckily, the handful of German soldiers mixed in with Tataie's unit were good at building fires.

Then, one evening, as they prepared to make camp, a call rang out that Tataie couldn't understand. One of his countrymen translated.

"Something's there. Up ahead."

Switching on his flat, rectangle-shaped light, which was clipped to his uniform, Tataie went deeper into the trees, relieved that his battery was still working. When he approached the ruins of what once was a house, yellow flashlight beams came in rhythmic waves over fallen walls and a gray, broken door. The air was quiet but for the patter of snowflakes and the whir of tiny, mechanical wheels. The Germans' lights were brass with hand pumps. Soldiers walked the perimeter, peeking inside. Most of the men became bored and moved on. Only three people lingered—Tataie, another Romanian man, and the German soldier who'd held the gasoline.

Something shifted inside the house. Someone made a noise.

The soldiers exchanged looks and approached. They pulled aside fallen boards and found a way to squeeze into the rubble. At the corner of what had once been a living room, crouched beneath what had once been a table, Tataie's light fell on a naked woman. Her hair hung from her face in long, greasy ropes. Her body was mottled with dark patches of bruises and dirt. A torn blanket was draped over her shoulders, but it slid down her back when she put her hands up to cover her eyes. She shivered as the snow settled, melting on her skin.

"Is she a Jew?" asked my grandfather's countryman, crossing himself.

The German shifted his weight but stayed silent.

"Are you a Jew?" the Romanian asked. "Are you helping the resisters in Odessa?" The woman didn't respond. Another few moments passed in stillness. "Should we kill her?"

Tataie flinched.

The German spat, then looked up through the half-collapsed roof at the snow coming down from the black sky. "She's already dead."

But no one moved to leave.

"She could give up our location," said Tataie's countryman, scrunching his nose.

"She could," the German agreed. And, after a moment longer, he took a deep breath and unholstered his gun.

Tataie reached down into his pocket.

"Wait," he said, and in the palm of his hand were two of his three silver coins. They glinted even there in the dark. They clinked together, singing like chimes. "Leave us. I'll take care of it."

The Romanian and the German looked at each other. They looked at the coins in Tataie's hand. The German reached forward and pinched one between his fingers.

"Be quick," he said.

Tataie's countryman paused before taking the other.

The two soldiers climbed back through the rubble, my grandfather still as stone till he could no longer hear their footsteps crunching through the woods. The snow came harder. The wind picked up. He moved forward, the image of the naked woman dimming as the battery in his light died.

"There's a small fishing village to the south," he finally

said. "They seemed like good people, but we ate through much of their meat and wine. They'll be in need of a means to restock for the winter. They'll not turn down good silver."

He took out his last coin and set it on the edge of the table.

Tataie's light flickered and went out. The woman lowered her hands from her face. He got his bearings and pointed.

"That way," he said, tipping his hat.

Alone in the dark, he walked back to camp.

It would not be till three years later that my grandfather found his way home. He had survived the Siege of Odessa and the Battle of Stalingrad. He had marched what felt like the length of the world. But then the Red Army forced its way past our borders, and when the tides turned against us, our young king led a coup against our prime minister. Our soldiers were informed we'd switched sides. They were told that the men they'd been valiantly dying beside, they now had to valiantly kill.

After Romania changed from Axis to Allies, the Americans flew over in planes and dropped bombs on our cities to free them from German control. My grandfather led a troop of young men and liberated small villages by foot. Winter came earlier in the mountains of the Old Kingdom than down by the sea. The ground frosted before mid-September. The first flurries arrived after dawn, just briefly, two weeks later. By the end of October, Tataie and his men were stamping their feet in the cold, a thin sheet of white on the ground. Once the snow began truly falling, it did not seem to know how to stop. Stretches of mountain range became impassable. Bridges collapsed under the weight of ice. Other soldiers would not have known how to travel such treacherous roads, but Tataie had learned the lay of this land as a boy.

One evening, while making camp in the forest, he realized he was only a day's walk from his village—a day's walk from the cottage at the top of the hill that he would inherit. So late, late that night, when the snowfall finally stilled, when the moon glowed high above the dark pines, Tataie walked out beneath the trees all alone. He stared up the mountain, searching for lights. He feared what he would find. He feared what would already be gone.

Behind him, a slide was pulled back, the echo of metal scraping metal muffled in the snowy clearing. Something frozen and hard pressed against the nape of Tataie's neck, and he went rigid with fear.

"Turn around. Slow," said a voice thick with accent.

Tataie did as he was told, his eyes widening as he realized who it was who might kill him.

The bin holder. The gasoline pumper.

The German's eyes widened too, but he didn't lower his pistol.

"They say it's almost over. The war," Tataie whispered. When the German didn't speak, he gestured up the mountain with a nod. "My home is just there, in a valley between the tallest peaks. I'd never left before, never seen anything else. Now I've seen so much, I fear it won't look the same."

When he was still met with silence, Tataie wondered if he'd been mistaken, if this wasn't the same man he knew. But then the German's expression changed.

His lip curled as he asked, "The woman. The naked one in the forest. What did you do when we left? What did you pay to keep secret?"

My grandfather stared down the barrel of the gun, then turned his head to look back up the mountain a last time. A flame flickered to life in the distance. First one. Then another. So close he felt he could reach up and take them.

"I gave her my last silver coin," Tataie said. "I pointed the way to the sea."

The wind shifted through the snow-covered trees. An owl called out in the night. Finally, my grandfather looked back at the soldier.

But in the white, moonlit clearing, he was alone.

The First Snow

Mamaie was superstitious of everything, though this hadn't always been true. When I was sick, she made a fuss if I looked at my nails or turned my face to the wall. She chased stray dogs out of our yard with her broom, screaming like they were devils.

"It's a full-time job in this house," she complained, "keeping the bad omens away."

If ever someone said I was cute—and they didn't pinch my cheeks and make a *puh-puh-puh* noise—she would have a conniption, sure I'd been charmed.

"Hasn't your mother taught you anything?" she'd ask, furiously braiding red string for a bracelet in hopes of protecting me from the evil eye.

I couldn't blow out candles, and I'd sooner be caught dead than whistling inside. If I brought her a bundle of flowers, she'd only accept them after making sure there was an odd number. If I sat at the corner of the table, she'd panic and scoot me to the center, swearing I'd never be wed. Mamaie always kept a piece of thread in her mouth while she sewed. She got excited when her palm started to itch. On Tuesdays she made sure not to wash her hair.

"And never, never, never, Ileana, look back at the house after you've left," she insisted.

I thought Mamaie's superstitions were fun, but I had a hard time keeping up with them all. Constantly, in the middle of the simplest things—like wiping water off the floor with a rag under my foot—she'd race in fast as a brush fire, sputtering wild prayers and setting things right. I figured her mind had gone curly, but on the night of the harvest festival I realized the truth.

In the mountains, fall came earlier than it did in the city. School had only been in session for a short time before the first frost of the season dusted the farmlands in crystal. To celebrate the harvest, all the villagers came together on the first of October to share their favorite foods. The morning arrived bright and crisp. The wind whipped and whirled through the valley, drying colorful, wet leaves as they scattered. Men built fires in the center of town, and women were baking by dawn, filling the village with the scent of hot, crusty bread, hand-stuffed sausages, and baked pumpkin.

Sanda was cooking tripe soup with calf stomach, beef hocks, garlic, and vinegar. Mamaie usually made plum dumplings, but since I didn't like plums, she agreed to fry up some dough to fill with sweet cheese and top with powdered sugar. It was amazing how much the villagers could do with so little. Because it was Sunday and I didn't have school, I helped in the kitchen and tended to chores, but the sense of community made me want to contribute in some more meaningful way. After digging around near my schoolbag, I found where I'd hidden my chunk of chocolate when I arrived. I brought it to Mamaie and unwrapped it. Some of the edges had whitened, but otherwise it was still perfect.

"I want to share," I said. "But it's too small for everyone, no matter how we divide it."

"That's nonsense," my grandmother said. And then she heated up some water in a pot and melted the chocolate in a bowl placed on top. After that she drizzled and dripped it over her fried pastries. "See there? Now we can all have a taste. You're becoming a real villager, Ileana."

I couldn't help smiling as I picked up the tray of sweets to bring down the hill. Before I could go, though, my mamaie caught my sleeve, gesturing to a crack in the table.

"Have you seen that before?" she asked, worry lines creasing her brow.

I shook my head.

"Oh my. Oh no, no, no." She started wringing her hands. "Go on, then. Off with you. I need to find your tataie."

Down in the valley, men were dragging long wooden benches into the street, and women were setting up goods to barter—homemade clothing, walnut jam, painted dishes, and leather. Mr. Sala and Mr. Ursu had a pig turning over a spit. Corn roasted on metal racks. Stray dogs ran everywhere, begging for scraps. There was a whole table of cheese: stinky cheese, smoked cheese, cheese aged in fir bark. Tonight there would be music and dancing and games, and maybe even a chance that someone would start telling stories.

Earlier that morning I'd asked Mamaie if someone might tell the story that could not be told, and she'd smacked me on the back of my hand.

"You promised your grandfather you wouldn't bring that up again!"

Outside Gabi's house, my friend and her mother were lugging their great covered pot of tripe soup, so I ran over to help.

"Did you see who's here?" Gabi whispered, head motioning toward a table near the well.

There, smoking cigarettes and watching the villagers, was the strange man from the inn. Beside him were two companions. Since they'd arrived, questions had gone from casual to confrontational. More than once Mr. Bălan had lost his temper, demanding that the men pay their bills and be gone, which of course only worsened the problem. The strangers had stopped playing pleasant. They'd stopped pretending to be on a countryside vacation entirely.

It was obvious to everyone that the men were Securitate. But only me and Gabi and my grandparents and Sanda knew they were searching for my uncle. Rumors said soldiers from the Land Forces had been spotted in other villages too—that they might be headed our way. Surely, this had something to do with my uncle as well, though we couldn't guess what.

After setting down the pot, I took a long look around the village, fear filling the pit of my stomach. When Sanda went to talk to another adult, I said to my friend, "The owl in our yard has been flying around during the day."

Gabi made a face. "Are you getting weird like your mamaie?"

"No," I said defensively. "But this morning there was a new crack in our table. . . ."

Gabi slapped her palm to her forehead. "You *are* getting weird like your mamaie."

"You're the one who thinks Old Constanta's a witch."

"Because witches are *real*," Gabi said.

By the time the sun was past the midpoint in the sky, everyone was down in the village. I avoided Mrs. Sala, who was tsk-tsking each time she saw me—after my terrible summer-homework grades, things had only gotten worse. Squeezing through the crowds, I found Tataie playing his fiddle with a group of other musicians. Nearby, women danced in a circle, holding hands. The circle cinched together and stretched apart, the women's feet matching in time as they went forward, left, forward, then back and right. I tried to find the pattern, impressed that they could all remember so many steps. Gabi joined in and did a wonderful job.

On the tables lining the street, there was more food than I'd ever seen in my life—except, of course, in American movies, like the secret ones I'd watched with my father. I wondered where the villagers had found it all. The backs of cabinets? The corners of attics? Beneath loose wooden planks in the floor? I wondered what had been traded and sacrificed to acquire the ingredients for the small frosted cake on a metal folding table to my left, the beef salad decorated with eggs and olives and roasted red peppers on my right. Even though I was a picky eater, I ate enough to stay full for a week. The chocolate-drizzled pastries were, of course, a success.

Everywhere people were having such a good time, clinking cups and tasting a bit of this or that, joking with loved ones and admiring neighbors' wares, that I started to forget about Mamaie's superstitions. It wasn't till I was sitting beside her, helping barter her pillows and blankets, that I remembered how worried she was.

"All around us there's trouble," she said, eyes on the Securitate. "We have to stay vigilant. I'm always telling you, aren't I? Heed the signs."

I stared, searching, but the only sign I saw was that the three strange men had had too much to drink. Early batches of *țuică* were the culprit. The plum brandy was being passed cup by cup, hand to hand. A drunk villager had even offered a glass to me, which my mamaie smacked away. It looked like the Securitate were competing to see who could reach a big pear trapped at the bottom of a bottle they were sharing, but when Mr. Ursu began carving the last bits of meat off the pig on the spit, their attention shifted. One of the men wobbled over.

"I want some of that," he said.

The old butcher kept carving, as if he hadn't heard. Next to him Ioan was holding a plate. His eyes widened when Mr. Ursu gave him the last of the meat and patted him on the back.

"Go enjoy," he said.

"Didn't you hear me?" the stranger spat, swaying.

"I heard you just fine," said Mr. Ursu, wiping his long carving knife on his apron. "But you've had enough of our food these past weeks. Doesn't seem right, you stealing meat from the innkeeper's boy when you haven't paid his father for your stay or your drinks or your constant questions."

"'Stealing meat'?" repeated the stranger, and his companions started to rise, joining him by the spit. The man gestured to the tables full of food. "All of this belongs to the state. That pig you slaughtered *belongs to the state*. Way I see it, *you're* the one stealing."

Mamaie's hand flitted to mine. Tataie, across the street, put down his fiddle. Ioan, who'd grown incredibly pale, took a shaking step forward and offered his plate to the stranger, but the old butcher put a hand on Ioan's chest.

"Come to think of it," one of the other Securitate said, "isn't this the same fellow with the radio in his shop? The one with the illegal antenna?"

The third stranger nodded, smudging out a cigarette butt with the toe of his boot. "Heard rumors he's been tuning in to the wrong kind of stations."

There was murmuring now, people crowding around the Securitate and Mr. Ursu, who was gripping his carving knife tighter and tighter. The skin on his neck went taut. He started sweating, started breathing all funny. His wife came up behind, looking worried.

"Mamaie," I said anxiously, "something's wrong."

She shushed me, rising, and pulled me away from the table just as a villager was pushed into it. I cried out. There was shouting. Ioan's father, Mr. Bălan, nose red as a beet, forced his way through the crowd, yelling at the Securitate and shaking his fist.

The old butcher clutched at his chest and fell to the ground.

My grandmother gasped, turning my face to her, covering my eyes with her hand. I could still see through her fingers, though—Tataie and Sanda rushing to help, Mrs. Ursu sobbing and squeezing her husband's arm, the Securitate and the crowd moving away. My insides clenched in fear.

Mr. Ursu did not get up.

When they carried his body into his house, still and breathless and pale, Mamaie stood with me outside in the garden, fussing with the collar on my blouse. People were carrying baskets of half-eaten food back to their homes, eyes darting to the Ursus' open door as they passed. There would be no games tonight. No more music. No stories.

Mamaie blotted her eyes. "I should have trusted the signs! A week ago, a painting fell off the wall in the bedroom. And that crack in the table this morning!"

When Tataie came out to meet us, shaking his head solemnly, a heavy sadness washed over me. My grandmother took a deep, trembling breath, stuck out her chin, and went into the house. Watching the villagers clean up the street, I was struck by how quickly things had changed. One moment we'd all been happy, laughing and dancing and carrying on. Now the whole town was silent and mourning. I saw how, in a breath, everything could be taken away—just like when I found the bug in my dresser, when I stepped on the train and left my family behind.

Since Mamaie was one of Mrs. Ursu's closest friends, that night she helped with the wake preparations. They washed the butcher's body and dressed him. They left a bowl of water at his feet so his spirit could bathe. They put a candle and a coin in his hands to light his way and pay for his boat ride into the next world. Inside the house, they turned all the mirrors and clocks toward the wall. They opened the windows and doors and laid the dead butcher on the kitchen table.

For two nights the Ursu family would have to stay up to keep watch, because if an animal got inside and walked under the body, it might become possessed with his soul. And of course, if he wasn't properly guarded, there was also a chance Mr. Ursu could turn into a strigoi mort and haunt the family forever.

Early the next morning, old women holding candles faced east and sang the "Song of the Dawn," begging the sun to rise slowly. Villagers brought Mrs. Ursu food and wine, and that night Mamaie and Tataie took me down to pay our respects. I froze at the little gate outside the garden. I'd never seen a dead body before. Not even my bunica or bunicu. And the truth is, I was frightened. Though I told stories about ghosts and death all the time, the reality was that they scared me.

"Do you want to go back?" my grandfather asked, noting the look on my face.

Mamaie put a firm hand on my shoulder and led me toward the door before I could say yes.

The light inside was brighter than I'd expected. It was late, so only a handful of people were there, family and very close friends. I tried not to look at Mr. Ursu. Instead I went and stood by one of the girls from school, his great-niece, hoping I could think of something kind to say.

"I'm sorry," I finally muttered, which I knew was maybe worse than staying quiet.

She just stared, not really looking at me, not really in the same room.

Tataie kept in a corner, nodding as another man talked. Mamaie stood with Mrs. Ursu, who would not leave her husband's body alone. She kept stroking his hand. She kept kissing his cheeks. I couldn't hear anything in my head except for her wail. Anxiety filled me up like a house in a flood taking on water. I thought about my uncle and father and mother. I thought about all the things that I feared—all the things out of my control.

Mrs. Ursu kept putting her face near her husband's, and Mamaie kept pulling her back.

"Don't let your tears fall on him or you'll drown his soul," my grandmother whispered.

And then I spotted a radio tucked behind a chair—a small, portable radio, the one the butcher sometimes took into his shop—and I pictured my mother leaning over the counter to change the station when he wasn't looking.

"She thought I didn't see her," Mr. Ursu had told me, winking. "Wasn't always smart, letting her play the music she liked, but it made life a bit better, listening to her sing. Such a wonderful voice."

I walked out of the room. I walked right out of the house.

Don't look back. Don't look back. Don't look back.

But when I heard the door open, I turned—and I saw straight through to the kitchen, straight through to the table, where someone stepped out of the way. I looked right at the butcher's body. His skin was waxy and swollen and fake. My head filled with air.

"That was very rude," Mamaie scolded, catching up after I was well down the street. Tataie hobbled behind. "If you were ready to leave, you should have told Mrs. Ursu goodbye."

While we walked back through the town and up the hill in the dark, my grandmother talked about all the things that still had to be done.

There was a sweet bread and a boiled wheat-grain dish to make.

There was a branch to decorate with dried fruit.

There were crowns of flowers to prepare for the grave.

The funeral, to take place on the third day before sunset, would happen in a neighboring village, since we didn't have a church in our own. We would have to carry the body on our shoulders and drape towels over our arms. We would have to halt at least three times on the way, passing special items across the top of the coffin. If we came to any bridges, we would need to be sure to lay down cloth for the whole procession to walk over. Mr. Ursu had to enter the church before anyone else. He had to be placed right in the center. And when the burial was done and we left, we could not forget to wash our hands at the cemetery. We could not forget to walk home taking a different route than we'd come.

Then, of course, were the forty days after death, all with their own items and lamentations and rituals.

My head spun again, as the first flurries of the year fluttered down from the dark sky above.

"Mamaie," I said, "I don't think I can do it. I don't think I can remember all this."

I started to cry.

Tataie stopped and reached down to comfort me, but my grandmother waved him away. She took my hand and kept walking. She held her head high and her eyes straight ahead.

"Then write it in your notebook," she said, squeezing my fingers. "Someone has to remember. How else can we keep the world from falling apart?"

I caught my breath, swallowed, and stuck out my chin.

Mamaie and the Evil Box

There once was a small village down below the mountains, near the train station at the end of the world. In that village lived a family of shoemakers with three beautiful daughters. Though the oldest daughter was certainly more beautiful than any other girl for many hundreds of miles, the middle daughter was even more beautiful than her, and the youngest daughter was more beautiful than both her sisters. In fact the youngest daughter was so beautiful that long before she'd come of age, she'd already been proposed to dozens of times. Her wild dark hair and big eyes were striking enough to make anyone stop and take a second look.

Much later in life, though she hardly could have

known, the youngest daughter would grow up and grow old and have a daughter of her own, twice as lovely as her. And someday that daughter would have me, not even half as pretty as the eldest sister. I, of course, would never have any daughters at all, except for my stories, which—much like girls—should never be judged by their looks.

In her youth, my mamaie did not think about daughters. She did not think about sons, either. Or boys in general. Or anything much except her embroidery and weaving, which she practiced every day. So when Mamaie came of age to be wed, she turned down every suitor who knocked at her door. Her eldest sister was married, then her middle sister, and Mamaie's parents started to fret. By the approach of her twentieth birthday, they were downright terrified.

"She'll never be married," they mourned. "She'll be an old maid."

It was around this same time that the first Roma family moved into Mamaie's village. Unfortunately, the other villagers weren't always nice to those who seemed different, and rumors started to spread that one young unmarried woman practiced magic. Mamaie didn't believe a bit in superstitions or spells, but the other villagers were so frightened of the Roma girl that finally she just had to meet her for herself.

When she arrived at the little house, the woman greeted her in the doorway.

"Is it true you read fortunes?" asked Mamaie.

The woman nodded, her dark hair bound under a red scarf. She wasn't at all like the villagers had said. Not ugly. Not tall. Not hunched or foul-smelling or with eyes like a serpent. She was rather unremarkable, in fact: somewhat thin, with a round nose and a long, tattered skirt.

Mamaie offered some coins. "If you read my fortune, I'll pay you."

The woman hesitated but took the money and led her inside. My mamaie was brought to a quaint little table by the stove, and when she sat, she placed her bag on the floor.

The Roma woman picked it right up and put it on the table.

"Never do that," she explained, "or someday you'll be poor."

Mamaie hid a smirk under her hand.

While the cards were being sorted before her, my grandmother sipped coffee—a rare treat, even though it was thin as water—and noted an unusual feeling. It was as if she were becoming reacquainted with somewhere famil-iar. Mamaie's eyes wandered to a plucked chicken, to a cloth filled with sheep's cheese hanging from the ceiling. Whey dripped rhythmically into a wooden bucket below. And then she noticed the half-finished embroidered vest draped over a chair near the wall.

What intricate, colorful patterns!

Where had the Roma woman found such fine thread?

How did she work with such tiny designs?

My grandmother started to chatter, talking tools of the trade, talking projects, asking if she might see other work. The Roma woman loosened and smiled, chatting back. The cards were forgotten between them. Before either realized, two hours had passed, long after Mamaie was expected for supper.

"It's been just lovely," my grandmother said, setting down her empty cup, "but I really should be getting back home."

"I didn't tell you your fortune," the Roma woman replied.

"Oh, no trouble. I know it's only a trick."

The woman's brow lowered. Her mouth puckered into a frown. "And here we were getting along."

"Don't try to convince me you believe it." Mamaie laughed. "There's no reason for secrets between friends. We all have to survive. I understand."

The Roma woman slid Mamaie's coins back across the table. "Keep your money and get out of my house."

"Now you're just being silly. Fine, then. Tell me my fortune."

There was a long moment of staring—all the mirth gone from the room—but then, finally, the Roma woman looked down at the cards. Her eyes narrowed. She took Mamaie's coffee cup and swirled the sediment around and around before turning it upside down on the table. Then she picked it back up and peered inside, eyes narrowing further. She looked at my grandmother.

"Let me guess," said Mamaie. "Soon I will meet a wonderful man and get married?"

"Yes," said the Roma woman, "but there's something else."

Mamaie rolled her eyes, crossing her arms. However, in the pit of her stomach was a knot.

"Can you feel it?" asked the woman. "The connection between us? There's a reason you came through my door. One day—I cannot say when—but one day great tragedy will befall you. Heed the signs. Send for me when they're clear. And trust me when I arrive. More than your life will depend on it."

Mamaie tried to laugh, but the sound caught in her

throat. It felt like someone was squeezing all the air from her chest. She stood up at once, gathered her things, and left without even saying good-bye.

Days passed. Then months. And my mamaie mostly forgot the premonition. Her parents continued to pester her about getting married, and after a while longer the idea sounded tolerable. In fact she'd become rather lonely. With her sisters both gone, there was no one to talk to while she worked the loom or stitched pinpoint flowers. She told herself that this was the reason she'd chatted with the Roma woman—this was why she'd felt so comfortable inside her home. She was craving a friend. Nothing more.

Not long after that, Tataie came into town. He'd traveled from his village in the mountains looking for someone who might help him fix up an old cottage he'd inherited. Tataie was older than my mamaie by more than a decade, something her parents would find most appropriate. He was also quite handsome, in a worn, unconventional way. The marks of the war were in his words, his demeanor, a ragged scar on his forearm. They were in the muscles that still lingered at his shoulders, his legs, and his broad chest.

And though since he'd returned home, Tataie had never again seen the world through the same eyes—though he had very much planned to live alone in his cottage till he lost the life he'd bought with three silver coins—at the sight of Mamaie's beauty he found himself unable to look away.

They became fast friends. And for two years they traveled up and down the mountains to meet, to have lunch, to chat and share news.

Mamaie liked that Tataie preferred goats to most people. She liked that he listened more than he talked, that he thought hard about the words he would say, always giving straight, simple answers. She liked how carefree he looked when he took out his fiddle—how his laugh rumbled before breaking, unexpected and rare.

Tataie liked that Mamaie didn't want to get married, even though he had begun to think that he did. He liked that she was always speaking her mind and giving advice, whether people would heed her or no. He admired her embroidery and weaving, often bringing tunics for her to decorate, or orders for pillows and blankets. He was her first and best customer, paying much more for her work than was fair.

When they finally agreed that it would be more convenient to marry—no more traveling up and down mountains to meet—Mamaie's parents nearly died from relief. The ceremony was plain and quiet, and they moved into his cottage right after. It wasn't long till my young grand-mother was round and glowing, soon to give birth to my mother.

In the last three months of her pregnancy, life seemed perfect.

If Mamaie had read stories, she would have realized that things were about to go horribly wrong.

At first the signs would have been easy to miss, even for someone quite careful. A twitching left eye. A tickling nose. A crow landing on the front porch.

But then came strange animal calls from the forest. Then came the storm that took part of the roof. Mamaie remembered then what the Roma woman had told her, but still she did not heed the warnings. It wasn't long before the goats and the well had gone dry. Soon after that, wolves got half of the chickens, and the crops in the field where Tataie worked rotted in mushy brown rows.

Finally, my grandmother began to have pains—sharp pains, staggering pains—far too soon. The village midwife was no help beyond recognizing the danger.

One morning, while Tataie was away, searching desper-ately down the mountains for a doctor, a knock came at the cottage door.

"Be off with you," Mamaie called.

"Please," replied a voice. "I'm starving. Haven't you got any food?"

Mamaie knew they hardly had any to spare, but she hated the thought of someone hungry, so she crossed the room, bracing herself with the wall, and opened the door. A Roma woman stood on her porch, head wrapped tight with a scarf. Though it had been years since their meeting, Mamaie recognized her at once.

"You," she breathed.

The woman's eyes widened. "So this is the way that fate tied us."

Mamaie snatched some bread from the cupboard and pushed it into the Roma woman's hands. "Take this and go. I have no need for your fortunes."

But the woman wouldn't stop staring, eyes tracing Mamaie's taut belly, her pained expression, the skinny goats in their pen, the damaged roof.

"You're in trouble," she said.

"Anyone with sight could tell," said Mamaie. "But there's nothing you can do."

"Why haven't you heeded the signs?" asked the Roma woman. "Why haven't you sent for me?"

Mamaie snorted, then grimaced. "To spare myself exactly this nonsense."

The woman shook her head, gaze narrowing. "Trust me now, like I warned. It's clear as day you've been cursed."

Mamaie laughed out of spite, then slammed the door closed in her face. But the Roma woman refused to be off. She stood there pounding and pacing and causing a racket. Finally, unable to rest, my young grandmother swung the door back open.

"What can I do to get you to leave?" she asked.

"Let me help. That's all. Then I'll go."

So Mamaie followed the Roma woman out into the yard, where they walked to the back of the house. The woman closed her eyes and knelt to the ground, touched the grass, then scraped the hard-packed dirt by the back wall with her nails.

"A shovel," she said. "Where can I find one?"

Mamaie told her, and when the woman returned, she started digging at once. Hard. Fast. She was strong. The late afternoon sun sank over the trees. The shadows grew long and dark. When the hole was big enough, the Roma woman crawled inside, reaching deep, deep under the foundation of the house. She called for Mamaie to pull her back out and emerged with a large, dirty wooden box in her arms. Purple and black markings were painted all over, from bottom to top. The lid was held shut with rusted, bent nails.

"What is it?" Mamaie asked, quite surprised.

"Evil," replied the woman.

For the first time, Mamaie felt frightened. She told herself that she still didn't believe. But the box had been deep under the house, so deep that it must have been buried before the cottage was built, decades and decades and decades ago. It made no sense that the Roma woman would have known it was there. Slowly Mamaie reached out to touch the half-rotted lid, but a pain struck like lightning through her womb, and she wrenched away. The other woman pried the box open with a tool, and together they peered inside.

Mamaie's eyes widened. The Roma woman's face tightened in terror.

Herbs, bundled and burned. Dark stains and scratches, as if something had clawed, trying to get out. Shriveled, rotten black pieces of what might have been flesh long ago.

And bones. Small bones. So many. Mamaie tried to convince herself they belonged to a bird. To a rabbit. A cat.

"Why would someone do this?" Mamaie asked, her voice shaking.

The Roma woman pursed her lips. "People hurt other

people for all sorts of reasons. The best we can do is stay watchful—keep our eyes open to protect those we care for."

Lifting her head high, Mamaie said, "Tell me how I can fix this."

That evening, as the last light faded from the sky, Mamaie brought the Roma woman a chicken and cut off its head. Its body shuddered and blood speckled the grass, painting the bones in the box. My grandmother held the animal as still as she could, keeping its wings tight together, and as the corpse drained, the Roma woman chanted, swaying and singing. In the dark they burned the box and the dead hen, then filled the hole under the house.

When they were through, Mamaie offered the coins she and Tataie had saved for the doctor, but the Roma woman just shook her head.

"Take care of yourself and your husband," she said. And then she glanced down with a smile. "Take care of your daughter as well."

She left that night and did not return.

In the morning, Mamaie's pain was gone and the goats were full to bursting with milk.

The Funeral

Three days after the butcher's death, just as planned, everyone in the valley made the long trek through the forest to the next town. Our village was left empty behind us, not a soul breathing the air apart from bedridden Old Constanta. Even the three strangers were gone. They'd left in the night without paying their bill, much to Mr. Bălan's great fury.

As we traveled down the road out of town, the casket carried over the shoulders of men up ahead, flurries turned into snowflakes. The ground was still too warm for them to stick, so our boots clumped up with mud and stringy brown grass. Women wailed, their sorrowed voices carrying over the mountains alongside the trumpeting of long, straight *buciume*, the same horns used to guide flocks of sheep. The horns played the "Song of Death" while we walked.

When we finally made it to the church, there was a sermon from a man with a black hood, and then the procession carried Mr. Ursu's body to the cemetery, where the man spoke again. After the butcher's casket was covered with crowns of flowers and lowered into the earth, we returned to the church, where the people from our village drank wine and sang songs and danced with colorful masks. Then everyone started to tell stories about Mr. Ursu. And as I sat laughing, listening to Tataie talk about one of Mr. Ursu's clever tricks, I realized that joy had found its way back into the world. Sometimes a good story can help keep people close to you after they're gone.

Emboldened, I stood up and asked to go next.

Mrs. Sala led me to the front of the room. It was the first time I'd spoken before an audience since the Great Tome was burned. And when one of the other village kids started to tease, I got anxious. But then Gabi noisily readied a loogie, which made everyone go quiet, and I gathered my nerve. Once the story started, there was no stopping it. I told the rest of the church how, even though I'd only met the butcher that summer, my mother's memories had long ago made him a part of my life. For several minutes I shared stories of radios and sheep and fake bloody hands. After I was finished and went back to my seat, Tataie pulled me into a hug, and the weight of sadness in my heart lifted.

When the funeral was over, we walked home a different way than we'd come. The sun set as we journeyed. The air grew frigid, snowflakes coming down harder and faster, but my tataie just took off his white sheepskin coat and draped it over my shoulders. It was heavy and long—so big that the sheepherders used the same kind as beds. I didn't mind, though, because it was warm and smelled like my grandfather.

"Won't you get cold?" I asked, looking up.

Tataie stretched, sucking in a deep breath, and smiled. "Yes, but I like it. Don't you?"

My mamaie started tittering and fussing, and I laughed.

After all the months I'd been lonely and scared—after all the time I'd wished only to return to the city—I finally felt content being just where I was. I finally felt like I belonged. Seeing the villagers come together had filled me with hope, and listening to their stories had given me strength.

The Securitate would forget all about my uncle, just like he'd promised. They would give up and leave my family alone. And when my mother and father came to get me—which would surely be any day—maybe I could convince them to move to a city near the mountains so I could stay close to all the people I'd come to love.

I glowed, feeling like nothing could shatter my mood.

But then at the front of the procession, a few of the younger men started calling out and picking up their pace. My grandparents looked at each other and began hurrying too. It wasn't till we rounded the road to the valley, though, that we saw what was causing the commotion.

Trucks parked in the road. Big green ones. Lots of them.

Lights dancing through the streets and the windows and doorways of homes.

Soldiers from the Land Forces were searching the village.

I froze, a rock in the stream of villagers running now toward town. If they found me, would they take me away? Would they put me in a cell like my uncle? I turned my eyes toward the hill with my grandparents' cottage, where flashlights were sweeping the trees, and I remembered the manifesto under the floorboards. My heart leaped into my throat as I realized how many others were in danger if the papers were found.

A hand on each of my shoulders—my grandparents—got me moving forward again. Terrified, I followed the mass of people to the schoolhouse, where everyone was being herded like cattle.

"Keep in line. No pushing. No reason for alarm," an official in a brown suit said, smiling as the building filled with our bodies. The three Securitate officers from before were standing outside with him, watching.

Shoulder to shoulder we squeezed in. Wall to wall. I was sure they couldn't fit any more of us, but they did. And when we were all stuffed inside—adults sitting on desks, children propped up on shoulders—the man in the brown suit skirted toward the front of the room and stood up in Mrs. Sala's chair. Somehow, Gabi found me in the crowd as he started to talk. I must have been pale, I must have been trembling, because she looked at me strangely and whispered, "Are you about to puke?"

I was so scared that I could have.

The official in the brown suit explained that recent incidents had brought the state's attention to the village. At first I was sure he meant me, and for the longest breath I'd ever held in my life, I waited for my name to be called.

Instead, though, the man said, "Your mountains are infested with terrorists. Anti-Communist foreigners who have no love for our country have been spotted in these very woods. If you have any information the state would find useful, you're obligated by law to speak up."

The schoolhouse filled with murmurs and frightened noises, but no one raised a voice above the rest. The man in the brown suit nodded, as though he had expected as much.

"No reason to fret. We'll stay till the issue's resolved. You're entirely safe," he said.

Of course, this brought only more worried glances.

"But there's other business as well." The man pulled an envelope from his jacket and took out a folded sheet of paper. Bone white. Black, typed letters. A red stamp. He wiggled it in the air till the room quieted. "An official announcement from the Supreme Leader himself!"

He opened the paper and read it out loud.

When he got to the part about the village being chosen for systemization, the adults in the room started yelling and shouting from all sides. I didn't know what the word meant, but I knew from the panicked reaction that it was bad.

"Everyone! Can't you see the opportunity your country is giving you?" The man spread out his hands, palms up, and smiled. "Life in these mountains is brutal. Your farmland's frozen for most of the year. The rest of Romania is moving forward without you!"

"We've always done just as you told us," cried Mr. Sala, shocked. "We send the crops down each year, right on time!"

"Eh," said the man in the brown suit, scrunching his nose. "But it seems, now and then, there's a bit off the top, yes? Those pigs you and your wife raise in the backyard, they don't all make it down the mountains, do they?"

Mrs. Sala started to sob. It was the first time I'd ever seen a teacher do such a thing, and it shook me right to the core.

"Many of you will still keep your professions," said the man. "I hear you have a talented veterinarian here? Even has a skill for tending people in an emergency, so it's rumored." He smiled at Sanda, who went white. "Those of you who have experience farming will simply be relocated to more productive communities."

"And what about the rest of us?" demanded Mr. Bălan.

"Why, you'll go to the cities, where you'll serve your country from the factory lines," the man said.

Voices rose again. The crowd began to get rowdy, eyes darting to the soldiers stationed at the door. Mrs. Ursu, face still puffy from crying, walked up and spat at the man's feet. He pursed his lips as her neighbors pulled her away.

"The Leader wants everyone gone by the new year," the man said over the rumble. "You should start taking apart your houses as soon as possible. We'll be recycling the materials for future projects, and the sooner you get to work, the sooner your country can too. Besides, you wouldn't want to get stuck outside pulling nails in a snow-storm, right? I hear this place can get pretty cold!"

As if on cue—as if the government could control even the weather—a gust of snow rushed past the windows, pushing hard on the glass. Mr. Bălan shoved his way to the front of the room, thumping his chest with the heel of his hand.

"Ten generations," he said. "My family's been here ten generations! You think I'll just pick up and leave?"

"Yes, I do." The man smiled again, bigger this time.

"And what if I won't? What if I tell you to go to hell? You can't force me to tear down my own house." The inn-keeper leveled his gaze. Ioan, standing next to him, tugged his father's hand but was ignored.

"You see what effect living like this has on good people?" The man in the brown suit gestured, addressing the rest of the room. "You're too distanced from modern society. You forget how the world works. If you won't do as you're asked, you place the burden on others, who then have to do the job for you." He shook his head at Mr. Bălan, who was still flushed, fists knotted beside his potbelly. "We'll be ordering machinery to help with any troublesome structures. When it arrives, your inn will be the first building to go."

Everyone was dismissed. In a mass exodus the villagers were shooed out the door—all except the innkeeper and his family. As I stepped outside, I could hear Mr. Bălan start pleading with the official. His fire was gone, pinched right out. I didn't want to look back. I knew that I shouldn't. But I did. Ioan had sat down on the floor right where he'd been standing. His mother was sobbing nearby. His father dropped to his knees, begging at the man's shiny brown shoes.

In the snow, still dressed all in black for mourning, the villagers returned to their houses.

Into the House of the Witch

The next day, after school, Gabi followed me up the hill and we crawled under the cottage to talk.

"Are you a terrorist?" she asked.

"No," I said.

"Is your uncle?"

"I don't think so. Unless . . . are poets terrorists?"

Gabi just shrugged. "So why did you look like you were about to be sick last night?"

I hesitated. Keeping my secrets completely to myself was the only sure way to be safe, but with things getting so serious, I knew I might not be able to save everyone all on my own. Besides, Gabi was my best friend. I trusted her.

So I told her my story from beginning to end. I told

her about "The Baker's Boy." I told her about the electrician. I even told her about the manifesto buried under the floor.

"I've got to protect it," I said. "Will you help me?"

Gabi bit her bottom lip. "How about we just get rid of it? Then no one could find it and see all the names. We could light it on fire or something."

"No!" I gasped, taking her wrists. "My uncle almost *died* bringing it here. Those words are worth more than our lives!"

"Okay, okay," she said, shaking me off. "Don't freak out. So what do we do?"

"First we find out what the soldiers are up to. Then we make a plan to protect the people we love."

My friend shook her head, uncertain. "We're just kids, Ileana."

"Yeah. *We're just kids.* Think about it. No one's going to suspect *we'll* do anything. I mean, has an adult ever come up to you and asked you strange questions? Like what your mom's reading, or what kind of things the teacher's saying in class?"

Gabi nodded.

"That's because they're trying to make you a spy," I said. "Just like in the story that got me in trouble. Kids are really good spies, because adults don't think about what they're doing when they're around us."

"You want to spy on the soldiers?" Gabi asked. After a moment she smiled. "I guess that could be pretty fun."

We got right to work as the rest of October crept forward. The wind gushed down from the peaks of the mountains, heaping snow-crusted leaves all over the cottage's yard. The great owl that nested nearby continued to call from our rooftop, night after night. I watched from the porch as she circled, hunting, fattening up for the cold months ahead.

I was fattening up too, but not with food.

Each day, I stuffed my little notebook into my jacket and filled it with writing about everything that I saw. When the soldiers put tents in the valley and took up residence in people's attics and kitchens, I made a list of who was sleeping where. When they started to go on routine security checks, I noted the route they walked and when they would break for a snack.

Gabi was in charge of the drawings. She mapped the whole village and added the new military structures, like the roadblock and the mysterious, growing pile of metal boxes—always covered with a black tarp. It was hard work, paying attention to so much all at once, but it seemed like the right thing to do.

By the end of the month, things started to get strange at school. More than one family had already left town, taking their children with them, and the empty desks in our classroom were an unhappy reminder each day. Mrs. Sala was acting weird too. Most mornings she looked like a plump little bird perched on a sill, head perking up at every small sound. She'd write a word on the board, then erase it, then go back and write the same one. The only good thing about her distracted demeanor was that she stopped assigning us homework. Gabi and I wondered why she bothered to stay, why she kept teaching, but I guess, when it came down to it, we were all just trying to act normal.

One day after school, Gabi and I planned to go to the abandoned church to exchange notes. We often met there when we had dangerous things to discuss, and we had stashed all sorts of secret lists and drawings in the debris of its broken chairs and crumbling tiles. When we scurried down the schoolhouse steps together, though, Sanda started calling from up the street.

"She's gonna make me stick thermometers up cow butts, I just know it," Gabi whined. "We'll meet later, okay?"

I waved good-bye as she ran off, then watched the other children walk home. It had stopped snowing for a few days, but the ground was still covered in white, the sky puffy and gray overhead. A group of men in uniforms was sitting outside the tavern, playing cards. They kicked at stray dogs when the animals wandered too close. I'd have to pass the men alone if I went back to the cottage, and just the thought of that made me sweat.

I turned, hurrying toward the church—and walked straight into a Securitate officer.

"Whoa there, little one!" he said, putting a hand on my shoulder.

I looked up and my eyes widened. It was the man who'd yelled at Mr. Ursu about the pig. My mamaie blamed him for the butcher's death. I wanted to be angry—to tell him to get his hand off me—but all I felt was afraid.

"Where are you off to so fast?" the officer asked, looking around.

Besides the ruins of the church, there was nothing in the direction I was headed except for Old Constanta's house. I opened my mouth, planning to say something incredibly cunning, but the words wouldn't come out.

After a moment the officer squinted, looking closer, and asked, "Whose daughter are you? Which family are you from?"

Considering all the times I'd pictured this interrogation—all the imagined scenarios—surely, I should have had a quick answer. But it was like my brain wasn't working. It was like I'd been cursed. The notebook in my coat pocket dug into my side, and I wondered if he could see its shape through the fabric. My mouth moved, soundless. I was trembling.

The officer tilted his head.

I was sure he would ask, "Are your parents Liza and Lucian? Is your uncle named Andrei? Where is he now? Have you hidden him? Have you hidden something for him?" I was sure he'd reach right into my coat and yank out all my notes and my stories, scattering them as he shouted, "What's this you've been writing? Did you think we wouldn't find out?"

But before anything like that could happen, a familiar sensation tingled right up my spine.

Someone was watching.

I turned and my eyes landed on Old Constanta's window. When I saw the hunched figure standing at her glass, the temperature dropped ten degrees. I remained perfectly still, my heart thudding, as the shadow vanished and the curtains were yanked shut.

Mamaie said Old Constanta could not rise from her bed.

She said the woman was so sick and so frail that other

people—neighbors and nurses and distant relatives—had to bathe her and feed her and help her use the toilet. Mamaie said every time they tried to take Old Constanta to live in a hospital down at the bottom of the mountain, she went wild and scratched and bit like an animal.

The wind rushed past my ears and flurries dusted the edge of my coat, whirling and skirting at my feet.

Old Constanta's front door creaked open.

"Hey, Earth to kid. You still with me?" the officer asked, jiggling my shoulder.

I spun away and ran toward the widow's yellow house, crunching through her dead, frozen grass, dashing up her front porch, and slamming the door closed once I was inside. Panting, I pressed my back to the wood, then scooted along the wall to peek out through the curtains. The officer had a confused look on his face, but after a moment he just shook his head and made his way up the street toward the tavern. I knew I needed to sneak behind the houses and back up the hill in case the man changed his mind, but my heart was still pounding, so I slumped to the floor, catching my breath.

And then I realized where I was.

The house was totally dark, all the curtains drawn over the windows.

"Hello?" I whispered, barely audible, my voice still lost somewhere far away.

Some of the other children said that Old Constanta was a witch, a *strigoaică*, and that if you didn't keep your promises, or if you tattled to the teacher when someone cheated off your test, or if you didn't share your best food at lunch, she would snatch you out of your bed and drag you back to her house to cook you up in her sour soup. They said she could put a spell on you so that even if you screamed while you boiled, no one would hear.

Something shifted near the far wall. Something crouched in the corner. Claws extended from gnarled, rotting fingers. Dry, slit lips pulled back over pointed, glistening teeth.

I squeezed my eyes shut hard, desperately wanting to run.

There was a faint, rattling laugh. "Come nearer, child, and I'll light a candle."

My eyes opened wide. It sounded like a witch's trick, just like something the Mother of the Forest would say, but I rose from the floor, peering into the darkness. I edged one of my feet a step closer, fists gripping the straps of my schoolbag.

A match was struck and a flame seemed to float in the air on the far side of the room. When the candle caught and flickered to life, I shielded my face with a hand. Old

Constanta was lying in bed, eyes closed, a quilt up to her neck. Her skin was so thin I could see her veins under the surface. Her hair—what was left of it—was so white it looked like misplaced tufts of down on her embroidered pillow. I squinted till I was certain. My mamaie's work.

The comfort of the familiar sight faded quickly. The old widow had not moved, had not breathed since I could see her in the light. For all I could tell, she was asleep or dead or a fake—a doll made of sugar, perhaps, meant to lure me closer till it was too late. Every nerve in my body told me to open the door and run, but when my eyes wandered the room, I spotted something that made my feet stick in place.

I needed to speak to the old woman. I hadn't realized it till now—till I'd seen what was sitting on top of her table.

"Have you lost your tongue?" a voice asked.

I turned back fast, but her eyes were still closed, her body still hidden under the quilt.

"No," I whispered.

"Speak up, girl."

"No," I said, louder, clenching my jaw.

"I thought you'd be a brave one, coming into the witch's house on your own," she wheezed. "But you sound frightened as a mouse."

I swallowed hard. Had her lips moved? I couldn't tell

beneath the shadows dancing over her bed. She turned her head to look at me, and her eyes were pale and foggy. I held my straps tighter.

"I am brave," I said. The rattling laugh again. I took a step closer. "And you're not really a witch."

The edge of what might have once been a smile appeared at the old woman's mouth. "What am I, then?"

"You're the one who brought the baskets to my uncle when he was sick."

She lifted the bald place where her eyebrows should have been. "Me? A crippled, dying old thing? I can't even get out of bed. There's a metal pan on the chair here beside me. Do you know what it's for? Would you like to find out?"

I took another step forward. "The wicker basket, the one that you used, it's right there on the table, with the same cloth and everything. You wanted me to come in here. You wanted me to see."

This time the laugh turned into a wet hacking. "It'll get your legs chopped off, that curiosity. I could lay a wolf trap at the feet of a girl like you, and you'd still stomp toward the bait. You're as bad as your mother or worse."

A smile spread across my face. "So it's true, then, the story about her and you. You went up the mountain together?"

"All stories are true in some way," she said.

"Did you really meet wolves in the forest?"

At this, her eyes widened. "Oh yes. And not just any wolves. Your mother went up the mountain many times. The White Wolf always followed her. He was always watching." When I didn't say anything, she continued with a smirk. "You've seen him too. I can tell. It's a great honor. He's the guardian of these mountains, you know. The rest of the world, they've forgotten him. They sacrificed their wolves to the Romans and he abandoned them. But not here. Not us."

The snow was coming down harder outside. When I peeked out the curtains, I could see the soldiers at the tavern, still playing cards. The Securitate officer had joined them, but he kept looking over at the house.

I knew that the smart thing to do was go home, but the taste of a forbidden story had filled my mouth. My bag slipped from my shoulders.

"Old Constanta," I asked, "do you know the story that cannot be told?"

"Every story can be told."

"Not this one. It's too dangerous."

"Don't be ridiculous," she said.

And then, before I knew what was happening, she

started to speak. The words of the story were right there, right in my ears, filling up my whole head. My fingers itched, wanting something to write with. I wouldn't remember the details, not all of them. When she was through, I waited in silence for something to happen, hairs standing up on the back of my neck. The story that could not be told had been let free in the room. I felt it there, hanging between us. But the walls didn't cave in. The floorboards didn't split open under my feet.

"I swear I won't tell anyone else," I finally said.

"Why not?" Old Constanta asked. "It isn't a good enough story for you? Can't suffer these old peasants' tales?"

"No! It's just . . . Mamaie and Tataie made me promise." And then, in case she really was a witch, I added quickly, "And I'm not the kind of person who breaks promises."

"Suit yourself," said Old Constanta, and her eyes closed again. I thought she'd fallen asleep till she whispered, "It's a code, child. That's why they want it kept secret."

I frowned. "A code? Like spies use in the American movies?"

My lips clamped shut and I heard my father shushing me, hissing that the movies we'd seen together could get us in trouble. If the old woman noticed my slip, though, she didn't care.

"They use the story to tell one another when unwanted guests—like your soldiers—are on their way to the village. The White Wolf protects us. If people say he's near, it means there's something coming that we need protection from."

For a while I stood there thinking. If it was a code, of course they wouldn't want just anyone telling it. It made sense that it was kept secret.

"Thanks for the story," I said, picking up my schoolbag. "And thank you for helping before, even if you won't admit that you did."

The candle fluttered. I opened the door a crack, making sure we were still alone.

"Old Constanta," I said, looking back at her once more, "do you think they'll really do it? Do you think they'll destroy the whole village?"

Her eyes opened a final time, facing the ceiling as if in prayer.

"They'll try," she said. "They'll tear down our homes and make us scatter like rats. They'll find your poor uncle, too."

My heart caught in my chest. My hand tightened around the door handle.

"But then," she said, her breath shaking like there were stones in her lungs, "then the White Wolf will come down with his armies. He'll come down and he'll rip off the beast's head."

Cunning Ileana and the Mother of the Forest

When news about the monarch's campaign of terror finally reached the mountain castle, it was clear that things weren't going so well for the three princesses' father. The monarch had begun to question the emperor's loyalty, concerned that his supposed ally had had some part in the very rumors they were out silencing. In response, the monarch had sent troops to the castle to spy on the girls. His soldiers were noisy and brutish—not very good spies at all—and they spent all day playing cards and drinking wine and being generally awful houseguests.

Fortunately, the youngest princess had made a new friend—a quick-witted girl knight clad in fantastic, hand-carved metal armor. Ileana and the knight began hiding stockpiles of swords and arrows and catapults, just in case things got bad.

One day, while reviewing the castle's diminishing stores of provisions, Cunning Ileana heard the middle princess crying. She ran at once to her room and threw open the doors, thinking the soldiers were up to no good. Instead, though, she found her sister tucked in bed, stinking something foul.

Sweet, sweet Ileana, the middle princess croaked, *I've fallen deathly ill and smell really bad! At this rate the boys will run away before I even start chasing them!*

Ileana gagged, clutching her throat through her chain mail. It only took a quick glance around the room to see that the middle princess had hidden onions and garlic in every possible crevice.

Have you got any idea what's to blame? Ileana asked, but the sarcasm must have been lost in her gasping.

Heartache, said the middle princess. *You know my string of pearls twined with golden flowers? The one my first crush gave me?*

Not really, said Ileana.

Well, I was flinging it around and it broke! said her sister. *Only a witch can rethread it, since it's enchanted, so I begged my beloved to take it to the Mother of the Forest.*

How incredibly stupid, said Ileana.

Listen, won't you! He's been gone for three days and I just know something terrible has happened!

At this the middle princess started crying again, and Ileana sighed.

Don't worry. All right? I'll go find the Mother of the Forest, she said. For even though Ileana knew this too was a trick, she still loved her sister dearly and would have done anything for her sake.

After packing a basket for her journey, Cunning Ileana headed off into the black woods. It wasn't long till things started to get pretty creepy. In the dark, hollow spaces of tree trunks, eyes followed each step that she took. Mist wisped along the mossy forest floor. The call of an ancient owl echoed through the dusk. By the time Ileana reached a dreadful little house in the woods, nestled beside a gurgling river of pitch, every hair on the princess's skin was standing up straight. She knocked once, and when she heard a muffled cry for help inside, she pulled an axe from her basket and chopped down the door.

There, tied to a chair and gagged, was the Mother of the Forest, skin sucked to her old bones like a skeleton, wormlike hair squirming around her loose, ragged garb. At her bare, wrinkled feet was the middle princess's pearl necklace, all fixed. Cunning Ileana hurried to the old woman's side and began undoing her gag. When the Mother of the Forest could speak, she reached her bound, shaking hands toward the princess's basket.

I'm starving, she managed to whimper. *If I don't have some food, I'll die.*

I've got some bread with jam, said Ileana, and she took her own rations and fed them to the witch.

Just then there was a great flash of light, and the Mother of the Forest began spewing strange, glowing words. Cunning Ileana shielded her eyes with a hand till the curse had been cast. When she dared to peek between her fingers again, though, everything looked quite normal.

What was that all about? Ileana asked. Or at least she would have, if she'd still had a voice. Her eyes went wide in terror and she grasped at her throat.

Oh, child, said the Mother of the Forest, still bound to the chair. *Oh, you poor, poor dear. I didn't mean for that to happen. I'm not really as bad as they say. If you're kind to my trees and you leave me to my prayers, I'm usually a mild, sensible woman. But a few days back, this vile prince captured me, and you know how that sort of thing ends—I had to grant him a wish. Can you believe he wished that the first person who offered me help would go mute? I shouldn't have*

been caught in the first place, but I'd found this broken pearl necklace outside my door, and he snuck in the back while I was busy rethreading it.

Ileana pinched the bridge of her nose and then reached into her basket to pull out a quill and pad of yellowed parchment. She wrote, *If you really feel that bad about it, you'll help me.*

Ehhh, said the Mother of the Forest. *You can't expect me to give wisdom out for free. Every cursed princess from here to Japan will come knocking. Think about my reputation!*

Cunning Ileana rolled her eyes and reached again into her basket for the jug of magical saliva from the balaur.

Is that what I think it is? asked the Mother of the Forest.

The youngest princess nodded.

Now, that's what I'm talking about! said the witch. *Since I can see you're such a generous girl, I'll let you have a fairy log from my river. That way, if you're ever in trouble, you can escape in a hurry. Go ahead and take my pearl necklace, too. It's caused me nothing but drama, and it's gaudy anyhow.*

When the Mother of the Forest finished explaining the finer points of fairy logs, Cunning Ileana did her best not to look irritated and wrote, *This is really great, but how exactly do I reverse the spell?*

Oh, dear girl, don't you know? Someone can steal your

voice, *but they can't give it back. If you want it, you'll have to find it yourself,* said the witch.

The princess sighed, but then she noticed movement down the hall—a shadow the size and shape of the middle prince. She wrote, *The boy who caused all this trouble is hiding in your back room.*

Then Ileana undid the rest of the old woman's bindings and went right out the front door. While she was choosing a fairy log from the river of pitch, a great flash of light filled the cottage, followed by screams of sheer anguish. Ileana didn't even once look over her shoulder.

At home, the youngest princess gave her middle sister the enchanted necklace, good as new.

Holy cow! It's totally fixed! said the middle princess, rosy with glee. After a moment, though, she bit her bottom lip and asked, *Um, you didn't happen to run into my boyfriend, did you?*

Cunning Ileana really wanted to say something rude, but since her voice wasn't working, she just made an inappropriate gesture.

When the second prince arrived back at his palace covered in warts and boils and missing all his teeth, the youngest son of the monarch fell into an absolute tizzy of rage. He sent a third message to the elder princesses, demanding they lure Ileana to his palace and help him take revenge. If they didn't, the monarch's sons would absolutely love them no longer. In fact, the three princesses from the castle of the king in the south were growing more beautiful by the day.

The two elder daughters of the emperor became worried. Even as dense as they were, and so stricken with love, they could no longer deny that the princes were outrageously evil.

The middle sister tried to rationalize it. *It's her own fault,* she said, swallowing hard.

She'll thank us when she's happily wed, the oldest sister added sheepishly.

For the last time, they agreed to trick Ileana.

The Ural Owl

When winter arrived, my grandparents were sure the gray Ural owl would leave. All year she'd lived in a rotted tree trunk near the yard, snatching up mice and lizards and songbirds. She liked to sit on the thatched roof of the cottage, staring down just like the eye in our attic. Her face was cute and round, and her feathers were fluffy, but her dark talons were sharp as paring knives. Mamaie always covered her head when the owl flew past.

"Watch her now," she warned. "That bird's a death omen and violent, too. Those claws could shred you to rags."

Tataie shook his head when my grandmother left. "She won't hurt you. She's just protecting her family."

At dusk I would watch the Ural hunt. Graceful and

fierce, she'd dive toward the brush, then swoop up with a shrieking dormouse or hare. Sometimes her mate came to join her, gliding over the trees with his dark-barred tail feathers fanned wide. He was much less impressive. Her wingspan was longer than his—more than a meter across—and she dwarfed him in size. Clearly, she loved him for his voice. "Wuhu huwu-huwuwu," he'd sing, deep and rhythmic. She'd bark back, hoarse and high-pitched, their duet echoing over the mountains.

Winter settled in the village. November arrived in a bluster of snow, and my grandparents insisted the Ural owl would soon be gone, but she stayed.

"Oh, that call," my mamaie fretted. "Heed the signs, Ileana. There's blood in the air."

"If we heeded every sign that you saw, we'd think the whole world was doomed," sighed Tataie.

My grandmother looked out the kitchen window at the valley below, where the soldiers were gathered around a great fire—the smoldering remains of a cottage.

"We'll find out soon enough if it is," she said.

That month, many more of the villagers left town. They pulled the nails out of their houses. They tore the doors right from their frames. The soldiers picked through what was left of the skeletons like carrion birds.

The only bit of luck we got came from the snow. It seemed to have no end, piling up on top of the cottage and covering the whole world in white. This caused trouble for the Land Forces and Securitate officers, who didn't know how to manage the weather as well as the villagers. The men were always grumpy, complaining about the cold, and their bulldozer got stuck coming up the mountains. Everyone in my country was used to snow, of course. In Bucharest it came every year, but not so early and never so much.

"Winter's just getting started," said Tataie.

"Did you catch any falling leaves this autumn?" Mamaie asked. "That should help keep you warm."

I hadn't, but when I fretted about it to Gabi, she just rolled her eyes.

"Superstitions," she said. "Your grandparents' stove is what will keep you warm."

As usual she was right. When wood burned in the kitchen, it heated up the whole cottage.

The snow changed life a great deal in the mountains. I had to bundle up till I waddled every time I went outside. It took a lot of effort to keep the animals dry and fed and make sure their water didn't freeze. Sometimes we had to use blankets to cover the goats. Not watching your step could be treacherous too—snowdrifts were often deeper than they looked, and icy patches were everywhere. As long as we were careful and dressed right, though—like in my tataie's white sheepskin coat, which was big enough to cover us both—spying on the soldiers became much easier for Gabi and me. We could drop down out of sight or dip behind a snowdrift in a heartbeat.

Unfortunately, the snow and the late arrival of the bull-dozer did little to help the poor Bălans. The man in the brown suit made their tavern and inn his base of opera-tions, eventually forcing the family to leave. Gabi and I watched from her doorway on the day that an army truck came to drive Ioan and his family away.

"I know he wasn't always nice," I said, "but I still feel bad for him."

My friend nodded as the innkeeper loaded the last box of things into the truck. They could take only what they could carry. They'd only been given a day.

Just before Ioan climbed up into the cab, he spotted us and told his father to wait, running over. My friend went stiff as a board.

"You two are planning something, aren't you?" Ioan said. "I've seen you darting around, whispering all the time."

Gabi stepped behind me, so I puffed out my chest. "If you want us to tell you our secrets, we won't."

Ioan shoved a piece of crumpled paper into my hand.

"I don't want your secrets," he said. "But you can have mine. These are directions. Some of the older boys and I were going to fight off the soldiers, but I'm the last one left. You've got to take over. You've got to make them leave. I hope you're as tough as you act, Ileana."

Gabi and I looked at each other when Ioan was gone. Later that day, we followed the notes scribbled on the paper, walking first down to the half-frozen stream, then farther out into the woods. Finally, in a small cave under drooping evergreen branches, we found what the boys had been hiding: weapons. A stash of good throwing rocks, some of them already stuffed into snowballs, which were heaped in a great pile. Homemade slingshots and sticks sharpened to points. Our eyes widened.

For the rest of the afternoon, Gabi and I sat in the cave and made plans. Attacking the soldiers head-on would be foolish, but at the very least we needed to be ready for them to attack us. Since I'd nearly been caught outside Old Constanta's, we'd been too scared to keep meeting in the church, so we made the cave our new headquarters. Gabi drew diagrams and sketches. I organized all my notes, searching for clues. We perfected birdcalls as signals. Mine was a female Ural owl's warning bark. Hers was the male's mating song. We took the boys' weapons and hid them all over town. There were some by the schoolhouse, some at the hill by my grandparents' cottage. The best stick— the one with the strongest wood and pointiest tip—was just inside Gabi's yard, tucked in the snow-covered bushes up next to the fence. Sometimes, on days when Mrs. Sala didn't open the school—which were becoming ever more frequent—we'd sneak to the barren fields and practice fighting.

"So if this was the tavern and someone came from around here"—I gestured, motioning to an icy tower of hay—"then you could knock the gun out of his hands."

I demonstrated with a stick.

"And if you were over here by the store," Gabi added, "then you could fire a rock at his head."

She demonstrated with a slingshot. Her aim was very good.

Gabi's map had all sorts of symbols, like for our stock-piles of weapons or the places to hide if things got really bad. She wouldn't draw a key, in case the paper fell into enemy hands, so we had to memorize all the meanings. Spying on the soldiers continued to go well. One man always smoked four cigarettes back to back, lighting each with the tip of another. One had an allergy to dairy products and got angry if anyone offered him cheese. The Securitate officer who'd stopped me sometimes whistled folk songs when he was alone. This all seemed like very important information.

No matter how much we planned, though, most things we couldn't control.

The officer in the brown suit ordered the remaining villagers to the tavern one by one. When Mrs. Ursu finished her talk with him—still dressed in black from her head scarf to her shoes—she went straight to her house, got a bag, and walked right out of town. A soldier offered her a ride, but she cursed at him and he backed away. The man in the brown suit was still feigning patience with stubborn old farmers like my grandparents, who simply refused outright to leave—though quite a bit more delicately than Mr. Bălan had done. The man nodded a lot and expressed sympathy, insincere as it was. He told them to spend some time coming to terms with the situation, hinting about consequences if they weren't gone by the new year.

The truth was, if the soldiers needed the rest of the villagers out, they could have forced us to go at any moment. Their real focus was on something entirely unrelated. Gabi and I donned my grandfather's sheepskin coat when we went out to collect clues. It was hard to perfect our movement together beneath it, but over time we became experts—able to blend perfectly into the snow at a moment's notice. We watched as groups of men disappeared into the forest, sometimes not returning for days. There was also a wall inside the tavern you could see through the window that had a map of the mountains all marked up. More suspicious than even that, the mysterious tarp-covered pile of metal boxes kept growing. Every week it got taller and taller.

"I know it's a dangerous mission, but we've got to find out what it is," I told my friend.

She agreed.

That evening, when my grandparents were cleaning up from supper, I lied about having forgotten something for school and managed to get permission to go down the hill. I took a flashlight and met Gabi near the edge of the woods. She kept watch while I burrowed through the snow on my belly. When I was close enough to the pile, I rolled onto my back and read the word spray-painted with stencils onto the boxes: AMMUNITION.

"Do you think there really are terrorists in the woods?" Gabi asked after we were safe.

"My uncle's pretty hard-core, but he's no Rambo," I said. "I can't imagine all that's for him."

Gabi gave me a weird look. "Who's Rambo?"

"A really angry guy with a bandanna."

On top of everything else, things were happening in other parts of our country. Sometimes my tataie and mamaie and I would go to Sanda and Gabi's to listen to the news. The veterinarian would check outside to make sure we were alone, and then she'd go down to the basement to retrieve Mr. Ursu's portable radio, which his wife had left behind. Sanda would thread a long, thin wire out the window so we could catch illegal programs broadcast by the Americans. There was news of a student protest in the capital, of civil unrest at one of the Leader's speeches— something almost too extreme for us to believe. The adults didn't know what to make of it.

"What do you think's going on?" Sanda whispered.

"Could all this here be related?" Mamaie asked.

"Please, please, put away the radio," Gabi begged, tugging her mother's sleeve.

She hated when the adults took it out, certain the soldiers would find us—that they'd brought all those bullets for just this kind of thing.

"Don't worry so much," I told her one evening after

we'd gone back into her room. "If they attack, we've got our plan."

"I don't know, Ileana," said Gabi. "I mean, look." She pointed to an empty box on the floor. "Even my mom's talking now about going. And think about it. Seriously. It's just you and me. Are we gonna fight all those men? Won't they only send more if we do?"

"So what?" I shrugged.

My friend stared at me like a cat at a calendar, but I couldn't say anything more. I couldn't tell her about my visit with Old Constanta, because no matter what the old widow had said, I didn't feel right repeating the story that could not be told. I still wasn't sure what to think of the White Wolf—except for a few stories about ghosts, which of course were all real, I didn't really believe in my fairy tales anymore. But Old Constanta had been quite convincing. And hoping for the White Wolf to come save us was better than not hoping at all.

When the bulldozer arrived, though, the last of my optimism vanished.

Gabi and I were standing at the schoolhouse, stomping our feet, waiting for Mrs. Sala to unlock the door. From down by the roadblock at the edge of town came a great mechanical whir, followed by cracking branches and ice. A black metal beast emerged from the forest, barreling straight ahead—straight toward our teacher's house. Mrs. Sala cried out, rushing down the road, slipping on snow and skinning her knee through her long skirt.

"Stop! Stop, will you!" she cried.

The bulldozer trampled over her fence, splintering the wood all to bits, before coming to a halt at her front door. A young soldier with a mustache came up behind us, breathing hot air onto his fingerless gloves as we stood staring.

"They were supposed to start with the empty ones." He smirked. "Oh well. Seems you're on early holiday. Lucky, huh?"

I didn't smirk back, and as we walked home, I realized Gabi looked scared.

"I told you," she said, squeezing my hand. "We can't win against something like that. It's impossible."

When I made it up the hill and told my grandparents what had happened, Mamaie began to collect woven blankets and set them in different stacks by the door, organized by how much she loved them. The same system went into effect for her embroidered pillows.

"This place is a filthy hovel," she told Tataie. "I'm just tidying up."

My grandfather's face fell. He buttoned his vest and put on his hat and his coat and excused himself to go outside. From the porch, through the bare trees, he watched the bulldozer start tearing up houses below. I wanted to go stand with him, but my mamaie caught me by the arm.

"Let him have his air," she said. "This cottage was built by his father, you know? Your great-grandfather. He's got deep roots in this mountain."

"They can't make us leave," I said. "I'll fight off the soldiers myself if I have to."

Mamaie tsked, smacking my hand. "Where do you get these ideas? And here I was starting to think you were clever."

"I just want to protect the people I love," I said, crossing my arms. At the window I watched through the bare trees as the front wall of Mr. Ursu's butcher shop caved in. Mamaie came over and sighed, stroking my hair, which was long enough now to be braided.

"Sometimes," she said, "the best way to protect someone is to hide them or help them get away. I hate it as much as your grandfather, but the truth is, we may have to leave."

I clenched my jaw, but deep down I knew she was right. Gabi was too. I couldn't fight all these soldiers. When faced with just the one, I hadn't even been able to speak.

Scanning the frosty branches of the trees in our yard, I searched for dark silhouettes, but the Ural owl was nowhere to be found. With an ache I realized I hadn't heard her in days.

Winter was here and she'd left, just like they'd said.

"What about me?" I asked quietly. "What if my parents never come? What if they're dead or in prison? What if the soldiers figure out who I am and take me away too?"

Mamaie shushed me, squeezing my shoulder.

"Don't you worry about *any* of that," she said, so sharp she sounded angry. "Your parents are safe. And no matter what happens, you'll be safe too."

Late that night, sitting up in the dark by the glow of the stove, I x-ed out on Gabi's map all the houses in the valley that were now demolished or abandoned. Tataie was so quiet creeping in from the bedroom that I didn't notice him till he lowered himself down in his chair. I looked up, surprised, and stuffed my papers under the covers.

"Do you know why Old Constanta went up the mountain each week before dawn?" he asked, looking into the fire.

I blinked, then answered softly, "To pray?"

Tataie clasped his hands between his legs and bent down his head.

"Long before you were born, right after the Second World War, Romania was under great pressure to change—in many ways not for the better—but there were those who refused to give in. They collected guns from the forest floor, where the Germans had dropped them as they retreated. The resisters went into hiding in these very mountains, sneaking out in the dark to fight against the same government they'd just finished fighting to save. Little villages like ours tried to help. We snuck them food and clothes, dug up ammunition buried under our houses. But the state's soldiers kept coming, and the Securitate found out who was where, giving what. Many of the resisters gave themselves up to save the people who'd helped them. They were shot in the streets right in front of the farmers and bakers and children who'd risked their lives to smuggle blankets and bread. Their bodies were thrown in mass graves."

I was still as a stone, my lips dry.

"Sometimes I wonder," Tataie said, "if we hadn't tried to help them, would more have survived? Would they have won in the end? You can never really know what the right choice is. No matter what, you always take risks." He turned to me then, head lifting, and in the firelight and shadows he seemed younger. "Old Constanta went up that mountain each week to do much more than pray."

Eyes wide, I whispered, "There were resisters in the monastery with the monks."

"The very last of them," Tataie said. "The fighting had been over a long time, but they had nowhere else to go, I suppose. Old Constanta brought them news. Carried messages. Sometimes she toted food and supplies hidden in baskets or up under her shawl. It made her look stooped and feeble." He shook his head. "But there were eyes for the Securitate in our village. There are eyes everywhere—you know that. And when they began to suspect even an old, lonely widow, she found someone new to start helping: a young girl who could steal potatoes and milk and run secret errands, traveling up the mountain in the dark to deliver letters and medicine."

I couldn't help the smile that crept to the edge of my mouth. "My mother did all of that?"

Tataie nodded. "I suppose she's never really stopped, has she? Copying those poems for your uncle. Risks, like I said. Not just to her, either. Look what it's done to your family. Look at the ruin it's brought here."

My eyes fell to my toes, ashamed, because it was true. If my uncle hadn't come, the Securitate wouldn't have followed. The village might never have found its way onto the Leader's systemization list. Dim, warm light from the stove flickered for a long time between us, and when my tataie spoke again, the words came from somewhere distant.

"You can never really be sure how stories will end, Ileana. The only thing certain in the whole world is that the whole world will change."

I looked back up at him and saw his lips purse.

He said in a low, sad, sad voice, "They've found your uncle. Your mamaie didn't want to tell you, but I thought that wasn't fair."

My eyes widened, and I thought I would cry, but I didn't. I suppose I'd only been waiting to hear it out loud. I lifted my knees and wrapped my arms around my legs, looking away.

"I know you've been keeping some secrets," my grandfather continued. "I won't tell you what to think or how to act. We all have to do what we believe is right, and those are choices no one else can make for you. But know that there are people who love you dearly. And know that everything has consequences. Everything has a cost."

For a moment my heart froze in my chest. I thought he had discovered the plan. It would have been easy, I realized—to peek into my notebook, to stumble across a stash of weapons hidden somewhere in the yard. But Tataie's eyes had fallen on something nearby, and I followed his gaze with my own.

The loose floorboard, barely peeking out from under my pallet.

"I understand you have a responsibility to your family," he said, "but remember that part of that responsibility is keeping yourself out of harm's way."

When my tataie went back to bed, I lay awake by the light of the stove, watching the last of the coals turn cold and black.

Had I imagined it? The connection between my uncle and the tale about Old Constanta? Had Tataie intended to reveal it at all?

Like in Mamaie's phone call to my mother, all those months ago, were there words hidden in my grandfather's story?

Above my head came a scratching and tapping on top of the roof. Snow, disturbed from the frozen, stiff hay, slid down in great, noisy heaps, thunking onto the hard ground below.

Clack-clack-clack. A hoarse, high-pitched bark.

She had not abandoned us, our owl.

And even though I'd lost my voice, I would not abandon him, either. Not now. Not ever.

Not when I knew exactly where my uncle was.

Snowbound

In early December, more Securitate and army trucks arrived in a swarm. Huge vehicles crowded the dirt road through town, giant guns built right into their backs.

"What is all this?" Mamaie hissed, watching the soldiers march by as we walked down the hill. "Who are they planning to fight?"

I glanced at Tataie, but kept my mouth closed.

Besides my grandparents and Sanda and Gabi, only a dozen or so villagers were left: a few stubborn farmers and, of course, Old Constanta. Several relatives had tried to get her to leave, but the widow refused to be moved. Soldiers had even gone in, meaning to carry her out, but Old Constanta spat and clawed and bit and swore till the men stumbled from the yellow house bleeding and furious. When her last caretaker left town, Mamaie and Sanda started checking on the old woman each day, feeding her broth and making sure she was warm.

"If we go," my grandmother said, glancing at my grandfather, "and I'm not saying we will, but if we do, we'll have to make sure she comes with us. We've got to think of a way to convince her."

Unfortunately we had run out of time.

The man in the brown suit discarded his pleasantries and his feigned patience. He came to everyone's house one by one and explained—in no vague terms—that we needed to leave. The deadline had been moved up. We'd been given more than enough time already. The Securitate would begin picking apart the remaining buildings to use for firewood and supplies. The bulldozer would take care of the rest—whether the owners had vacated or not.

Sanda came up the next day with Gabi to tell us they'd decided to go.

"I'm so sorry," the veterinarian said, rubbing her tired face. "We wanted to hold out, but they've knocked down the house two doors over. I don't want to be there when they roll that machine through my yard and trample my kitchen to crumbs. I want to have time to save all our pictures of Petre, you know?"

Mamaie looked to my grandfather. He nodded—a curt, subtle gesture—then turned away.

"We understand," my grandmother said, patting Sanda's hand. "Let's all go together. We'll talk to Constanta in the morning."

Gabi and I caught eyes and our expressions fell. All the training, the preparations and planning, gone to waste. No hope was left for the village. No hope was left for my uncle.

After packing my schoolbag, I helped my grandparents clean the cottage, sweeping out cobwebs and scraping ash from the stove. Even if they meant to bulldoze the house to the ground, my mamaie refused to let strangers see it a mess. Every time I walked over the loose floorboard, I glanced down, wondering how we'd hide the manifesto as we traveled. Would we sew it into our jackets? Would we cut it up into scraps to be pasted back together later? Never once did I think we'd leave it behind. My grandfather went down the hill to make arrangements with the man in the brown suit for us to leave the next day.

But the mountain had other ideas.

That afternoon, it started to snow. It did not stop all through the evening. It did not stop all through the night.

It did not stop when the sun tried to rise, turning the whole world into a blinding white blur.

"A storm," said my tataie, looking out at the window. "Big one, too. Trucks won't be driving in that."

He couldn't hide the smirk at his mouth.

My grandfather and I went out to take care of the animals, but we couldn't risk a trip down the hill. The stone steps were a cascade of ice. The wind whipped from the top of the mountain all the way to the valley, piling great drifts of snow against our cottage. In some places it was deep enough to cover the windows. Surely, everyone in town—Sanda and Gabi and the soldiers, too—was stuck just like us.

Days passed without sign of the storm letting up. At night Tataie kept the wood-burning stove hot and we all stayed close together, telling stories to ward off the cold. So cut off from the rest of the world, others might have starved right away, but Mamaie just dug into the cupboard for dusty glass jars of tomatoes and pickled cabbage and cucumbers. She emptied her pot of lard, where she stored sausages in the summer, then climbed the attic ladder for smoked pork. She scraped bits right off the bones and then used those, too. With all of that, plus our eggs and goat milk, we were doing just fine.

That is, until one night, after more than a week trapped inside, when we heard a strange cracking noise in the forest. The first time it happened, only I seemed to notice, but when it came once again—a rhythmic burst of percussion, followed by a thunderous boom—all three of us went still and quiet. My mamaie's eyes lifted from her embroidery to the shuttered windows.

"The wind," she whispered. "Falling branches."

My tataie shook his head slowly.

"Gunshots," he said. "An explosion."

The next morning there was a knock at our door. When we opened it, we found a Securitate officer shaking and covered in snow. My grandparents let him inside, so I scurried into the back room and listened through the wall. The man had come to tell us our chickens and goats were illegal. We were stealing milk and eggs and meat from the state. The police would turn a blind eye only on the condition that we start helping feed the soldiers down in the valley.

Of course, there wasn't really a choice.

After that, shots continued in the distance each night, and the officers and soldiers came to the door every morning, looking more and more haggard. Tataie would go out in the snow and come back with a bucket full of warm milk and what few eggs he could find. Sometimes the men left us the little wind eggs, which had no yolks. Mostly they left us with nothing.

Finally they showed up asking for the chickens themselves.

I put on my coat and slipped past my grandfather.

"They're my responsibility," I said, and he watched as I went behind the house to the coop. I pulled a hen out of her nest, stroked her speckled feathers, kissed her on top of the head. I held her out to the officer and looked him right in the eye. "This one's Mirabela."

A different man came the next time.

"This one's Pongo," I said.

A different man came the day after that.

"This one's Wicket."

"This one's Jonesy."

"This one's Duchess."

When the chickens were gone, they came for the goats, dragging them out of their pen down the hill. The soldiers told me to stop helping, so on those days I watched from the porch and glared. I remembered their faces. I made little notes in my book.

Once the animals were all gone, even with the resourcefulness of my grandmother we started to run out of food.

It wasn't hard for me to go back to old habits. I turned my nose up at plate after plate.

"I don't like it," I said. "I'm not hungry. Someone else can eat what's left."

Just like at home, someone always did.

When Sanda trudged up through the snow to check on us and found the animals gone—our food almost run out—she insisted we follow her back down the hill. She and Gabi had enough potatoes and cornmeal to share, and by some miracle they even still had electricity.

"We'll be safer if we all stick together," Sanda said, and I knew she wasn't just talking about the storm.

I put on my backpack and took a pile of blankets, but my eyes fell to the floorboards. Tataie followed my gaze, then shook his head.

"No one will bother the cottage till the weather lets up," he said.

I hesitated, but then took my mamaie's hand to help her down the porch. The snow was coming so heavy it was hard to see past my arms. With great care, the four of us made it down the steep stone steps to the valley, and, in a line just like schoolchildren, we turned our faces from the wind and walked toward town. When the street between the houses was in sight, I halted with a gasp.

Many of the buildings were gone—little more than piles of rubble.

And there, right in front of the veterinarian's house, was a massive black beast, half buried in snow. I squinted, trying to make out the dark shape, certain I could see fangs as long as daggers and at least four or five heads. It wasn't till Mamaie pulled me closer that I realized it was the bulldozer, abandoned and covered in icicles and debris. The machine had stalled right in front of Sanda's garden.

Once inside the house, I ran straight to Gabi's room, where I found her on the floor, drawing maps.

"Ileana!" my friend gasped, jumping up. "I was just making plans to come save you!"

"It's okay. We made it," I said. "Did you know there's a balaur outside your house?"

"You mean the bulldozer?" She smirked, but then her face fell. "It was headed straight for us."

I hugged her. "I promise it won't tear your home down."

Gabi still looked worried, though. "It's not just that. It's the soldiers. They're everywhere now. Always watching us. They're up to something. I know it."

That night Sanda took out the radio, and we all sat around it, bunched up under blankets and eating mămăligă. The volume was low, so the five of us had to lean in. Through the static came news.

Three days ago, in a city called Timişoara, far away, the Securitate had tried to arrest a pastor who'd spoken out against the Leader. Thousands had gone marching. Soldiers had arrived to suppress them. Armored cars after that. Helicopters circling overhead. Shots were fired into the crowds. Cars went up in flames. The bodies piled and piled. People broke into government buildings and bashed out all the windows, throwing documents into the streets to burn. And now the factory workers were striking, swarming the town square and singing as they began to push back the soldiers.

As the rest of us bent close, holding our breath, Gabi leaned back.

"We have to get rid of it," she said.

"What's that?" her mother asked, surprised.

"The radio. They're going to find it. We're going to all get in trouble."

Sanda just patted her hand and adjusted the frequency.

By midnight the snowfall was so heavy again that we could barely see out the door. The storm surged and swelled, howling as we cuddled together, trying to sleep. By noon the next day, though, for the first time in forever, the sky finally seemed to run out of breath.

We all stepped outside, blinking in a world frozen and glistening, the sun bright behind a layer of clouds. Tataie shoveled the walkway while Mamaie and Sanda started cooking. Gabi and I dug tunnels in the yard to reach our stashes of weapons, just in case we still needed them. Down the street, soldiers and Securitate officers peeped out from the inn windows, surveying the unfamiliar new landscape.

"Once the snow's clear, it's all over," my friend said, her eyes full of worry.

I yanked our best sharpened stick free from the ice and propped it back up against the fence.

"I won't stop fighting if you don't," I said.

Gabi bit her lip, but she nodded.

That afternoon, while my grandparents and Sanda carried fried peasant potatoes to Old Constanta and the remaining neighbors, we crawled around in our tunnels and stuffed rocks into the bulldozer's exhaust pipes. Then we practiced with the slingshot in the front yard. I wasn't much better than I'd ever been, but my friend hit her mark every time. When I started to get frustrated, I suggested we go in for a while. I much preferred preparation for battle that involved books.

"Just a little longer," Gabi said.

I told her I'd meet her inside. Alone in the house, I took off my mittens and jacket, rubbing my fingers to get warm.

That was when the knock came at the back door.

"Ileana," a voice called in a whisper. "Ileana, open up."

For a long time, I stood staring. For a long time, I didn't do so much as breathe.

It had been almost half a year, but that didn't matter at all. A thousand years could have passed and I'd still know his voice. Somehow, I made my way down the hall. Somehow, I undid the lock.

There, standing in the snow, was my father.

The End of Adventures

On my eighth birthday, my tata promised to show me something spectacular. He made me swear on my life to keep it secret. We kissed my mother good-bye and said we wouldn't be too long, just a couple of hours for stories by the light of the construction cranes at the palace, forever still being built. This was only mostly a lie.

To the boulevard we walked, its great, empty cobbled streets lined with lampposts taller than trees. I paused and tugged on my father's sleeve. He pointed and whispered, "There—it was just over there," and I pictured our old apartment building with the frothy cream walls, with the double doors and round awning and pantry. I heard the explosion, saw the rust-red roof crumbling down, and imagined my mother's piano turning to dust.

"You had a little window in the room with your crib," my father said of the home I didn't remember. "It had a little seat with the pillows your mamaie embroidered. That's where I would rock you."

He squeezed my hand as the sun fell below the skeleton of the gargantuan palace, lights twinkling to life on the cranes. The machines were lifting enormous pale pillars of stone and magnificent slabs of marble for vast ballroom floors. The Leader's greatest achievement. The largest building in all the world, so massive it could be seen from the moon.

"It's haunted," my father told me, and I begged him for more of the story. "They tore down ancient monasteries to build it. They laid the foundation right on a graveyard— sliced off the top of a hill and looked inside and saw that the dirt was packed with bodies, hundreds and hundreds of bodies, all killed by the Black Death. But they kept building."

"Didn't the Leader know it would be haunted?" I asked, full of fear and pleasure. I'd memorized this story already, but it tasted so much better when I said my lines just right.

"I suppose he didn't care," said my father.

Most nights on such walks, we would stop at a bench

and read side by side, but tonight my father turned away from the boulevard and kept going. We wove between gray concrete buildings in identical rows down the street. The factories pumped smog into the air, clouding the sky as it darkened.

I realized what direction we were heading. On my last birthday Tata had taken me to the theater and we'd seen a Bollywood film. I'd liked all the dancing, but the ending hadn't gone the way that I'd hoped.

But then we passed the turn that led to the theater. I twisted, looking over my shoulder. "We're going the wrong way. Where are you taking us?"

My father cleared his throat as a couple walked by on the other side of the street. He nodded at them with a smile.

"Be patient," he said. "And keep your voice down."

My excitement swelled instantly. We were doing something we weren't supposed to.

My father turned into an alley and led me to an apartment complex. We went up a flight of rusted stairs that swayed as we walked, then entered through a lonely back door. The light was orange in the hallway and the wallpaper was torn, the carpet worn through to the cement underneath. I gripped my father's hand tighter. I tried not to make a face at the smell of mold. Door after door passed on both sides till we turned a corner and stopped. My tata knocked two times, then waited and knocked again.

"Who is it?" someone asked.

"Lucian," he replied.

The door opened a crack, still with the chain on, and a person peeked out before pulling it wide. "Professor! Come in. So good to see you."

We were hurried into the apartment, and the man began chattering about classes. I realized he was one of my father's graduate students.

"We just started," the man said. "Is this your daughter? Hello, there! She's very cute. Would you like a drink, Professor? You can have my chair, if you want, or there's some space on the floor."

We passed through a small, dirty kitchen and emerged in a dark little living room. Somehow more than a dozen people had squeezed inside. They were seated on mismatched chairs, plastic and metal and wood. Some were pressed together on a plaid couch near the back wall. Not a single person turned his or her head to greet us. They were all fixated on the TV, the blue light tinting their skin and reflecting in their wide eyes.

"The floor is fine," my father said.

He handed the student some money and it was slipped into a pocket, both gestures quick, practiced. Then we made our way to the front and sat down on a thin rug. I blinked in the light, squinting at the black, whirring box below the screen. A little red dot glowed on its face. I'd never seen a real VCR, though a couple of the kids from the Pioneer club said they had them. I'd always assumed their parents informed for the Securitate. VCRs were extremely expensive, but if you managed to get some of the big plastic tapes, the machines could play movies right on your TV. It seemed likely this student or his parents were informants, because not only did he have a Sharp VCR and tapes, but he had a color TV. I didn't even have any friends who lied about one of those. It must have cost someone a fortune. It must have cost much more than money.

My eyes flitted up to the glass. Someone in a weird metal helmet was sneaking through a dark palace, trying to rescue a man made of stone. When the stranger took off the helmet, revealing a hidden face, I gasped.

"Tata, it's a girl!"

He shushed me, smiling.

When I found out the girl was also a princess, I was totally hooked. It took a while to understand what was happening in the film, and even then it wasn't always clear who was good and who was bad, but I figured out the main characters were fighting a dark lord who was trying to control the whole galaxy. I'd never seen anything like this. I was enraptured by the costumes and sets. I was swept away by the score. The colors alone were enough to leave my mouth hanging open.

The actors and actresses all spoke in English, a language I wouldn't get to study in school till fifth grade. But it didn't matter that I couldn't understand what they said, because as soon as they started talking, another voice spoke for them in Romanian, high-pitched and fast. When they got sad, she would get sad. When they were angry and screaming, she'd say, "Go to hell!" I pictured her with long legs and permed hair and shoulder pads in her jacket like my mother sometimes wore. It was as if she were sitting there with me, translating over my shoulder.

When the film finished, the lights came on in the room and people exchanged quiet good-byes. My father's student thanked us for coming and asked me what I'd thought of the movie. I wasn't able to speak, so I just stood there, as dazed as if I'd traveled through a portal from another dimension.

"Uh-oh! She's a shy one," the student laughed. He looked up at my father and spoke more softly. "I'll let you know about the next showing."

On the way back to our apartment, my father shook me by the arm. I frowned, still feeling strange.

"Are you getting sick? No one's ever mistaken you for shy," he said, suspicious.

"Tata," I said, mind whirling. "What we just did, it could get us in trouble."

"It could."

I thought a moment, my voice growing stronger. "My teacher told us that in America, it's not safe like here. She said Americans will jump on you and steal your things just for walking down the street."

"Is that so?"

"The movie. It was from America, right? The people there don't think like we do."

"That's what they say."

We turned a corner, and our apartment complex was in sight now, just up ahead.

"You didn't tell Mama because she wouldn't want us to go. Because it's too dangerous." This time he only nodded, and I squeezed his hand. "I swear I won't tell. Not anyone." And then, after a moment, I added, "Do you think, though, when he lets you know the next showing, that you might bring me again?"

"We'll just have to see," he replied.

No more than a week later, we took another walk to the palace. We had to finish dinner as if everything was normal, so my mother wouldn't get too suspicious. Out of anxiety I ate all my stuffed peppers.

At the door, Mama raised her brow. "Are these walks to escape me?"

"Just father-daughter bonding," my father replied, planting a kiss on her cheek.

"Is this becoming a habit?"

"I sure hope so!" I said, grabbing my jacket and running down the hall.

On the way, Tata scolded me for my eagerness.

"You'll give us up!" he said. "And then I won't be able to go see them either."

"You've been watching movies for a while now," I accused him. "You've been saying you're working late when you aren't."

"Ileana," he replied, "if you get any more cunning, you'll ruin us all."

At first, I couldn't figure out why he'd take such a risk. Maybe it was the stress of worrying about so many loved ones for so long. Maybe it was just as he'd lied—a desire to be closer to me. But eventually I realized that, after a lifetime of caution, of keeping his head down, my father

longed for rebellion—just like his brother, just like my
mother—and he'd chosen to share his adventures with
me. Our secret screenings became prefaced with special
phrases and gestures. He'd arrive home from work and
catch my eye, tapping his watch, and I'd know. We'd
eat our dinner in a rush, my stomach fluttering till
every part of me tingled, and he'd bring up the topic so
casually.

"I was thinking of a walk, Ileana. Want to join?"

One night we saw a movie about some guys fighting
ghosts in New York. But it wasn't the ghosts that haunted
my dreams. It was the skyscrapers. Were they really that
tall? How did they keep on so many lights? Did all American women really dress in those clothes? Did people really
drive in those cars?

Action films, dramas, comedies. The same woman's
voice every time. She went with me to places I'd never
dreamed I might go. Martial-arts tournaments. An
empty, snowbound hotel. Spaceships full of frightening aliens. In that tiny living room I blushed through
love scenes I was too young to be seeing, hid my eyes
from guts and gore. I gaped at refrigerators packed
with food, grocery stores without a single empty shelf.
People bought milk in huge plastic jugs. They ate two

tiny bites of a chocolate bar and threw the rest away.

My father knew the risks we took, but he believed it was worth it to show me the world outside our gray concrete city. He believed it was worth it to show me what could have been, what might yet be.

Then, one night, we were rushing down the hallway to the student's apartment, late as always. There was only one more corner to turn.

But at the sound of a scream, we both stopped.

My father didn't seem to know what to do. I clung to his arm, barely breathing. Someone else yelled. Something thudded into a wall.

"Line up!" a man shouted as a door was thrown open out of sight, the noise growing louder. "Identification! All of you!"

There was a resounding crash. The television must have been knocked to the floor. The cords of the VCR must have ripped right out of their sockets.

"Why are you doing this?" The student's voice now. "It's just films! Only films!"

"Where do you get them? Who do you know?"

I realized in that moment that no one was safe. Not even the spies.

Handcuffs clinked closed over wrists. More Securitate

were spitting commands. A woman was crying. Finally, my father was in motion, pulling me back the way we'd come. Too late. Too slow. We'd only made it four doors down when a man in a uniform came around the corner, scribbling into a notebook.

"Stop. Where are you going?" he called.

My father halted, looking petrified. He glanced down at me with only his eyes, then turned around, sliding his keys from his pocket before the officer could see.

"Good evening. Just on our way home. Heard the commotion. Something happened?"

"Nothing serious," replied the officer, a mustache hiding his upper lip. The skin around his eyes was so tight, I could believe that he'd never once laughed.

"I hope it all gets sorted out," my father said.

The officer's eyes were on the keys in Tata's hand, then the door we stood beside.

"You never know what sort of people are trading in contraband these days," the man said. "Students. Neighbors. Even parents." He gestured to the door. "Don't let me keep you."

My father nodded, forcing a smile. Anyone could have seen through it. He lifted his keys to the door and tried the first one on the ring. It was so much larger than the keyhole, it wouldn't even slide in. He laughed as if to himself, hand shaking.

"It's been a long day," he said.

I stared at the handle, terrified it would turn, that the real occupant would come out. My heart raced as I realized my father would be caught in his lie.

"Tata!" I cried out, patting my stomach, my arms, turning in a circle and looking frantically all over the floor. "Tata! My doll! I've forgotten her! She's still at the park." I tugged, pulling him away from the apartment door. "We have to go! Someone will take her!"

My father let me drag him. "Are you sure you brought her with you? Ileana, don't pull!"

He looked back at the officer as we made for the rusted stairwell.

"Excuse us," Tata called apologetically. "Have a good night, sir!"

And then we were free. I tried to leap down the steps three at a time, but my father caught me by the sleeve and made me slow down. I kept peeking over my shoulder till he put a hand on the back of my head and I realized at once how suspicious I looked.

When we reached the boulevard, I said with a grin, "Wasn't I clever? A doll. Ha!"

But my father didn't answer right away. And when he did, he sounded upset. "That was dangerous, not clever."

I frowned. I squeezed his hand.

"But he believed my story. He believed me 'cause I'm a little girl."

My father's eyes were still pointed forward. The light of the palace gleamed ghostly on his skin, making him appear gaunt and lifeless.

"You won't always be," he said. "You can't always count on stories to save you."

I searched his face, confused. The adrenaline seeped out of me till I felt empty and hopeless. We would never see another movie. He would never take another risk again in his life. I knew it right in that moment, more certain than I'd ever been about anything.

"He didn't believe you, Ileana," said my father. His voice was so weak, so frightened, that I cringed and recoiled. "He just let us go."

Traitor

My father stood just inside Sanda's doorway, his hair covered in snow. His long nose was red, his lips tinting blue. When he saw me, his eyes lit up and he wrapped me at once in his arms. He smelled the same, felt the same, but I wasn't entirely sure he was real. I stood there, hands by my sides, staring.

"I've just walked several kilometers," he said, out of breath. "Is anyone else here? I waited till I saw people leaving, but I couldn't be sure."

I shook my head, and he glanced outside, then closed the door behind him.

"I don't have long to talk," he said. "They're probably looking for me already."

"Where's Mama?" I asked, frightened.

"She's safe. The Securitate have had us with them in another village for a couple of months now. When this is all over, they promised to bring you down."

I gaped, trying to make sense of what he was saying. "The Securitate know where I am?"

My father's mouth opened, but he hesitated before nodding. "Right after you left, they came to the apartment, asking about your uncle and what your mother did. We wouldn't talk. . . ." He hesitated again, looking distressed. "But they showed us photos. Photos of you on the train."

I felt as if my head had filled up with air, as if I were going to float away any moment.

"We wanted to come get you, but they wouldn't let us," he continued, his voice anguished. "We couldn't even call. Andrei had escaped from a nearby prison and they thought . . . they thought he might come to the village if he found out you were here. So we cooperated. We came with them to the mountains."

I could hardly believe what my father was saying. His haggard face went out of focus as I braced myself against a small table by the door.

The whole pretense of my stay had been false.

The Securitate had known who I was all along. They

didn't care about the stories I'd told. They didn't care about the Great Tome. My father had burned it for no reason.

The only person I'd ever been a real danger to was the one I most wanted to protect.

"Was he here, Ileana? Did you see him?" my father asked, and there was hope somewhere in his voice. "He had something they're looking for. If they get it, they might leave our family alone."

I wondered what threats had been made. I wondered how many. Concerning me, surely, no question in that. Nothing else could have made him sound so afraid. But as much as I knew my father had suffered—as much as I loved him, even after what he had done—I couldn't stop myself from putting the pieces together. Even with so many gaps in the story, I already had a feeling about how it would end.

Tata put his hand on my cheek and my body went stiff. I didn't have far to look up to stare straight into his eyes. I'd grown taller since I'd been gone.

"You know, don't you?" I asked, quiet. "You know they've caught him?"

Tata's lips parted, and then, finally, he said, "Yes."

I started to breathe faster, shaking my head. "You said you cooperated with the police. What does that mean?

How did they know where to find Uncle Andrei?"

"Ileana . . . ," my father said slowly, apologetically, and my eyes widened as I heard everything hidden beneath my name. When he reached out for me, I jerked away.

"You told them!" I shouted.

"I didn't tell anyone anything! I answered a phone call. That was it."

"You're a traitor! You're a coward and a traitor!"

"Ileana!" my father snapped. "Calm down right this instant!"

"He's family. *He's your family!*" Now I was crying and gasping.

"So are you. So is your mother." My father reached for me again, and I wrenched away so hard that I stumbled into the wall. "You're just a child! You don't know what they can do!"

"I do too! I do know," I spat. "They'll make him eat rotted meat and pee on the floor where he sleeps. They'll break all the bones in his hands."

My father's mouth fell open, and for a moment he just stared.

"You saw him," he finally said.

I swallowed. I took a shaking breath. "If you loved me at all, you'd go save him."

Tata stared as if he hadn't heard right, and then he started laughing, incredulous. "I don't even know where he is!"

"The Securitate are holding him prisoner at the top of the mountain. He was hiding in an old monastery where the resisters stayed with the monks. That's why he came to the village. He's been gathering people to fight so we don't have to live like this anymore. He was trying to save us! But the Securitate found him and it's all your fault!"

My father's expression turned angry.

"No more of this, Ileana. No more stories. It's over. This isn't a fairy tale! Do you want me to die? Because if I go climbing that mountain alone, they'll put a bullet right in my head!"

"I hate you! I hate you! *I hate you!*"

The words spat out before I could catch them, and both of us stood there surprised in the wake. I wiped my eyes with my sleeve and Tata crossed his arms, looking away. There was a long spell of silence between us before he said, "The manifesto, Ileana. Do you know where it is?"

I looked up, and the blood drained from my face.

"You do, then," he said. Suddenly there was desperation in his voice. "Did he say something to you? Did he show you?"

My heart started to thrum.

"Whatever you know, you have to tell me right now. Every day they ask me. Every day. It's the only thing keeping him alive. If we bring them the papers—if I find them first—maybe . . . maybe they'll let him go back to the prison. Maybe they'll let him live."

It had always been so hard to tell what my father really believed. And I didn't know which risk was the right one to take. I didn't know which betrayal was worse. But when I recalled my name signed to the manifesto, my jaw set. The space between us blurred as my eyes filled up again, narrowing.

"I'll never forgive you for burning my tome. I'll never forgive you for helping the Securitate."

I opened the door, waiting for him to leave, my heart breaking all over again. It hurt so much, I couldn't breathe. This time he hadn't just betrayed me. He'd betrayed everyone I cared for—everything I believed in.

I wasn't even sure the father I loved was inside him anymore.

Tata stood there gaping, but from the way his eyes glazed over, I might as well have been a ghost. When he turned and walked outside, I shut the door behind him and bolted it. I pressed my back to the wood, breathing deep. Seconds passed. Minutes. Panic swelled up. Heartache. Regret. But I didn't open the door to see if he'd left. I didn't call out for him in the snow.

Alone in the house, I just sank to the floor.

Cunning Ileana and the Golden Apples

Winter in the mountains was brutal. Snow whipped down from the glaciers and piled up taller than giants. Wind beat at the castle walls with such force that already two of its three frozen towers had fallen. Ileana and her knight friend rallied every able servant and guard to brace the stone foundations and keep the great fires burning, but they worried that their efforts were in vain. The monarch had decided, without doubt, that it was the emperor who'd said all those humiliating things about his teeth, and he'd turned on the princesses' father in the middle of battle.

The fight was hardly fair. Somehow the vile ruler had learned a whole bunch of the emperor's secrets, like where his soldiers' armor was weakest and what time he let everyone go on break for a snack. On the battlefield the monarch decimated the emperor's troops.

Whispers were spreading that the other kingdoms had about had enough, though. They were fed up with the monarch being such a jerk all the time. It was said that armies were amassing to help the emperor fight back.

But if help was on the way, it was nowhere in sight.

The soldiers stationed at the mountain castle had orders to imprison the emperor's daughters. They were scaling the ramparts and ramming the doors. Since everyone else was busy with the blizzard, Ileana and the knight had to fight off all the monarch's soldiers themselves. More than once, the youngest princess—still unable to speak—went to her two elder sisters for help, but each time the girls would ignore her and pretend they knew how to do needlepoint.

During the height of a particularly merciless onslaught full of lightning magic and poison arrows and utter chaos, Ileana heard screams in the throne room. Fearing that the monarch's soldiers had finally breached the castle's defenses, she got the knight's attention and together they ran full speed through the halls. When they made it into the throne room, Ileana found her two sisters collapsed on their father's chair, faces painted pale and armpits rubbed with onions, making a scene by hacking and coughing up loogies.

Now, that's just gross, said the knight, pulling down the face shield on her helmet.

Sweet, sweet, Ileana! the two princesses called. *You have to help us! We're dying!*

You know what? Ileana said with sign language—she'd become quite the expert. *I don't care.*

The two elder princesses weren't clever enough to learn sign language, though, so they just thought their sister was making shadow puppets with her hands.

Is it supposed to be a goat? Slow down! said the middle princess.

We don't have time for this! cried the eldest. *Do you see the state of my hair? We each have to eat a golden apple from the monarch's palace garden by morning or we're done for!*

Ileana threw her hands up, turning to leave, but the knight caught her by the shoulder.

Look, said her friend, *of course it's a trick, but a bite from a golden apple is supposed to heal anything. What if it can give you back your voice?*

Ileana's eyes widened at the thought, but then a massive fireball exploded through the nearest wall and soldiers came pouring in. The knight raised a mace in one hand

and a crossbow in the other, not looking the slightest bit concerned.

I've got this, she said. *You go.*

Ileana pursed her lips and turned to the two elder princesses, who were cowering in the corner.

My dear sisters, signed Ileana, *I would travel the world for your sake. How much more willingly will I go to your princes.*

Down the mountains and to the west she rode her steed fast as a storm, a basket of provisions beside her. Cunning Ileana reached the monarch's palace by nightfall and tiptoed through the garden. Under the tree with the shining golden apples, the youngest prince had buried knives and spears and other sharp things and disguised them with flower beds. The princess spotted the danger at once. She also spotted the youngest prince behind some decorative shrubbery, hoping to watch her gruesome death. Ileana leaped over the trap and pulled herself up into the tree.

Below, the prince revealed himself. *How glad I am to see you in my garden, little sister.*

Ileana glanced down, feigning surprise. She scribbled a note onto a piece of parchment, folded it into a heart, and tossed it to him.

My prince! the note read. *Only your father's golden apples can heal my poor sick sisters. But this fruit is terribly hard to* reach! *Since you are so handsome and brave, perhaps you can give me a hand?*

Only if you give me yours first, the prince said, smiling a villainous smile.

Cunning Ileana smiled back, reading in his eyes the wicked plan to pull her down into the blades. When she reached toward the prince, sure enough he grabbed her wrist with both hands, yanking as hard as he could. But Ileana was stronger, and with one arm she lifted the prince into the air, then plucked his fingers off one by one till he dropped into his own death pit.

Oops! Ileana signed as he writhed, screaming. *What a simple girl I must be!*

Just then the monarch's palace guards burst forth from hiding. When the princess saw she was surrounded, she plucked several golden apples from the tree and retrieved the fairy log out of her basket. Grabbing on just like the witch had explained, she wished as hard as she could, just as the soldiers dove toward her.

There was a flash of light, and then Ileana found herself back at the mountain castle.

Immediately she knew that something horrible had happened.

Everything was silent and still. The battle had ceased.

Even the blizzard had relented. There wasn't a single other person in sight. Cunning Ileana crept through the halls, eating a golden apple on the way. She cleared her throat, trying to speak, but the words stayed stuck in her mouth. When she heard a noise in the dungeon, the princess took the stairs two at a time.

To her horror she discovered her father, lifeless, on the floor of a dirty cell.

Tata! Ileana cried without sound, dropping her basket.

She ran to him, but realized at once her mistake. It wasn't the emperor in the cell after all, but a dummy meant to lure her into a trap. The youngest princess spun around just as the iron door slammed shut. With a ridiculous laugh, the monarch emerged from the shadows, Cunning Ileana's father beside him.

Hello, sweetheart, the emperor said.

Ileana grasped the bars with both hands. Behind her father were the courageous knight and her two sisters, all three gagged and bound. The emperor tried to smile.

The thing is, darling, the monarch's right, you know. His teeth are just the best. And it's really totally fair how mean he is and how his sons steal secrets from everyone. I've been such a fool. So we've got to make it up to him, he said. *Since you've kept such good faith, unlike your sisters, I've given my blessing for you to marry the monarch's youngest son.*

Ileana gripped the bars tighter, eyes widening as she shook her head.

We've sent for the prince already and will host the wedding as soon as he arrives. Unless, of course, you refuse?

Cunning Ileana screamed at the top of her lungs. She kicked the cell door, shouting every bad word in the book. Of course, there was no sound at all. After allowing this to continue for some time, the monarch nudged the emperor, and the princesses' father smiled again.

Okay, then, he said. *It's settled. We'll get the cooks started on the wedding feast right away!*

Alone in the dungeon, Cunning Ileana sank to the cell floor.

The Radio

When Gabi came inside, she could tell at once that something was wrong.

"Why are you sitting in the hallway?" she asked, and then her brow lifted. "Have you been crying?"

I wiped my nose and used the wall to stand. "I was just thinking about my favorite goat, Scaparici."

"Oh, Ileana." Gabi came over and hugged me. "Your heart's too big for this world."

When my grandparents and Sanda returned, the veterinarian called us into the kitchen.

"Did someone come by the house?" she asked. "There are boot prints leading to the back door."

"No," I said. "We were playing in the yard, though. So maybe we didn't hear."

Lies are much easier the second time you tell them.

Sanda turned to Mamaie, scowling. "Those damned Securitate. Wait till I catch them peeping on our girls."

Though the snow had stopped, the wind picked up again after dark. All night it howled through the valley, muffling the crackle of machine guns in the distance. I clutched my blanket to my chin, barely able to sleep.

The next day, the green phone rang on the wall. Mamaie answered.

"Liza?" she said into the receiver, her eyes widening. I perked up from the sofa nearby. "Liza, is that you? Where are you, darling? The call's breaking up." After a heartbeat my grandmother's eyes turned to me. She hesitated before saying, "Yes, she's here, but we haven't seen her father. When did he go missing? Yesterday morning?"

I wandered into the kitchen, feeling sick. My mamaie passed me the receiver, concerned.

"Mama?" I said, clutching the phone to my head.

"Baby," my mother replied, already crying. Just the sound of her voice was enough to take away the breath from my lungs. "Are you all right? I'm so sorry I haven't been able to call."

I pressed the plastic to my ear till it hurt.

"Mama," I said, my voice breaking. "Are you coming to the village? Are you coming to bring me back home?"

"I'm trying," she said. "But right now I have to find your father. Your mamaie says he hasn't stopped by. You're certain you haven't seen him?"

I squeezed my eyes shut and dug my nails into my palms, gripping the phone like I was holding on for my life. I told myself Tata had headed back down the mountain. I told myself he'd gotten stuck in the cold on the way, taken shelter in a little farmhouse or barn. I told myself that if he'd actually done as I'd begged him—if he'd really gone after my uncle—I couldn't risk saying the words. The Securitate would hear it over the phone. And if not, my grandparents, out of good intentions, might give him away. They might go to the officers, asking for help.

"If you come to the village, we could look for Tata together," I said. "Maybe he's somewhere nearby."

But it was like my mother couldn't hear me.

"Something's not right," she whispered, voice shaking. "He's done something reckless. I know it. I'm so sorry, Ileana. This is all my fault. I love you, you know that, don't you?"

I nodded, but I couldn't seem to make any sounds. I

kept gripping the phone tighter and tighter.

"Things are going to get better, you'll see. The whole world is going to change."

And just like that, the line went dead.

"Mama?" I said. "Mama!"

My grandmother pried the green phone from my fingers.

"There, there, now," she said, stroking my hair. "It's okay, child! Don't worry. Your father will turn up, I promise. And look at this! We know your mother is safe."

Mamaie glanced at Tataie, but her expression wasn't as optimistic as her words.

A couple of hours after the phone cut off, the power went out, so that evening Gabi and I had to light candles before setting the table for dinner. However, hungry as we all were, no one seemed particularly interested in eating more potatoes, especially the adults. They were clearly desperate for news, so they barely had two bites before moving to the living room.

"Something's happening," Sanda said. Since she couldn't plug in the portable radio, she'd had to scrounge up an old pack of batteries in the basement. "All this secrecy and then Liza just gives everything away? Our country is boiling and we're the frog in the pot."

The veterinarian checked first for soldiers, then threaded

the antenna wire out the window. Gabi and I finished our food and went to sit on the floor behind the couch. We looked at our map by the light of the woodstove, but it was hard to concentrate through all the gasping and whispers.

Protests had spread over all of Romania. That morning, in response, the Leader had given a televised speech from my city. Foreign fascists were blamed for Timișoara. The crowd booed and shouted. The Leader raised his hand to silence them, gaping in shock, but at the sound of gunshots, chaos erupted. A hundred thousand grew to hundreds of thousands, and in the University Square a student ripped a hole in our flag as the masses swayed and sang, "Down with the dictator! Death to the criminal!"

The Leader responded with tanks.

Chaos was everywhere now. There was bloodshed on the streets near my apartment.

I rose from behind the couch, heart pounding.

"They're saying the people are fighting back." Sanda put her ear close to the speaker as the broadcast came in waves. "They're saying it's only a matter of time."

I stared at the little gray radio, blinking as the adults whispered in excitement and fright. The fire blazed behind the iron door of the stove, warming the air so the windows fogged up in the corners.

I tried not to think. I tried not to picture my tower-block concrete apartment, explosions going off outside my bedroom. My fingers clutched the side of the couch.

I tried not to picture my father shielding his head from gunfire—his nose red, his lips blue, his hair covered in snow. He'd walked such a long way in the cold to come see me—to see I was safe and to do the best that he could to keep my mother safe too.

I tried to keep my feet, tried to keep the words in my head, but for all my effort I couldn't. Mamaie and Tataie and Sanda must have sensed something was wrong. They turned to me, and my eyes filled with tears. I lowered myself to my knees.

"I know where he is." My voice trembled. "Tata's trying to rescue Uncle Andrei. He's gone to the top of the mountain."

The room went quiet but for the crackling wood and the static on the fading broadcast. Gabi peeked over the back of the couch.

"I made him go. I called him a traitor and a coward." The tears spilled, running down my flushed cheeks. "He's out there in the mountains all alone. It's freezing and dark. They've probably caught him." My voice dropped to barely a breath. "He said the Securitate wanted the manifesto.

He said that was the only reason Uncle Andrei was alive. But I didn't tell him where it was. And now maybe they'll both die because of me."

For a long time, no one said anything. Sanda's hand was at her mouth.

Mamaie took a big breath and let it out slowly. "We have to do something," she said.

"I'll go get the papers," said Tataie. "I'll try bartering with the officers across the street. Make a trade. Half now. Release them. Half later."

Something flickered at the corner of my eye, drawing my attention to the front hall.

"That's a terrible plan," Sanda said, her voice hushed. "How can you trust them? They might take half the papers, then grab someone as a hostage. Or they might say sure, agree to release her father and uncle, but shoot anyway when they have what they want."

The flicker came again—lights outside the window. I wiped my nose, rising, and made my way across the room.

"There's just one choice," said Mamaie. "One of us has to go up there ourselves. Offer the trade right at the source."

"It could still turn out bad," said Tataie. "And how do we decide who will go? I'll say me; you'll say you. We'll talk in circles all night."

The adults and Gabi were still distracted when I reached the door. They didn't see me open it. They didn't see me freeze in place.

Flashlights dancing in houses all down the street.

Flashlights in the yard.

A beam cast right in my face, blinding me as I turned back inside, door still open. Everyone in the living room was looking my way now, but I couldn't make myself move. I couldn't do anything but drop my eyes to the radio. Only seconds to hide it. Soldiers merely footsteps away. Soldiers who could hear every word I might use. Only a code would be enough to warn them in time.

"What is it?" asked my mamaie, frightened by my expression.

I opened my mouth, but the story that could not be told stuck in my throat.

Behind me, armed men burst through the door.

The Rescuer

We all cried out as the soldiers rushed in, pointing flashlights and shouting commands. I ran to Mamaie and grabbed her arm, clutching tight as they circled around us. A Securitate officer picked up the radio and started yelling to the rest of the men as they turned over furniture and pulled up rugs. We stumbled our way through the living room and were marched into the street before we could even put on our coats. Soldiers barked orders as we were herded down the dark road. I wrapped my arms around myself, shaking. There was a similar commotion up ahead, yelling and lights reflecting off snow. I realized where we were headed when I saw the glow of lamps through the windows of the schoolhouse.

Inside, the stove had not been lit. A layer of frost covered the chalkboard. Desks and chairs were all shoved to the walls. Books toppled from shelves as people bumped by, pages torn under feet. All the villagers who remained, less than fifteen, were made to sit in the center of the room on the floor. I heard one Securitate ask another about the nasty bedridden woman who lived across from the church. Whatever response he got made him smile.

The villagers were restless, muttering and panicked as the soldiers paced back and forth, standing guard at the door, their guns pointed toward us like a firing squad. Even I could tell, though, that some of the uniformed men looked incredibly anxious.

"Surely by now they've heard," whispered Sanda. "They must know what's happening in the cities."

For a long time we sat there, for hours, freezing on that hard classroom floor. But then, finally, the man in the brown suit came bustling in. He emptied a box of things from villagers' houses onto Mrs. Sala's wooden desk. A cookbook from Italy. A collection of tapes—Elvis Costello, Michael Jackson, Madonna. Mr. Ursu's portable radio with its long, thin wire. The man knelt down in front of Tataie.

"Are you in league with the fascists?"

My grandfather blinked. "The fascists?"

"The ones in the forest. You've been caught with terrorist contraband. What other explanation could there be?"

"The radio is mine," Sanda spoke up. "I was listening for news from Bucharest."

The man in the brown suit narrowed his eyes. He moved so that he was standing right above her, looking down. "And what does the news say?"

The veterinarian hesitated, glancing at her daughter. "There are protests everywhere. There's fighting."

The man in the brown suit smiled his awful smile. "Lies. The trouble is contained. The last of it will be over by morning, I assure you."

Gabi's back was pressed against mine. She started breathing heavily, in and out through her nose.

"But for you," the man said to the room, "for you things are not looking well. Contraband. Illegal activities. We know you've been supporting the terrorists in these mountains."

When someone started to protest, the man yanked a gun from the arms of a soldier beside him and fired it repeatedly into the roof. People shouted. Chunks of ceiling dropped down to the floor. One of the old farmers started to cry.

Gabi began coughing.

"You have one chance. There is a document. A manifesto with names." The man in the brown suit lowered the gun and his voice. "One chance. That's it. Tell us where it's hidden. Otherwise, those resisters you're helping will die, and in the morning we'll burn down the rest of your homes—perhaps even with you inside them."

There was commotion then. The crying grew louder. People tried to stand, yelling. More shots were fired.

Through it all, the only thing I could hear was my friend beside me, gasping for air.

"Help! Help her!" I screamed.

Sanda turned to her daughter and caught her by her shoulders. She looked into her eyes.

"My medicine," Gabi said to her mother. She was wheezing, convulsing.

"Help her!" I cried again. "She's just a kid!"

The other noise quieted down. Sanda got on her knees, crawling forward.

"Please, I'm begging you. Sir, please. Her medicine! She needs her medicine!"

The officer's face didn't change. "The manifesto. Where is it?"

"It could be in a few places. I'm not sure. We'll tell you

everything we know, I swear, but how can we trust that you won't still harm us if you let my little girl die! I need to help her back to the house. Please. I'm begging you, *please*."

Sanda started to sob. Gabi's eyes turned up into her skull. The man looked at her brace, then at me.

"You. Take your friend to her house. Come right back," he said.

He motioned to one of the Securitate officers, who pulled us to our feet. I stood, blinking, my limbs weak, as Gabi grabbed onto my neck. For some reason, though, even as I helped my friend to the door, the fear in Sanda's eyes only grew. I realized the look had spread to Mamaie and Tataie as well.

"She's just a child. She won't know how to administer—" Sanda started.

The man in the suit took Gabi's arm. He shook her till she almost slipped out from under me.

"Do you want her to get medicine or not?" he shouted.

Sanda lowered herself back to the floor. My tataie took my mamaie's hand.

"You don't have to go. It's your choice," he said to me, and this time I was certain he was hiding something else in his words. I looked at him, confused, till Gabi started coughing again and I led her away.

Out in the cold, the night was black, the sky full of clouds overhead, but the ground was so white that I could still make out the houses and the frozen tunnels we'd dug in the yard. The officer trailed along as we staggered through the snow. I hadn't realized who he was till just then—the same man who'd taken my voice the afternoon Old Constanta had saved me. He didn't offer to help even once as Gabi leaned into my shoulder, and that, more than anything else, made me furious.

When we got back to the house, my friend seemed much better already, hardly gasping at all. The officer paused in the foyer with his flashlight.

"Hurry up now. It's cold," he said.

Gabi shook her head. "We can't see." Her voice was raw. "And I'm scared."

The man made a face, rolled his eyes, and handed over the light. Then he went in the kitchen to poke through what was left of our food. I helped Gabi to her bedroom, skirting the mess the soldiers had made. After her door was mostly shut, she let go of me and ran to a pile of clothes on the floor, tossing over pieces, one by one.

"Mittens," she said. "Double pair. And put these long johns on under your pants. You'll need a hat, too. This one will fit over your big ears."

I stared at her, gaping. "What about your medicine?"

She looked over her shoulder like I'd sprouted corn from my nose.

"I don't take any *medicine*."

My eyes widened. "You were pretending."

"You have to get the manifesto." She tossed me her hat. "You have to save your uncle and father. The Securitate are going to find the papers. Don't you get it? That's why they've been tearing apart all the houses."

I shook my head, astonished. It was one thing to tell stories, to make plans, to play the heroine in your dreams. It was another thing to be brave in real life.

"The resisters will find us," I said. "They'll realize and come to our rescue."

"What resisters? The ones the Securitate are holding hostage? The ones in the city hours and hours away, who've never even been to a village? No one's coming to rescue us, Ileana. That's *you*. You're the rescuer. Didn't you hear that guy? What he said? He's not playing around." And then something sad passed through her eyes. "Your tata might already be dead. Really, he might. But maybe not. I know you're still mad at him, but you'll miss him forever if he dies. I promise you will. You've got to try. You've got to go now."

I nodded once, then again, then over and over. Then

I was putting on clothes, layer on top of layer, like my mamaie had taught me. The officer down the hallway called after us. It must have been late—closer to morning than midnight. When we came out of the bedroom, we went straight for our coats.

"Feeling better?" the officer asked, but not like he cared. He put his hand out. "My flashlight."

"Can't I just hold it on the way back?" I asked.

"Give it here."

"Please," Gabi begged. "It's so dark. We really were frightened on the way over."

The man put a hand to his forehead and rubbed. He closed his eyes and motioned for us to go out the front door. When I stepped into the yard, I glanced at Gabi a last time. She squeezed my hand.

And then I switched off the light.

I dove straight into a tunnel, wiggling like mad. I heard the man shout as Gabi ran in the opposite direction. He hesitated only a moment before choosing to go after her first. She looked like she'd be slow, after all. But Gabi was fast—faster than all the boys and girls in our class, snow on the ground and short leg and everything. At the end of the tunnel I snatched up the best stick and made a break for my grandparents' hill.

In the Dark Before Dawn

I took the stone steps up the hill two at a time, the beams from the flashlight reflecting off ice. I was worried about someone from the village seeing me, but even with the light on, I kept slipping. I fell more than once, bruising my shin. I pressed on, forcing my legs to go faster, my feet to stick when they slid. By the time I reached flat ground, I was panting, stumbling through the snow in my grandparents' yard. I opened the gate and got up the stairs, crossed the porch, and let myself into the house. I tried to catch my breath as I stared.

The kitchen had been turned upside down.

My mamaie's dishes were smashed. Her pots and pans were all over the floor. The benches and chairs were flipped over, in pieces. A glance into my grandparents' bedroom showed more of the same.

I closed the door behind me, but the bolt had been broken. I got down on my knees, set aside my pointed stick, and dug through the mess. Underneath it all, on the cold wooden boards, was the pallet where I slept. I moved my favorite of Mamaie's embroidered pillows, the one I'd brought all the way here from home—dark green with a black border and a big, round-faced bird. I scooted the blankets aside and revealed the loose plank beneath. My hands shook as I lifted it, fearing the papers had already been found or that my grandparents had moved them somewhere else. I pointed the flashlight inside.

The manifesto seemed to shine in the dark.

I pulled it out carefully, folding until it was too thick to fold anymore. I stuffed the papers into my coat pocket and reached for the plank to re-cover the hole.

There was a hoarse warning bark overhead on the roof. It came again, echoing.

I switched off the light, froze, and listened, trying my best not to breathe. Instead of the plank, my fingers wrapped around my weapon. I scooted till I was under the window, just in time to see the man who'd chased Gabi peer inside. He spotted the rustled blankets and exposed hole in the floor.

My heart raced. If he was here, something had happened to her. I thought of my friend lying in the snow, still and alone, nobody coming to save her.

When the officer moved away from the glass, I squeezed my eyes shut and dashed across the room, quiet as I could be. I crouched, my pulse racing, as the door swung open slowly. Behind it, I waited—flashlight in one hand, stick tight in the other. The officer stepped into the cottage. No one followed. No one else was out in the yard. I readied my weapon. When he knelt by the hole in the floor, I took a step forward, then another to get around the open door, then backed out of the house.

I was all the way on the porch when he glanced over his shoulder.

We both went still. The officer blinked in surprise. And then I took off down the stairs, missing the last step and falling face-first in the yard. I climbed to my knees, feeling around for my stick in the snow, but all my hands found was the flashlight. By then the officer was standing at the top of the porch, a pistol pointed right at me.

"The game is over. Give me the papers or I'll shoot you."

My lip was bleeding. I couldn't seem to catch my breath. The flashlight—still off—shook as I pointed it toward him.

Ileana gives up the manifesto. She is shot in the head any-
way. She cannot save the people she loves.

"Wuhu huwu-huwuwu!"

A male Ural owl's call. I looked up at the female on the
cottage's roof. Gritting my teeth, I flicked on the flashlight and shone it straight into the officer's eyes. In the
same moment, he was clipped in the side of the throat
with a stone. He cried out and fired haphazardly, shielding
his face. But by then I was already stumbling through the
yard toward the path.

"Stop!" he shouted, but I didn't. He aimed his gun.

The next rock missed, but the third struck him square
in the head.

I saw Gabi retreat into the woods. The officer was having trouble keeping his feet. He looked woozy, though
that didn't stop him from stretching out his long arm. He
fired in my direction. The bullet hit a nearby tree trunk,
spraying bark. I screamed, but I didn't look back.

Up the worn path into the forest. Higher and higher
and higher. The cottage vanished from sight. The sounds
of the Securitate officer pursuing me vanished with it.
Still I hurried, too frightened to pause. Soon I was farther than I'd ever been. I kept losing sight of the trail,

buried in white as it was. I kept shining my flashlight this way and that till I found it again.

The world was quiet, the soft snow here untouched. No one used this path anymore. Not for years. Branches had collapsed right across it. Bushes were smack in the middle of where you should walk. I climbed and I climbed and I climbed, always waiting for the moment when the man would catch up. But he didn't.

Finally, I slowed. Finally, I came to a stop. To the right the land sloped down and away. The lights of the village were distant, tiny stars in a sky full of pines, ashes, and firs. I looked up the path into the dark. And for the first time, I realized that I was deep in the woods all alone.

The story came back to me.

For an hour my mother had traveled this way, but after that hour she'd turned, journeying through the heart of the forest itself.

My flashlight dropped to my side, my heavy breathing the only sound in the stillness.

I had no idea where to go.

For a long time, I stood there on the path. I turned in a circle, shining my light, looking for something, anything I might have missed. I glanced back down the mountain, energy seeping right out of my limbs. I was so tired and cold.

Ileana sits down to think. She freezes to death. She cannot save the people she loves.

Something shifted in the darkness straight ahead—just up the mountain, hunched over by the side of the trail. I rubbed my eyes, squinting.

"Old Constanta?" I called out, bewildered.

The figure turned and looked right at me. Then she stepped off the path into the trees.

Adrenaline came back in a rush. I ran ahead, my feet eating the earth, and pushed my way through the dense undergrowth. Off the path there was no one, and for a moment I thought I'd imagined the whole thing. I swept my light across the forest floor, and it bounced off the snow into the boughs up above. Nothing. Nothing. And then, almost right in front of me, she was there, caught in the glare of the beam. She glanced over her shoulder and gestured.

I smiled, feeling righteous. I'd known all along that she'd been fooling the people in town. She'd been pretending to act sicker than she actually was. Hurrying forward, I pushed branches out of the way. The snow hadn't fallen as thick here as it had in the village, but without any path— forgotten or not—it was harder now to keep my feet.

"Wait for me, Old Constanta," I called. "You're going too fast!"

But the woman did not change her pace. Her bent, lumpy frame shuffled incessantly on, never bothered by bramble or rocky terrain. When I lagged too far behind, she only paused briefly, leaving me gasping as I strained to catch up. I climbed a great boulder she'd somehow avoided and slid down the other side, scraping my knees. At one particular ridge, I paced back and forth, calling her name. She'd already gotten to the top, out of sight, but I couldn't figure out how. The drop was straight up and down, taller than I could touch. I tossed my light first, then jumped till I caught hold of some roots and could pull myself over the ledge. I kicked wildly to gain traction, limbs trembling by the time I made it to level ground.

Again the old woman was ahead, waiting, always just out of reach.

Farther and farther we traveled away from the path and the stone stairs and my grandparents' cottage. Darker and darker the woods grew. The air felt light in my chest. I felt dizzy. I kept having to pause so I could breathe.

"Please, Constanta, slow down," I begged.

But whenever I'd start moving again, she'd be back at her original pace. I couldn't understand how she managed.

For the first time since I'd made my choice to go after her, something knotted deep in my gut.

What if it wasn't Old Constanta?

I hadn't gotten a close look at her face. The light had never lingered on her long enough for me to be sure.

A howl came in the distance. It echoed, repeating in every direction till I realized it wasn't an echo at all. It was many voices, not one.

Ileana follows a witch deep into the forest. She is eaten alive by the wolves. She cannot save the people she loves.

It was only then, as I peered through the dark, searching for the glint of yellow eyes with my light, that I realized something was wrong with the trees. Their trunks were all bent and twisted. Some spiraled round and round like a screw. Some had branches protruding out of their thick, exposed roots.

The flashlight turned off, just like that.

No dimming. No blinking. No fade to black. Instant darkness. And in that moment, I swore I heard the trees shuffling toward me.

Ileana gets lost. She is torn limb from limb by the monstrous forest. She cannot save the people she loves.

"Old Constanta!" I shouted, terrified. "Don't leave me!"

For a long time, there was nothing but night. The wolves

howled again, closer. But then my eyes adjusted, and the old woman was there. She reached out her hand, gesturing, and I could see now that she was smiling, toothless and wide.

"I thought you were brave," she croaked, sounding a thousand years old. "Come along. It always gets worse right at the end."

I dropped the dead flashlight in the snow and went after her. And, just as she said, it was not very much longer till moonlight appeared through the clouds, spearing the boughs in great shafts. The trees thinned, looking normal once more. We passed a white-faced rock jutting out of the earth.

When the ground flattened, opening up to reveal a huge clearing, it was a moment before I understood what lay before me. The stones of the high walls were covered in moss. They were split in haggard lines at the seams. The towers had crumbled decades before.

In the dark before dawn, the ancient monastery glistened.

I looked around, surprised that I'd finally gotten ahead of my companion. Somehow I'd walked right past her. I turned to ask what I should do next.

I was alone in the white moonlit clearing.

The Story That Cannot Be Told

Creeping forward through the snow, I searched the dark, empty windows and high walkways of the monastery. No one sniped me dead. No one shone down a spotlight and called out. I made it to the nearest wall and snuck up to the edge of an opening—the ruins of a splintered wooden door. My heart was racing, so I reached into my coat pocket and touched the folded manifesto. I pictured its torn edges, its smeared black ink, its unfamiliar handwriting. I remembered my uncle's left fingers, fat and dark and twisted in all the wrong ways.

Making fists in my mittens, I ducked inside.

The hallway echoed. Melting ice dripped into a puddle somewhere out of sight. A rat squeaked and scurried away.

I tiptoed as slowly as I could. I turned one corner, then the next, and went down a short flight of stairs. The place was a labyrinth of abandonment. Broken bed frames were crumpled in corners. Tattered lengths of cloth sat in moldy, wet piles. I passed rooms with no ceiling, dead vines curtaining every wall. I passed a chapel with toppled lecterns and icon cases. Its benches were split down the middle. Its altar was scorched and charred.

When I heard voices, I paused, peeking down the next corridor. Light came from a great arched, open doorway. I crept forward till I could make out the shadows flickering on the opposite wall. A man paced back and forth, gun strapped to his back. I could hear his boots on the stone. I could hear radio static, a broadcast drifting in and away. Inch by inch, I scooted right up to the entrance.

"Some water. That's all I'm asking for. He isn't well."

My heart stopped—my father's voice. I put my back to the wall, digging my shoulder into a crack. Tiny rocks clattered out, bouncing along the floor and echoing like an avalanche. I squeezed my eyes shut, pressed my mittens to my mouth till I couldn't breathe.

Ileana reaches the ancient monastery at the top of the world. She cannot stay quiet for just once in her life and, after being discovered, dies a slow, gruesome death. She does not save the people she loves.

"He's not supposed to be well," the pacing man said to my father. "Neither are you. When the sun comes up, you're all dead anyway."

"Please. *Please.* If I knew where the papers were, I'd tell you. My brother could tell you if he weren't in this shape."

"Your brother had his chance to talk. Didn't seem interested."

There was coughing. Bodies shifted. A voice I didn't recognize said something incoherent. I realized my uncle and father were not the only ones being held hostage.

I took a breath and peeked around the edge of the arched entrance.

The vaulted room was lined with massive oak tables. Some were broken. Some were covered in maps and piles of books. Some were pushed out of the way to make room for mismatched cargo crates filled with provisions and weapons. Cots were stacked with blankets and winter clothes. In the center of the room was a fire. The soldier there was facing away from me. His fingers worked a handheld radio, scanning for broadcasts. On a nearby table was a plate with some bloody, half-eaten meat. A bottle of alcohol. A fork. A knife.

I tried to plot the upcoming scene. Across the vaulted room, the far left wall was partially collapsed. I could see into the moonlit, snow-covered clearing beyond. I could see into the dark forest. To my right, sitting on the stone floor, seven resisters were tied up—my uncle and father among them. If I caused a distraction and got the soldier to leave, I could free everyone, and we could escape through the hole in the wall.

I leaned back into the corridor, careful not to make any sound—though it wouldn't have mattered. Standing right in front of me was a second soldier, bigger than the first. He put both his hands on my shoulders, so heavy I felt myself sink into my boots.

"Did you know you were being spied on?" he called to his partner. It didn't take much of his strength to pull me away from the wall and walk me into the room.

The smaller man looked up, eyes wide. He set down the radio. "How long has he been here?"

"It's a she, I think."

"Ileana?" my father gasped.

Both men turned, and I shrugged out of the bigger one's grip, darting away toward the fire, the hostages at my back.

"I've come to make a trade," I said, my voice as loud as I could make it.

The two men looked at each other.

"A trade?"

"With us?"

I nodded. "I know where the manifesto is. And I'll tell you, but first you have to let everyone go."

I wouldn't have been surprised if they'd both started laughing, but I didn't expect the smaller man to swing around his rifle.

"How about you just tell us and we don't kill you?"

"For God's sake, she's a child!" my father shouted behind me.

I stared down the barrel, breath catching in my throat. The weight of the folded papers in my pocket grew and grew.

"Will you let them go after?" I managed to ask.

The man cocked the gun. "I don't think so."

"Ileana, tell them where it is *this instant*," my father said.

The Securitate hadn't cared about my Great Tome. They hadn't cared about any of the stories I'd told, because I was just a young girl. The only real danger I posed wasn't what I might do to someone else, but what someone else might do to me—how my safety might be played like a card.

Sometimes, though, who you are is the disguise.

Sometimes you have to take risks.

And the truth was, if I could only say the words, I might still change the end of this story.

Ileana is brave. Ileana does what she thinks is right. Ileana saves the people she loves.

"I can't just explain where the manifesto is," I started slowly. "I have to . . . I have to tell you something first. You'll have to listen real close."

The smaller man tapped his ear with the gun. "Listening. Go ahead."

I stood up straighter, fire hot at my back. I licked my chapped lips and tasted blood.

I had promised never to tell it, not even for my life, but my life was not the only one now at stake.

"Long, long ago, there lived an ancient, noble people. Among them was a priest with white hair and a white beard and white, unseeing eyes. He would travel from village to village, helping those in need and spreading the word of their god. But since he was blind, he would often get lost in the woods and have only the animals to preach to."

The smaller man's mouth fell open. "Is she telling us a story?"

The bigger man smirked, crossing his arms and shushing his partner.

"One day," I continued, "the god decided to offer the

priest a deal. The wolves, who loved the blind man best of all, needed someone to lead them. If he would agree to live with them and guide them till the end of all time, the god would give the priest back his sight. The blind man wanted so badly to see the world, and he cared for the wolves dearly, so he agreed to let their god do his will. In a flash of light he was turned into a great white wolf that would rule over all the land, and with a lap of milk from a wild red goat, he was able to see."

In the distance outside, a wolf's howl echoed over the monastery.

The hairs stood up on the back of my neck. The soldiers' eyes went wide. Both of them glanced out into the woods. Distracted, the smaller man lowered his gun.

"The people who worshipped this god," I said, speaking faster, "they loved the wolves too. They cried just like them in battle. They carried blazing flags with a white dragon's body and a wolf's head. They carved pictures of wolves into their doors. But though they were great warriors, there was one enemy too strong for them to defeat. The enemy's armies invaded their villages, burning their homes to the ground. Out of fear, the people betrayed the wolves, offering them as animal sacrifices, and lost the protection of their god. In return the enemy let them live, but they forced the people to look and act and think just like they said."

I narrowed my eyes, gritting my teeth. "There was one village, though, up high in these very same mountains, that refused to surrender. Instead of betraying the wolves, they fought beside them, retreating farther and farther north. Finally, hiding at the top of the world, they believed they were safe."

The soldiers were facing me again, listening closely, but I could still see through the opening in the wall behind them. A snowy blur darted across the clearing outside.

"But one evening, a hunter went out in the forest, and through the trees he saw the White Wolf." My voice dropped to a whisper. Movement again. Nearer this time. "He ran back to his people to warn them, and the villagers agreed it was a sign from their god. They prepared for battle at once. Sure enough, that very night, the enemy reached the peak of the mountain and attacked. They were more savage than ever before, determined to slaughter the last of the villagers."

A massive, white, fur-covered beast appeared at the gap in the wall, crawling over the fallen stones. Through the shadows, his yellow eyes glinted. The White Wolf. My mouth went dry, my limbs stiff. Silently, he crept closer.

"What? And what then?" asked the big man.

The smaller one rubbed his arms, the spell breaking. "Oh, come on! She's just stalling. She doesn't know where the papers are." He stepped forward, raising his rifle. "Story's over."

My hand darted into my pocket, heart pounding as I revealed the manifesto.

"Stop!" I shouted, holding the papers over the flames. My mitten caught fire almost at once, and the soldiers stepped back instinctively. I switched hands, got off the double pair of mittens, and tossed them, smoldering, to the floor. I dangled the papers higher. Behind the men, the wolf had gone still, but through the break in the wall was more movement—others closing in. "You want the manifesto? It's right here. But if you don't let me tell the rest of my story, I'll drop it into the fire. I swear that I will."

"All right, little girl, all right," said the big man. He put his hand on his partner's gun, pushing it down, and forced a smile. "Go on. We're both listening. You can finish."

My breath was shaking, my arm already growing tired. The heat from the flames was too much. My skin turned pink, burning. But the wolf was so close. He lowered his head into a prowl. Behind him, more white beasts appeared in the snow. My eyes filled with tears and everything blurred.

"Just when the people thought all hope was lost, a great cry came from the forest," I said, voice rising in pain. "The White Wolf had come, and with him was an incredible army—a thousand wolves at his back."

Another meter. Another few moments.

"The animals crashed into the enemy and ripped them to shreds, winning the battle."

The skin on my hand started to blister. The papers started to smoke.

"And ever since that day, when the people of our village see danger on the horizon, they whisper his name."

The beast was in place now, teeth bared. His brothers and sisters crept in through the wall at his back.

"Because they know that, every time, the White Wolf will save them."

The edge of the manifesto caught fire, and I couldn't hold it any longer. The papers dropped into the flames. The smaller man cried out, diving forward, but the wolf leaped, snatching him by the throat.

I blinked, shocked, unsure of what I was seeing.

He wasn't a wolf at all.

A big, gruff, potbellied resister in a white sheepskin coat was choking the soldier, shaking him like a rag doll.

"Mr. Bălan?" I gasped through tears.

The second, larger soldier cried out, reaching for his gun, but he was too slow. Another resister tackled him to the floor, pinning his arms.

I dashed to the nearby table and grabbed the knife. I fell to my knees by my father, cutting frantically at his ropes. My hand was burned so badly that I couldn't stop sobbing, but I kept sawing.

"Hurry!" my father yelled. "Hurry, Ileana!"

When he was free, Tata took the knife from my hand and pushed me behind him, staggering to his feet. He held out the weapon before us.

But there was no need.

The smaller officer took his last breath, falling to the floor on the other side of the fire. The bigger man was already gagged and bound.

The resisters had reclaimed their mountain.

Cunning Ileana and the Sugar Doll

In the depths of the mountain castle's darkest dungeon cell, Cunning Ileana awoke with a start. Someone was there, kneeling at the door, staring at her through the iron bars. At first she was sure it was a ghost, but then the figure offered some water and bread, and Ileana realized it was her father.

I'm so sorry, he said. In the moonlight she could see tears running down his long nose. *I thought he would hurt you if I didn't do as he wanted. For so long, I believed I could protect our family by helping the monarch, but I can see now that I was wrong.*

Princess Ileana climbed to her knees and crawled over. She ate the bread, drank the water, and tried to speak, but still the words wouldn't come. The princess tapped her throat, shaking her head, and her father went to get parchment and a quill.

Sometimes it isn't easy being so clever, she wrote. *After you betrayed me the first time, I knew you would do it again.* The emperor's head sank to his chest, but then Ileana continued. *I still love you, though. I always will.*

Oh, my baby girl, her father cried, reaching through the bars to put his palm on her cheek.

Even if you're not always brave, she wrote.

Yes, well . . .

And sometimes a bit of an idiot.

Thanks. I get the point.

Cunning Ileana smirked, but the light quickly faded from her eyes, *I can't marry the monarch's youngest son. He's the worst person on the planet, and he's definitely going to try to kill me again. You have to help me escape.*

I don't have the key to the cell, fretted her father. *The monarch carries it around his neck, and he's sworn not to let you out till tomorrow's ceremony. He's pretty upset about his boys getting dismembered and cursed and impaled. You . . . you didn't really do all that, did you?*

I might have had some small part, wrote Ileana.

I'll help you however you ask, said the emperor, *but I'm no good at these sorts of plans.*

The cunning princess looked across the cell at the fake body of her father, raising an eyebrow.

Are the cooks still in the kitchen? she wrote.

The next afternoon, the monarch sent the two elder sisters into the dungeon to dress Ileana in an outrageously ugly and glittering gown. When they were through, they led her upstairs to the ballroom, where a magnificent gathering of men and women from kingdoms far and wide had come to celebrate the holy union of the youngest prince and princess. In the hall outside the ballroom door, Ileana tugged her sisters to a halt and handed them detailed instructions. Their eyes widened as they read, and they glanced at each other in worry.

You owe me, Ileana mouthed, glaring.

During the ceremony, the guests were a bit surprised to find the youngest princess of the emperor entirely docile. Rumors said she was a rabid, unpredictable thing, so it was somewhat shocking to watch her smiling blankly at the priest for the whole wedding. When the prince and princess were announced husband and wife, the guests were equally surprised to see the monarch's youngest son—who was half-covered in bandages and missing an eye—slide a dagger from his formal attire and drive it into the princess's stomach.

That's for tempting me into your room so I'd fall into your father's vault, he snarled. Then he raised the blade again and cut the princess's throat.

That's for letting a balaur eat my elder brother's arms.

Then he slit the princess in half from head to foot.

That's for helping the Mother of the Forest to curse my middle brother.

Like a madman, the prince hacked and slashed without heed.

That's for dropping me into the pit beneath the apple tree.

Then the prince pulled back his blade a final time, offering his princess a cruel smile.

And this, he said, *this is for being a clever girl.*

With a scream, the youngest son of the monarch shoved his dagger straight into his wife's heart. Laughing like he'd totally lost it, he leaned forward and kissed her, but he immediately pulled back, licking his lips in confusion.

What's this? he said. *My love, Ileana! Sweeter in death than in life?*

By this point the wedding guests were in absolute chaos. They were running wildly all around the ballroom, yelling and knocking over expensive decorations. Of course, none of them thought to come help—not even when the prince figured out Ileana's final trick and his furious eyes turned on the emperor. With a roar, the youngest son dove, meaning to murder the princesses' father.

The elder sisters were hugging and crying.

The monarch was cackling at the back of the room, clapping his hands merrily.

But then, just as the sun set over the mountains, Cunning Ileana appeared from behind a colorful tapestry at the wall, wearing nothing but her undergarments. The bride the youngest prince had stabbed to bits was only a sugar doll, made to look like the princess, which the elder sisters had dressed in her hideous gown.

Stay away from my father, the real Ileana howled, voice finally returned, and from across the room her friend the knight tossed over a massive broadsword. The princess caught it mid-leap and in one swing beheaded her prince.

Of course, the monarch and his two living sons fled right after, along with whatever remained of the permanently scarred wedding guests. The emperor embraced his youngest daughter, and after a moment the two elder sisters joined in, everyone sobbing and making a scene. When the family reunion was through, Ileana ran to the knight, who caught her in a big bear hug.

Thanks for always protecting me, said the cunning princess.

That's what best friends are for, said the knight.

Later that evening, after the surrounding kingdoms received word that the monarch's son had attempted to murder Ileana and her father, they decided to band together to take down the cruel tyrant. With the emperor himself leading the battle, it wasn't long till the evil monarch was no more.

For the rest of her days, Cunning Ileana and her family lived in peace and happiness. And if they haven't died, they're still living.

To the Valley Below

My whole life I'd changed the endings of stories.

When I told them to my father on our walks to the park or to see movies in his student's apartment, he would keep his brow lifted, nodding from time to time. When I got the nerve to ask my uncle to look at the things that I'd written, I would sit right at his feet, watching his eyes scan the pages, trying to predict the line he'd just read that made him bring a finger up to tap his scruffy chin. No matter who it was, though, when the story was over, I'd revel in the look of surprise on their faces.

My father always gave gentle critiques.

"Have you thought about how this fits with the tone of the rest of the piece? Kind of jarring, isn't it?" he would ask. If we had reached our destination, if we had time, he'd take a seat and pull out the Great Tome from his bag. "Let's look at places where you might foreshadow to help things along."

My uncle, more often than not, simply didn't understand.

"But she's a princess."

"Yes," I'd agree.

"But she murdered her prince during their wedding."

"Yes. Isn't it great?"

"But that's not how these sort of stories go. It's a fairy tale. She's supposed to forgive him. Live happily ever after and all that."

I'd tilt my head, quite concerned, and touch the last lines with a finger, like maybe he'd missed them.

"She's totally happy. See here?"

Changing the endings of stories gave me control in a world where I had none. It gave me a voice where I'd have otherwise vanished. But I could not rewrite my life as it happened.

And on top of that mountain, when dawn rose, clear as the spring, no one was fooled. The hardest months of winter were ahead, not behind.

After my father and I and the other resisters helped

untie the rest of the hostages, we went through the crates for supplies and started taking care of the injured. Tata put ointment on my hand and wrapped it with a bandage. It still hurt, but I had stopped crying. While he gave his brother some water to drink, I helped tend Uncle Andrei's wounds, packing snow on his swollen ankle and finding sticks and cloth for a brace. Tata kept looking over as if he'd never seen me before.

"How did this happen without me realizing?" he asked. I glanced up from my work, confused. "When did you become such an adult?"

I rolled my eyes but couldn't hide my smile.

As daylight returned color to the world, the resisters began to discuss going back down the mountain. Just like the Securitate, they had their own spies. After they'd gotten word of the hostages in the schoolhouse, they'd planned a simultaneous rescue. Now, though, they were worried about the state sending reinforcements. While the adults argued, I crawled under a table and came out with the dead soldier's handheld radio. After twisting the dials through static, I turned up the volume when I found the Voice of America. Everyone in the vaulted room went quiet.

That morning, we listened as the world below changed

forever. The square in front of the palace in Bucharest flooded with protesters. The Leader declared martial law, but when our defense minister—who'd refused to order his men to shoot the civilians—turned up dead, our soldiers began to switch sides. The Romanians they'd been killing, they now armed with guns and supported with tanks. They fought back the loyalist Securitate. People were running to the soldiers in the streets with offerings of sweets and cigarettes.

Everyone in the room turned to the big uniformed man tied up at the far wall. His eyes were wide and blinking. Mr. Bălan went over and ungagged him.

"What is it?" the innkeeper asked. "Some sort of trick?"

The soldier shrugged, looking helpless. "I don't know. I just do what I'm told."

Mr. Bălan made a disgusted face. "I suppose nothing's left but to see for ourselves."

I had to help Tata carry Uncle Andrei as we trekked back down the mountain.

"I still don't understand," said my father, sunlight on his round glasses. "How did you get to us?"

"I walked," I replied.

"But how did you climb up the mountain in the snow? In the dark?"

"On two feet."

When he gave me a look, I explained about Old Constanta.

"I hope she's all right," Tata said, worried. "That's a hard journey for someone her age."

I flushed, because until then I hadn't thought about what might have happened to her. The whole way down, we looked for some sign of the old woman but found nothing.

"Maybe she made it back to her house," I said, and then lowered my voice. "I'm pretty sure she's a witch."

The resisters in their white sheepskin coats made slow progress with the injured to care for, but eventually the valley below was in sight. Uncle Andrei, who'd been mostly unresponsive, suddenly seemed to realize where he was.

"Lucian?" he asked. "Did you come rescue me?"

"Sort of," his brother replied, "but then Ileana had to rescue us both."

"And you let her?"

My father just smiled.

At the bottom of my grandparents' hill, on the side of the road, we met an old farmer holding a gun. That confirmed things had changed.

"I'm a lookout." The man beamed. "Haven't held one of these since 1945!"

The soldiers who hadn't fled were now working with the villagers to clear snow from the streets. Most of them had turned on the Securitate when the resisters had arrived. As for the man in the brown suit, he'd disappeared in the chaos.

Uncle Andrei spat and cursed. "And here I thought I'd get to repay him for his hospitality," he said, clenching and unclenching the fingers of his left hand.

When Mamaie spotted me coming down the road, she gathered her skirts and ran over, sobbing. She caught me, kissing my cheeks so many times my face hurt.

"We heard gunshots. Gabi wasn't sure if you'd been hit," she said into the neck of my coat. "But there was blood in the yard and I saw that cursed owl. Dogs started barking. I just knew something awful had happened!"

Tataie reached us and pulled me from her arms into his. "I never doubted you once."

"Of course you say that now," chided my grandmother. "He was in shambles, believe me."

I tried to ask about Old Constanta, but behind us my father cleared his throat, and I turned around in surprise.

"Oh," I said stepping back. "Tata, these are my grandparents. Mamaie, Tataie, this is my tata."

My father nodded, smiling apologetically.

"Thank you so much," he said. "I don't know how we'll ever repay you for taking care of her."

"She took care of us, mostly," said Tataie, winking at me.

Mamaie gasped at the sight of Uncle Andrei. "What's happened now to your ankle? Can you even see out of those eyes? Sanda's going to have a fit!"

I giggled, but the air was knocked out of me by a half-tackle hug.

"Ileana!" Gabi cried, squeezing my middle. "You're alive!"

I hugged my friend back, grinning. "I knew that officer wouldn't catch you," I said. "I've never seen anyone run so fast!"

Gabi explained how she'd lost the officer and then used a shortcut to double back so she could shoot him with her slingshot. After she'd helped me escape, she'd hidden in one of the spots from our map till Ioan found her and said it was safe. While she was talking, Sanda came out of her house, where she was tending the injured, and, as Mamaie had predicted, made a huge fuss over my uncle.

"Why did I even bother fixing you?" Sanda scolded. "And I always thought poets were such calm, rational people."

Beneath the dirt and the bruises Uncle Andrei smirked. "You haven't been reading the right poets."

When the adults left us to go help the wounded, Gabi gagged dramatically.

"I think my mom likes your uncle," she groaned.

I blinked, taken aback, before we both started laughing.

And then I noticed the figure walking up the road through the village. I went still, stunned as I realized who it was. Her long dark hair tumbled out from under a wool shawl. Her hazel eyes locked on to mine, her smile igniting. She was as beautiful as if she'd stepped out of a story.

"Mama," I breathed.

It took a moment more before I found my feet—before I ran to her. When she embraced me, it felt like the world was whole again. I shut my eyes, overwhelmed with relief.

"Oh, my sweet baby girl!" Mama cried into my hair. "Are you all right? Are you hurt?"

"I'm okay. Really. Tata too."

My mother pulled back, wiping tears from her wide eyes. "You found him?"

I nodded. "And Uncle Andrei. They got beat up pretty bad, but the veterinarian says they'll be fine. Everyone's in her house now getting help."

"The veterinarian?" asked my mother, confused.

"Sanda. Gabi's mom." I pointed at my friend, who did a little wave, her cheeks red in the cold. "She's my best friend."

"Hello, Gabi," said my mother; then she turned back to me, her brow raised. "I guess we have a lot to catch up on." She picked up my braid, shaking her head. "I think you've grown thirty centimeters. And look at this hair!"

A cheer rose up from inside Sanda's house and we turned. My heart clenched in excitement as voices started to shout, "Victory! Victory!"

That afternoon my mother reunited with her parents, sobbing and hugging and apologizing for the years that they'd lost. My father took care of his brother, forgiving him for all the danger he'd caused us. Gabi and Ioan and I ransacked the Securitate's abandoned rations and helped cook a feast for the whole village.

All the while, in other parts of our country, life as we knew it was changing forever.

The news coming in through the radio had been too much to believe, so when a soldier finally got our power working again, someone plugged in Sanda's TV. Nothing should have been airing. The daily national broadcast wasn't due to start for several more hours. But there it was—our one, state-run channel renamed Free Romanian Television. The studio in Bucharest had been taken over by resisters, and they were showing live coverage of what was now being called a revolution.

That morning, the Leader had tried to address his country one last time. He'd rained manifestos down into the crowds, telling the people to go home and enjoy feasts. Protestors, half-starved, had pelted him with stones, storming the building, and the People's Genius and his Scientist Spouse had barely escaped. For a brief moment they were trapped in an elevator, just out of reach of the angry, grasping hands, but the couple made it to the rooftop and into a helicopter. It was hard finding somewhere to land, though—someone who still wanted to save them. Eventually the pilot claimed they'd been spotted on radar and would be blown out of the sky, so the Leader ordered him to set down in a field.

"Are you serving the cause?" he asked the pilot before hijacking a car.

"Which cause should I serve?" asked the man.

Not long after that, the Leader and his wife were arrested, and on TV I watched an actor and a poet announce victory for Romania. There was marching in the streets, gunfire lighting the sky. There were shells exploding into the ground. We celebrated even as our country still burned.

That evening, everyone gathered around Sanda's stove. The adults talked and talked, laughing and drinking, but my heart still felt a bit heavy.

I dropped down beside Uncle Andrei, looking grim.

"What's with the sad face, princess?" he asked. "This is a day to be smiling!"

"I failed you," I said miserably. "I couldn't protect the manifesto. We fought so hard to save it, and I let it fall in the fire."

"That's what this sulking's about?" He laughed. "What fell in the fire was just words on paper. How those words made people feel is the thing that's important. What's happened today—here in the village and all over Romania—*this* is what we have to protect. We don't need the manifesto anymore."

I felt myself starting to smile as the weight lifted from my chest.

"Okay, Ileana. It's time," Gabi said from a few paces away. I looked up, uncertain. "We're ready to hear the whole thing. From the start."

Beside her, Ioan took a seat, and the adults began to pay attention too.

"Yeah, Ileana," said the innkeeper's son. "Tell us what happened last night. The truth. All of it."

And even though I was exhausted and aching, even though I just wanted to rest, I couldn't resist someone asking me for a story, so I sat up, looking around at my family and friends. For the first time, I told "Ileana and the White Wolf."

When I was through, I searched each person's face. As I'd expected, most of them were shocked by the end of the tale.

"That's the best one yet," whispered Gabi in awe.

"You know what?" asked Ioan. "I think you *are* as tough as you act."

"You do realize you could have been killed?" asked my father, aghast. My mother pursed her lips, staying quiet.

I shifted my eyes to my toes, then looked up, resolute. "It was a risk. But it was the right thing to do."

"My niece the storyteller," said Uncle Andrei. "It's a good one. You should write it down somewhere. People don't read enough folklore these days."

My heart fluttered with pride, but then fell in despair as I realized what he meant. I sighed, shaking my head. "That's the problem. It's not folklore. It's all true, but no one will believe me. I really did hear wolves in the forest. I swear it wasn't just the resisters who saved us."

"Some will believe," said Tataie. "I certainly do."

"There's just one part, though," said Mamaie, hesitant. "Are you sure it was Old Constanta who led you up the mountain?"

"Totally." Then my eyes opened wide as I panicked, realizing that in all the commotion I'd forgotten about the widow again. "Where is she? Hasn't anyone seen her? What if she's still out there in the cold!"

My grandmother glanced at the others. She reached over to calm me, taking my good hand.

"Old Constanta died last night, child," she said gently. "Before they even rounded us up."

How the Story Ends

When I tell my story now, when I insist that it happened, people are forced to believe one of two
unbelievable things: either a ghost led a child to an ancient
monastery at the top of the world, or the child made her
way there all alone through the dark and the snow.

To me, though, what remains the most unbelievable is
not my journey up the mountain, but the country that I
found down below it.

After helping with what we could in the village, my
father secured us a ride with some soldiers back to the
city. There was a great deal of crying during good-byes,
especially from Mamaie, who made my mother promise
there'd be no more silence between them.

"We'll be back in the spring to help you rebuild," said Mama, kissing my grandmother's cheek. "I'll call as soon as we get to the apartment."

"You could come stay with us while things settle down," offered my father, not for the first time. "We don't have much to offer, but it's the least we can do."

Tataie politely declined. He still had no intention of ever leaving his home.

As we loaded into the soldiers' truck, Gabi came to give me one last bear hug.

"Don't forget to draw pictures when you send me letters," I said. "And thanks again for saving my life."

"That's what best friends are for." Gabi smiled.

We drove home through the countryside, fires still smoldering on the horizon, and listened to the radio the whole ride. On Christmas Day—a holiday that for so long had been banned—our new government offered us a grisly present: The Leader and his wife were executed by a firing squad, their deaths broadcast all over the world. Some say that, right before he died, our oppressor started to sing.

In Romania, the revolution had been written with blood. We didn't really understand this till we saw for ourselves— till we came face-to-face with the devastation.

Bucharest looked like it had been at war.

Statues were toppled and crumbling. Government buildings were ransacked. The university library had burned to the ground. More than half a million books were destroyed. There was damage to radio and television stations. There was damage to our art museum and concert hall. No one was ever really sure who had kept shooting—"terrorists," they said, whatever that word now meant—but the fighting had continued for days.

In our apartment that first night, we cleaned up what we could. It would be a long time before we again had electricity, before we replaced all the broken windows and swept all the dust and ash from our floors. It would be a long time before Uncle Andrei stopped crying in his sleep. For years, he would be afraid to be alone.

But on that first night home in Bucharest, we wanted to pretend things were just as they'd been. So we cooked dinner and ate at the table. We talked about nothing important. I did the dishes, humming off-key, while my parents made my uncle a bed on the couch.

Sometimes, though, things can't go back to normal, no matter how much you wish that they could.

I closed the door to my room, feeling empty. For so long, I'd craved my home and my family, but it was as if on the day that I'd disappeared on the train, the home and family I'd known had disappeared too.

The truth is, sometimes it's not just the world, but your eyes that have changed.

Late that night, while I lay awake, unable to sleep, there came a knock at my door. And in the ruins of what had once been my apartment, in the debris of what had once been my room, my father came and sat on the edge of what had once been my bed. From his pocket he took out folded papers, and for a moment I thought he was holding the manifesto. But then I recognized the childish hand-writing, and my heart caught in my chest.

"I'm sorry, Ileana," Tata said.

My mother had spent her whole life taking risks. As a girl she'd carried messages up to the rebels in the moun-tains. She'd run away from home at just seventeen. She'd listened to illegal cassette tapes and sung illegal songs in a pub. She'd married a professor, a man who'd never farmed for a day in his life. When she'd had me, she'd tried her best to be mild and sensible. But then they had torn down her apartment with the pantry and the frothy cream walls. She hadn't had time to save her piano. So when my father and I had gone on our walks, my mother had copied dangerous poems. She'd organized. She'd collaborated. She'd helped get them published abroad.

Tata had taken risks too, though. They'd just been harder to see.

He'd risked his happiness when he stopped going to movies. He'd risked my love when he burned the Great Tome. He'd risked being called a coward and a traitor to make sure we stayed safe.

Every last risk that he'd taken had been for our family—for me.

"I'm so sorry," he said again.

In his hands was a retelling of "Cunning Ileana." Long, long ago, when I was small, he'd helped me bind it into the Great Tome. My first entry. It didn't have an ending, of course, but it was the story he'd most often asked me to read. Before he'd set my tome in the flames, he'd torn it out. And now he was giving it back.

I reached forward, eyes wide as my fingers brushed the old words. I folded the pages into his palm.

"Keep it," I said. "I wrote it for you."

"Can you ever forgive me?" he asked.

"I think so," I whispered, pulling the covers up to my chin, "but only on one condition."

A smile crept up to my father's round glasses. "I'll stay awake if you do," he said.

"On my life, I swear that I will."

And then he began.

"Once upon a time, something happened. If it hadn't happened, it wouldn't be told. There once was an emperor with three beautiful daughters, the most clever of whom was named Ileana. . . ."

Author's Note

As you know by now, this is a book about stories.

And the truth is, they aren't all entirely mine.

Let me explain.

Not so very long ago, I lived in Japan, where I taught at a school for children from all over the world. My classroom had students from Sri Lanka and Egypt and Denmark, and some of my very best friends were teachers from Romania. I didn't know much about Romania back then, so when we were together, I'd ask my friends about their home. If I was lucky, they'd tell me stories. And one day I got smart and started writing them down.

Recipes for sour soup were mixed in with notes about the Romanian Revolution. Fairy tales got swirled up with history. One friend had a grandfather who believed his life had been spared in World War II because he'd helped someone in need. She also had a grandmother who, with a Roma woman, found a buried curse box under her house.

Another friend told me about listening to the Voice of America on a radio her family kept hidden beneath the floorboards—about being frightened they'd get caught. She told me about living through austerity, when resources such as food and heat became scarce.

It wasn't long before I realized I was holding the pieces of a book. Sure, the book wasn't written yet. And, admittedly, it was a big, jumbled-up mess. But I knew it was there. I could feel it. And when I told my friends my idea—to take bits of their stories and bits of my stories and bits of history and folklore and turn everything into a novel about a little girl named Ileana—they thought it was wonderful. That was all the encouragement I needed.

For almost a year, before ever writing a word of *The Story That Cannot Be Told*, I researched Romania—its fairy tales, its history, and its revolution in 1989. When my friends were children, Nicolae Ceaușescu was the leader of the Romanian Communist government. In a Communist country, the main philosophy is that everyone should be equal. Property and goods and wealth of any kind should be owned by the community as a whole. The trouble in Romania, though, was that Ceaușescu himself was materialistic and power-hungry. He didn't care that while he was building his luxurious palace and holding celebrations in his own honor, families were starving and orphans were sleeping three to a bed with no heat.

Romania's government eventually became totalitarian, meaning it controlled most aspects of people's lives. Propaganda was everywhere, so it was difficult to find information that wasn't misleading, and all sources of media—like television, books, music, and movies—were strictly censored. The Securitate, the secret police, recruited half a million regular people to spy for them. These informers reported on their families, friends, classmates, and neighbors, making it very dangerous to speak your mind, no matter who was around. Anyone suspected of opposing Ceaușescu and his government faced serious repercussions: arrest, loss of employment, torture, or even death. People who had the power to convince others to turn against the regime—people such as writers, teachers, directors, and scientists—were frequent targets of the Securitate.

However, even during the hardest of times, Romanians persevered.

Uncles whispered jokes about Ceaușescu under their breath. Grandparents upheld their religious traditions in secret. At night, by the flicker of candles, parents and children recited poetry and sang songs and told stories that had long ago been banned.

In the 1980s, audiocassettes and videotapes, which were easily copied, flooded the Romanian black market with illegal music and movies. For the first time in decades, Romanians got an unfiltered look at the outside world, and it's hard not to believe that this contributed somehow to the revolution of 1989.

The Story That Cannot Be Told is grounded in the true history of a real time and place, but most of the novel is fiction. Much like someone we know, I took the stories I'd collected—from my friends, through my research—and I retold them. In a very old, lovely book titled *Roumanian Fairy Tales*, for example, I discovered the folktale "Cunning Ileana." However, if you go read the original story, it won't look quite the same. As much as I adored clever Ileana herself, I wasn't a fan of princesses marrying princes who'd treated them badly. And of course, everything is better with dragons.

Like Old Constanta said, though, in some ways all stories are true.

And mine are no exception.

Because many parts of this book—and perhaps not the ones you'd expect—came from the real lives of real people.

And at its heart is a little girl who, like Ileana, wanted all her life to be a writer.

Acknowledgments

Like all stories, the ones in this book were made possible only through the help of countless other people. At the heart of *The Story That Cannot Be Told* are three incredible Romanian women: Cristina Sologon, Ana Maria Fujimagari, and Cecilia Ioana. This novel is as much yours as mine, since without your friendship it never would have existed. Thank you for your countless hours of conversation, research, and remembering. Any historical or cultural inaccuracies that remain are entirely my own.

This book would never have found its true shape without my amazing editor, Reka Simonsen, who not only seems to know just the right words, but always says them in the kindest of ways. Thank you times a million to Yishai Seidman, my superhero agent, who championed *Story* from its earliest draft. I would be remiss not to mention the rest of my incredible team at Atheneum—Julia McCarthy, Justin Chanda, Clare McGlade, Michael McCartney, Tom

Daly, and Lili Feinberg, just to name a few—and the talented artist Isabella Mazzanti, who brought Ileana to life with her stunning cover illustration.

Thank you also to the University of Tennessee at Chattanooga, where I drafted this book as a graduate student. I am forever indebted to my friend and thesis director, Dr. Sarah Einstein, who believed in me and my writing from the beginning. Special gratitude is also due to several professors, peers, and friends who gave me thoughtful feedback on early drafts, including Dr. Kayla Wiggins, Sybil Baker, Jennifer Jones, and Bonné de Blas. I should also mention that this journey to publication would not have been the same without the support of my friends in Novel Nineteens, Class of 2K19, and JPST.

Thank you, Mom and Dad, for always reading to me when I was little and usually making it to the end of the story. You took my writing seriously even when it was still mostly pictures or typed entirely in green Comic Sans, and that love and support has shaped everything since.

And of course, thank you to my best friend and husband, Dustin Kramer, for being my first reader since we were sixteen years old and never thinking twice about helping me follow my dreams.

A READING GROUP GUIDE TO

The Story That Cannot Be Told

by J. Kasper Kramer

1. During the time when this story takes place, Romania was a communist country. What was life like for Romanians under the communist regime? Why would they want to rebel against their leader?

2. What was dangerous about Uncle Andrei's poetry? What "dangerous" ideas can you identify in the stories that Ileana writes in her Great Tome?

3. Why do you think the government installs surveillance equipment in Ileana's apartment? Do you think a government should have the right to use surveillance on citizens?

4. Why does Ileana's father destroy her Great Tome? Discuss whether or not you think he did the right thing. Do you think her father had other options in this situation?

5. Why do Ileana's parents decide to send her to live with her grandparents? Why don't her grandparents recognize her when she arrives in the village?

6. Describe the differences between Ileana's life with her parents in the city of Bucharest and her life with her grandparents in a rural mountain village. If you were Ileana, would you prefer living in Bucharest or the small village?

7. Why do you think the village children are cruel to Ileana when she first arrives? Why might the people in the village have a hard time trusting one another? What advice would you have for Ileana? How might you and your friends make a new person feel welcome?

8. In what ways do the people in the village come together to help one another? How does feeling like a part of a community begin to change Ileana? What people or places make you feel like you belong?

9. Ileana's grandmother has many superstitions. List and explain some of her superstitious beliefs. Do you or does

anyone you know believe in superstitions? Why do you think these notions exist?

10. Describe Ileana's friendship with Gabi. What brings them together? How do they work together? What do you think might have happened if Ileana had never trusted Gabi?

11. What do the Securitate mean when they tell the villagers that they have been "chosen for systemization"? How will this affect the villagers' lives?

12. Ileana's uncle trusts her with his manifesto for safekeeping. What is a manifesto? Why do you think someone would sign their name to a manifesto? What do you think the government would do if they had Uncle Andrei's manifesto?

13. Ileana's father tells her not to resist the Securitate. Why do you think he wants her to turn over the manifesto? Why does she refuse? What would you have done if you were in her position?

14. Summarize the story about Old Constanta. What parts of the story do you think are true? What does the

story reveal about Old Constanta? What does it reveal about Ileana's mother?

15. What is "The Story That Cannot Be Told" about? Refer to "Into the House of the Witch" as well. Explain what Old Constanta means when she says the story is a code. Why do you think the author chose to title her own book this way?

16. Why is it essential for a culture to have storytellers? Why might a government try to control which stories are allowed to be told? Can you think of any real-world examples?

Guide prepared by Amy Jurskis, English Department Chair at Oxbridge Academy.

ALONG A LIVELY RIVER LIVES A GIRL NAMED LUNA.

All her life she has heard about the old days when sprites danced in the waves and no one fell ill from a mouthful of river water. Luna thinks these are just stories, though—until her little sister gets sick. Now, Luna is determined to find a cure, no matter what it takes. Even if that means believing in magic . . .

★ "[A] delicate fantasy of sisterly love tested by separation and illness."
—*Publishers Weekly*, starred review

★ "A quiet story of perseverance and hope, exquisitely written with words and images that demand savoring."
—*Kirkus Reviews*, starred review

★ "Highlights the power of sisterly love in a truly enchanting way."
—*School Library Journal*, starred review

PRINT AND EBOOK EDITIONS AVAILABLE
simonandschuster.com/kids

ANYTHING MIGHT HAPPEN IN SARA-KATE'S BACKYARD.

FOR THAT MATTER, ANYTHING WAS HAPPENING.

Janet Taylor Lisle's captivating story explores how magic, like friendship, can emerge when you least expect it—and when you need it most. All you have to do is look deep.

atheneum
SIMONANDSCHUSTER.COM/KIDS
PRINT EDITION AVAILABLE

READ THE BOOK THAT TWO-TIME NEWBERY HONOR WINNER GARY SCHMIDT CALLS "A JOURNEY THAT EVERY READER NEEDS TO GO ON."

"An intelligent, imaginative, and moving tale, full of clever twists and surprises."

—STUART GIBBS, bestselling author of the Spy School and FunJungle series

Like every other kid in the world, Raul longs for Fridays, but not for the usual reasons. As soon as the other students at his boarding school go home for the weekend, Raul goes to the lighthouse deep in the heart of the woods. There, he waits for sunset—and the mysterious, magical phenomenon that allows him to go home, too.